I0710011

Only Ours

LYNDA TOMALIN

GlitterInk
PRESS

Text Copyright © 2024 Lynda Tomalin
Published by GlitterInk Press Ltd – New Zealand

All rights reserved. This book or any portion thereof may not be reproduced or used in any manner whatsoever without the express written permission of the publisher except for the use of brief quotations in a book review.

ISBN: 978-1-99-118057-5 (NZ Edition Paperback)
ISBN: 978-1-99-118058-2 (POD Paperback)
ISBN: 978-1-99-118059-9 (Epub)

Cover Design by Jennifer Rackham
Editing and proofreading by
Bellbird Words Proofreading, Editing, and Writing Services

www.lyndatomalinauthor.com
www.glitterinkpress.com

For my Soul SiStars,
Kelsey and Natalie
x

CHAPTER 1

Luke

I SHOULD BE THINKING about seeing my best friend
again.

I should be thinking about how it's going to be between us,
the first time together since we made up after our stupid
misunderstanding that changed everything.

I should be thinking about seven thousand different things
– none of which is the single thing I *am* thinking about, though.

Of course not.

No, instead of thinking about Jonathan and our recently
revived friendship, all I can think about is Dan.

I don't even know his last name. I've spent only a handful
of moments in his presence. It was weeks ago.

And yet I cannot stop thinking about him; especially now,
when I'm about to see him again.

I make my way slowly down the street, taking extra care
with my crutches on the footpath that's slippery after a shower
of rain. The last thing I need right now is a fall. With the way
my limbs are shaking I'm in danger of one regardless of how

wet the ground is, and if I go down I don't know if I'll be able to get up again. I'd rather expire in the street than ask for help.

I don't want Dan to see that.

I don't want Jonathan to either.

I take a deep breath and steady myself. I'm used to needing help now, nearly five months after a fall down a steep staircase that left me with a few mangled vertebrae and a concussion, but it doesn't mean I like it.

I especially don't like Jonathan seeing it, since he spent the months directly following the accident thinking it was his fault. I spent those same months thinking he hated me because he'd found out I'm gay – by walking in on me kissing another guy.

Super-fun times.

It turns out we were both wrong. Thank God.

At least the rain has passed now and there's a tiny bit of sun forcing its way through the clouds. I'm thankful it's cleared in time for me to walk to Jonathan's house so I don't arrive looking like a drowned rat.

I thought Jonathan would want to see his parents first, catch up with his sister, then come and find me when he was ready, but when I texted him yesterday to find out what time he'd be around, he insisted he wanted to see me straight away.

'Don't you want to see your family first?' I asked.

'Dude, you are my family,' was his response.

My breath catches at the memory of it, of the over-whelming feelings five simple words sent spiralling through me. Joy that we sorted our shit out, despair for the months we lost, pain for the everything we both endured.

He pretty much fled this place six weeks ago, bearing the guilt for my accident. He went to live on his aunt's farm four hours away.

He hasn't been home since, though his mum, sister Kristen and I went to visit last month, which is when we finally got over ourselves enough to talk it out.

I was hoping he'd come home again, but he'd met Hollie and her best friend, Dan, and despite being a farm boy now, Jonathan is happy. He deserves that.

I don't begrudge him a second of his happiness, though sometimes I wish it hadn't cost me so much for him to find it.

But I can still walk, even if it's slow, painful and awkward, so there's that. Everything else – brain included – is fully intact. Some days it feels like a miracle I got away with only the spinal injury and a concussion. I still can't recall the events right before the fall, but the rest of my head injury seems to have healed itself over time.

I turn into Jonathan's driveway and make my way up the short slope. There's a navy blue SUV, and leaning against the bonnet, his back to me, is Dan. My heart stutters.

Those damn curls of his. Dark blond, wild and haphazard. I've never seen hair like it on anyone. My need to touch it is desperate.

Last month Jonathan's mum and sister went to visit him, and at the last moment I decided to tag along. I was sick of hiding from him and I wanted to know what was going on between us; if I'd ever have my friend back.

My mum warned me it was a terrible idea. Not because she didn't want me to reconcile with Jonathan, but because sitting in a vehicle for four hours was going to be murder on my back.

She was right, but I'm not telling her that.

My legs were so stiff from sitting still for such a long time that when I tried to walk after climbing out of the car, I stumbled.

There was a flurry of tumbled gold and an arm around me, holding me up, before I even realised I was likely going to hit the ground hard. I have no idea how Dan got there so fast, but there he was, catching me before I could fall.

The deepest, warmest brown eyes met mine and I've been able to think about very little else since.

My crush on him was immediate and overwhelming.

And completely and utterly pointless, for so many reasons.

I pry my eyes away from Dan as the afternoon sun highlights the breadth of his shoulders, and for the first time I notice the people standing at the front door.

Jonathan, his mum, and Hollie.

Jonathan disentangles himself from his mother's embrace, and as she pulls Hollie into a hug, he turns enough to catch sight of me.

My panic and excitement over seeing Dan vanishes in an instant.

My best friend, the one whom for a while I thought I'd lost forever, is walking towards me, his face relaxed in an easy grin. There's the tiniest trace of tension around his eyes, but most people wouldn't notice it at all – only the ones who've known him since childhood.

He looks less polished than he did when he lived in the city, his hair is scruffier, his clothes somehow look more worn, his shoes more scuffed, but he looks so much better. He's so happy. Rural life clearly suits him.

I freeze where I am in the middle of the driveway, vaguely aware that Dan has turned to watch our reunion, that he's seen me.

But all of my focus is zeroed in on Jonathan. He stops in front of me and reaches out his arm, and I drop my right crutch in order to throw my arm around him. He squeezes tight for a second and I hold him just as fiercely, then he lets me go, retrieves my crutch, and hands it back to me without batting an eyelid.

I exhale, and all of the tension I've been holding until this moment rides the wave of my breath out of my body.

He's here, and the weeks of worrying that things would be different now, even after we cleared everything up, were for nothing. Because he's the same as he's always been: easy-going, relaxed, full of charm and swagger. It's truly one of those situations where I'd hate him if I didn't love him so much.

Jonathan's sister Kristen appears through the front door and stands on the porch, hands fisted on her hips. "Am I not worthy of a hello?" she calls to her brother.

"Eventually. Getting my priorities in order," he says back, which sets them off bickering.

I laugh at them and let any lingering trace of anxiety and worry about this reunion drop as Hollie finishes saying hello to Jonathan's mum and reaches his side. She gives me a gentle smile and says a quiet hello.

I bet she's freaking out, coming to spend several days with her boyfriend's family whom she's only briefly met. I give her what I hope is a reassuring smile and she relaxes a fraction, but that might be more to do with Jonathan sliding his arm around her waist and holding her close to his side.

Kristen stops bickering with Jonathan long enough to ask Hollie how she is before returning to ribbing her brother.

I've missed this. Missed these two together. The three of us spent so much time together before my accident.

Before I can fall into a melancholy daydream wishing we could be like that again, my attention is recaptured by Dan.

For a moment I forgot he was here. While I've been listening to Jonathan and Kristen, Dan has been saying hello to their mum. He grins at her, his smile wide and easy. His whole demeanour is easy, which I struggle to comprehend.

Dan is Hollie's best friend; that's how Jonathan always refers to him, anyway. I don't think Jonathan has ever called Dan his friend, always Hollie's, so I don't even know if they're actually friends. Yet Dan's here now, ready to stay with Jonathan's family. He's only met them once yet he looks like he fits in without a care in the world. I'm more stressed about this and I pretty much grew up in this house.

Then those dark brown eyes of his find mine across the expanse of driveway as he makes his way towards us, and the corner of his mouth kicks a little higher.

Heat rushes through my body, and all the carefully thought-out reasons why having a crush on him is a terrible idea are incinerated.

Apparently, I don't have a choice.

CHAPTER 2

Luke

ONCE WE ALL TROOP INSIDE, Jonathan's mum Carol fairly quickly banishes us to the downstairs rumpus room.

She loads snacks into Dan's and Jonathan's arms and directs us towards the stairs.

"Uh, I'm going to go around," I say after levering myself off the couch.

The internal stairs in Jonathan's house are steep and narrow and I'm fully aware of my limits. I get around these days with crutches and a deeply uncomfortable brace strapped around my waist. My mobility still isn't great, and it hurts a whole lot to simply exist most days, but it's improving – slowly.

I'm definitely not ready to tackle these stairs though, especially when I can go the long way around, down the sloping outdoor path and in through the downstairs door.

I catch a glance between Hollie and Jonathan. She silently takes his armful of snacks and follows Dan down the stairs. She's wearing a moon boot from a car accident that broke her leg recently, but her mobility is still a million times better than mine.

Jonathan heads for the front door and holds it open for me as I make my way outside.

We start the walk in silence, and I realise this is what I've been worried about. The silence between us when there never used to be any. I toss thoughts around in my head, wondering what I should say to him. I think of how we used to spend hours together, and how the only times we weren't talking were when we were playing music too loud to hear each other. Music is what brought us together. The majority of our friendship was based around learning to play new songs on our chosen instruments.

"Have you played yet?" I blurt out, referencing the guitar I took to him last month. The one he stopped playing after my accident.

He hesitates, then nods. "Yeah, I've picked it up once or twice."

I grin. "Good." Then I notice the look on his face. "Why do you look like that's a bad thing?"

He shrugs and fists a handful of hair. "It feels unfair that you had to give up so much."

I try not to react to his words. He's right. I've had to give up the two things I loved most in the world, the two things I could have turned into a career.

"I still want you to be happy." I nudge him with my elbow. "Write a song for Hollie. You can keep it in reserve for the next time you screw things up." I laugh and Jonathan laughs with me, but I can see he's worried.

"Going to have to write more than one, then. She'll get sick of hearing it otherwise."

I laugh, and Jonathan does too, but it all still feels a little awkward. I really, really hope things go back to normal again soon.

We reach the downstairs door and Dan unlocks it from the inside, pushing it open for us.

Jonathan heads straight for the chair where Hollie is sitting and scoops her up so they can both fit, her sprawled across his lap like it's the most natural thing in the world. She giggles.

The bitter taste of envy creeps up my throat. I wonder if I'll ever have that. I don't want to feel like this, especially not about my best friend. But they make it look easy, even though I know it's been anything but easy for them to get to this point.

"It's so sweet it's sickening, right?" Dan says, his voice low in my ear as he stands beside me.

I snort. "Completely revolting," I say, and feel a little spike of excitement when I see him flash a smile.

I head for the couch and lower myself down, letting out a sigh as I relax back into the cushions. Dan sits next to me and my heart rate increases, especially when he leans across me to take a bowl of chips from Hollie's outstretched hand. He offers them to me and I take a handful. I have to force myself to concentrate on the food and not just stare adoringly into Dan's eyes, which is not easy because he's *right there.*

I reach out to grab the game controllers sitting on the low table in front of us and pass one to Dan. While Hollie and Jonathan get lost in each other's eyes, I hope I can get lost in the game.

"All right, I'm out," I say, gathering my crutches and pulling myself off the couch.

Jonathan breaks off making out with Hollie long enough to look sheepish. Her face blooms a stunning pink before she buries it in Jonathan's shoulder, laughing.

"Do you need a ride home?" Jonathan asks.

"Nah, the walk does me good," I say, shaking my head. "I also wouldn't want to drag you away. I know it's been a long time since you saw Hollie."

Dan bursts out laughing beside me and the happy couple blush even harder. "Do you want some company?" Dan asks me.

My heart does a whole series of jumpy, skippy things and I wonder at what point it becomes a serious health concern. I clear my throat when the words stick, but finally manage to croak them out. "Yeah, sure." I glance at Jonathan and Hollie, then back at Dan. "Wouldn't be humane of me to inflict this on you anymore."

Dan laughs again and I marvel at the sound of it, at the way his eyes crinkle. "I've been overexposed already. I've developed immunity. They never stop."

A cushion bounces off Dan's shoulder and we turn to face Jonathan's smug face.

"You're just jealous," Jonathan says.

"Undoubtedly," Dan says.

"One hundred percent," I mutter, then we both turn for the door and leave our best friends to their own devices.

Once outside, Dan turns to me. "I don't actually have to come with you," he says. "I just needed an out." He pulls a face and I laugh. "I thought it would be weird me being around his family and stuff. I didn't consider they'd be making out in front of us. It's like they haven't got it out of their systems yet." He smiles fondly. I know from what Jonathan has said how much Dan loves Hollie and I know he's happy for them, but I can't help but wonder.

"When you said you're jealous…" I trail off.

"Of their relationship … yes. Of them specifically, no. Like, I'm not hung up on Hollie or anything. It's not like that with us."

I don't know why, but this makes my heart do weird things again. Him not being in love with Hollie doesn't mean *anything* except that he's not interested in dating his best friend. Which I get. I'm not interested in dating mine either.

"Well, whenever they get too much, you can come to mine," I say, suddenly feeling lightheaded as the words spill out. "I'm right around the corner." Does my voice even sound normal right now? I'm going to have to get a handle on how I behave around this guy, or who knows what he's going to think of me. Probably not what I'd like him to think of me, that's for sure.

Dan smiles. "Is that how you guys are friends? Like how you met?"

"It's not how we met, but the convenience probably made it easier for us to stay friends." It was definitely easier having him around the corner than four hours away, that's for sure.

We walk in silence for a while and I notice Dan watching the steady rhythm of my crutches and steps.

"You can talk about it," I say, my voice quiet.

"Oh," is all he says in response.

"I mean, I don't know how much Johnnie's said already, but I'm pretty used to talking about it." I didn't mean to sound that bitter about it. "Everyone always has questions."

Dan shrugs. "I don't."

I look at him, disbelieving.

"Okay, I have a lot of questions, but I'm not going to ask them. If you want to tell me about it, that's fine. If you don't want to, then it's none of my business."

"Oh, well … thanks," I say. His response is refreshing. I'm so used to people asking extremely inappropriate questions in the bluntest manner and being offended when I don't want to answer. Once a virtual stranger asked if I'd still be able to have kids one day. I managed to bite my tongue and not retort that it was unlikely but that it had far more to do with my total lack of interest in having sex with a girl than my injury.

I angle away from the footpath we've been making our way along, heading across the grass verge and up my driveway.

I pause for a moment and take in the house, wondering what someone like Dan thinks of it. Then I shrug off the thoughts, because when it all comes down to it, it doesn't really matter what Dan thinks of anything to do with my life.

I head for the garage attached to the side of the house, unlock the side door and swing it open, inviting Dan into my bedroom.

CHAPTER 3

Dan

LUKE STEPS ASIDE and waves for me to enter his garage.

It's not where I expected him to take me, but since I barely know him at all, maybe this is exactly the sort of place he'd take me. Maybe he doesn't want to go through the drama of me meeting his family, so he's sneaking me in the back.

I stare at him for a long moment, wondering how the heck I ended up here, standing outside this boy's house with my heart racing a billion times its normal speed.

When Hollie, Jonathan and I planned this trip, I knew I'd see him. Half the reason we came was to see Luke. Well, for Jonathan to see Luke.

I haven't yet mentioned that I also wanted to see him, so I can figure out if the way he set my blood on fire with one touch the first time we met was a blip, or if it's an actual thing.

When I turned around in Jonathan's driveway and laid eyes on Luke for the first time today, I knew for sure.

It's a thing. Definitely not a blip.

One look, and the hugest crush I've had in my life was confirmed.

Now he's standing here in front of me, waiting for me to step into his garage. I take in his grey eyes and dark hair, the way his hands grip the handles of his crutches. He's chewing on his bottom lip, looking decidedly nervous, like what's inside the garage is of significance.

So, I step forward, through the door – and realise it's not a garage at all anymore.

The room is lined with white painted plywood and there are pictures and posters stuck everywhere. Posters of mountain bikers and a wall full of photos, like my own one at home. There's a shelf running along one wall laden with trophies and medals, which at a brief glance look like mountain bike awards.

There's a double or queen-sized bed against one wall, a green duvet thrown messily across it. A TV is mounted on the wall with an Xbox below it. A laptop and a stack of books sit beside the bed. A really big stack of books.

Something in the corner catches my eye. There's something back there, hidden under a sheet. I study it covertly, trying to figure out what it could be.

Luke hovers awkwardly in the middle of the room.

"This is awesome," I say, turning to him, trying to ease the tension away.

"Ah yeah, I suppose. I had to move in here because I can't handle the stairs up to my old room. Jonathan's sister did most of the decorating." He winces a bit. "I wouldn't have bothered with most of it."

I don't say anything. I mean, what is there to say in response to that?

He sounds so resigned; not exactly bitter, but he's definitely not ecstatic about his current residence.

The desire to say the right thing in this moment, to make him feel okay about what he's been through, overwhelms me. I *need* to make him feel better.

I'm normally so much more in control of my words. I always know what to say in the face of pain or discontent. But not with Luke. With Luke I feel like a fumbling mess, like whatever I say is going to be wrong.

I'm not sure I've ever felt like this before.

I study some of the photos on the wall. The vast majority are of Luke and Jonathan. Sometimes Jonathan's sister, Kristen, sometimes other friends.

My attention is caught by another picture near the top corner of the collage. It's Luke, and the biggest grin I've ever seen is spread across his face. I've never seen him remotely close to grinning, let alone like that. I've barely even seen the guy smile. The photo reminds me of why I love photographing people so much. It's in moments like this, when joy is so enormous. Those moments should be captured.

In the picture he's sitting behind a brilliant blue drum set, and it hits me.

"Those are drums?" I spin around, pointing to the bulky shape in the corner.

"Uh, yeah."

"God, that's even more cool," I exclaim and head for the corner. "Can I look?"

"Um, sure," he says, and I hear his crutches making their way across the room. I fling the sheet back, and there they are. Gleaming and enticing. I've always loved the idea of playing drums.

"Can you play something for me?"

I glance up at him and freeze. He's staring down at those drums with a look that I can't decipher. It's not a good one, anyway. Most definitely bad. I've screwed up.

"I'm sorry," I say, trying to reach the sheet to cover up the set again. "I shouldn't have just barged into your life like this."

I don't know what's wrong with me. Like, aside from being excessively nervous. It's not every day I get to spend time with a boy with the prettiest eyes I've ever seen. A boy who made me realise that liking boys was an option for me.

Luke exhales this long slow breath and reaches up with a crutch to stop my grasping hand, fumbling with the edge of the fabric. I freeze again, the cool metal of his crutch against my skin, then after a moment let my hand drop to my side.

"I don't play anymore," he says quietly. "I..." he pauses and takes another shaky breath. "I can't."

"Oh," I murmur, again unsure what to say. Hollie would be gobsmacked. Me, speechless. She thinks that's an impossibility. And usually she's right. But with Luke all I seem to be doing is putting my foot in my mouth, so maybe I should stop opening it.

"I don't have enough control of my legs. I tell them to move and there's always this delay. I wouldn't be able to hold a beat anymore."

He glances up at me. A piece of hair has fallen over his eyes and it makes him look shy and adorable. And always gorgeous. My breath catches as those grey eyes lock on mine. "But you can have a go."

"Oh, no. No, it's all right," I stammer. "I don't play. I've just always wanted to be able to."

"Well, go for it." He indicates with his head towards the stool where a set of drumsticks lies.

"I'd murder them. I have no idea what I'm doing."

"Drag that chair over." He nods towards a chair in the corner. "Chuck the stuff on my bed."

I hesitate, wondering if he's putting himself in a painful situation only because I have all the subtlety of a monster truck. But when Luke gives me a nod, calm and sure, I grab the pile of clothes and toss it on the bed. I pull the chair over and put it behind the drums, next to the stool. He lowers himself into the chair and nods for me to sit on the stool.

Then he starts giving me a lesson.

He explains the names of the drums, the sounds they make, the best way to use them. He taps the drum sticks lightly against each drum as he speaks and I watch his hands, gently grasping the sticks.

There's a light in his eyes I haven't seen before and I realise this is something he truly loved. Loves, I suppose. That doesn't go away because you've had the ability to do it ripped away from you.

He holds the drumsticks out to me and I carefully take them.

I grip them, gazing down at the drum set before me, hyper aware of Luke's presence beside me.

I tap lightly at a drum, a gentle *tsk*. I press on the foot pedal and a thump reverberates around the room.

"Like this," Luke says, leaning closer. He wraps his hands around my wrists, sliding his fingertips along the inside. My heart thumps and I hope he can't feel my erratic pulse. His fingers hold mine and gently pry my grip away from the sticks. "Hold them softly." His voice is low and close beside me and I feel the brush of his breath. A shiver goes through me. His body is so close.

All this is … new. Different.

I used to get a fluttery stomach when I was around Hollie when I first got to know her, especially when I'd catch her eye, or I'd make her laugh, or best of all, when I made her blush. That feeling is gone now, faded into friendship, especially since she fell for Jonathan, but Luke being near me might actually be making my vision blurry. I can't breathe properly.

Holy crap he smells so good, like coffee and chocolate. Thank God he doesn't reek of cheap body spray like most teenage guys I know.

He's so big, and solid, not dainty like Hollie or Rebekah, the only person I've actually had a romantic relationship with. If you can call two fourteen-year-olds hanging out and holding hands a romantic relationship.

I've had crushes on other girls too, got giddy when they were around, tried to make our paths cross like it was some natural thing. I've never had those feelings about a guy before.

Not until Luke climbed out of that car at Jonathan's place and tripped.

In the moment I wasn't thinking about how good-looking he was; I was worried about him falling on his face and somehow I managed to catch him. How I actually did that is still a mystery to me, but I'm grateful for that moment of coordination and athleticism.

That first touch was electric, and when I looked up into his eyes to check he was okay, my heart started skipping beats all over the place.

I'd never considered being attracted to a guy, but Luke changed everything and I've spent too many nights lying awake thinking about it. About him. Even though I barely have any idea what my own preferences are, let alone his.

Luke finally releases his grip on me, his thumb trailing back up my wrist as he does so, and looks at me expectantly. "Now," he says, the corner of his mouth tilting upwards while I try very hard not to stare. "Play."

"Play?" I choke out. "What do I play?"

He shrugs stiffly. Not because he's feeling awkward – I don't think so anyway, god I hope I don't make him feel awkward – but because his body doesn't move easily anymore.

"Just bash at them until you get a feel for it."

"Really? Just bash them?"

He grins and nods, and after a gentle tap or two, the drumsticks looser in my hands, the ghost of Luke's touch still on them, I let rip.

CHAPTER 4

Luke

I DON'T KNOW what I'm doing, or who I even am.

I don't know how I ended up here with this boy in my room.

For a long time now I've not known who I am. I guess it happens a lot when you wake up one day in hospital with an injury you're not sure you'll ever recover from, especially when the two things you used to define yourself by are no longer possible.

And that's on top of the loss of your best friend.

But sitting here, on my bed, staring at this almost stranger absolutely thrashing my most prized possession, his face lit up like a beacon of joy, I wonder about everything in my life that has led me to this point.

Dan is the kind of guy I've always envied. He's like Jonathan. He's so carefree, confident, easy-going. While I was constantly training, pushing my body to the limits on mountain bike trails and in the gym, he was having fun, and now that I don't have the training part anymore I don't know how to do the fun part.

At least, that's how I described Jonathan before the accident that changed everything, in my life and in our friendship.

After the accident he turned into a bit of an idiot, trying to blame himself for the entire thing, when really I'd been drunk and confused and he'd been trying to help me. The guilt of the accident broke him down, but it seems like he's on the right track again. I hope so.

I'm still coming to terms with his admission that he believed the whole thing was his fault. That it was the reason he cut off contact, left town and moved to his aunt's horse farm. I thought he'd cut me off because he'd caught me making out with a guy. I should have trusted my best friend more.

I'm also still coming to terms with the idea of Jonathan living and working on a horse farm. I wouldn't believe it if I hadn't seen it with my own two eyes.

But, in moving there he met Hollie, who's helped him come back to himself a little. And her best friend is Dan.

Who is currently in the process of getting a noise complaint filed by the neighbours.

I watch him and munch on another square of dark chocolate. It's the only thing that keeps the nausea at bay from the pharmacy of painkillers and other medications I've been taking for the past four months.

I'm lying on my bed, which with him in the room is so awkward. It looks like I'm trying to be alluring and seductive or something. Which I'm really not. It's just the most comfortable place for me the vast majority of the time.

I used to worry that I didn't know if I was straight or gay or something else, and now with Dan thrashing my drums, occasionally breaking concentration to beam across the room at me from under his dark blonde curls, I have all the evidence I'll ever need.

I am most definitely not straight, because he is beautiful.

And when I touched him … I'm dizzy simply thinking about it.

With that realisation – the crystal-clear certainty of my crush on Dan, the one I can't deny anymore now that he's sitting right in front of me – comes the question of what the heck I'm going to do about it, if anything.

Having a crush on him is one thing, but acting on it, spending more time with him, trying to find out if he's interested in me in the same way – that's something else entirely.

With everything that's happened in the last few months, I really don't think a long distance "thing" with anyone is a good idea. I've got going back to school to contend with next week. That development is going to take everything out of me.

The drums silence abruptly, and it drags me from my thoughts. Dan is fishing his phone out of his pocket. He checks the screen then grins up at me.

"Hollie assures me it's safe to return," he says.

I laugh, but it feels hollow. I don't want this moment to end. I'd like to stay here in this little suspended reality, thanks.

Dan stands, picks up the sheet and flings it back over the drum set. He drags the chair back to where it was and leans on it, crossing his arms over the high back. He looks like he's thinking hard about something.

"This whole trip," he starts, studying the ceiling carefully, "it's kind of a fine balancing act."

I'm not exactly sure what he means, or where he's going with this, so I lean back into my pillows and say nothing.

He continues. "I want to make sure Jonathan gets what he needs out of it. Enough time with his parents, with you." His eyes finally meet mine as he sucks in a deep breath. "But, I could try to rearrange some things so we can hang out again…"

My own breath catches as I realise what he's getting at. He's asking to spend more time with me.

"That is, only if you want to," he says in a rush before I have a chance to answer.

I push myself upright and climb off the bed. It's agonisingly slow especially with him watching, but eventually I'm standing in front of him.

I clear my throat because for some reason it won't work. "Yeah, I want to," I say, and hope he can't hear the nervous waver in my voice. "I don't know how it'll work, though."

He's only here for two full days. I'm spending most of tomorrow with Jonathan while Dan and Hollie do … something, though I have no idea what. All four of us are hanging out tomorrow night. The following day is filled with a bunch of rehab and specialist appointments I couldn't reschedule when I heard about Jonathan's visit, and there is absolutely no way I'm inviting him to come to those with me. He leaves the following morning.

The biggest obstacle to seeing Dan again is that I don't want anyone to know how much I want this. How much I want to see him – alone.

It's a dumb thing to think, but it's where my mind goes.

I'm not ready to face the fallout from this thing that I know can never go anywhere, so I can't simply tell Jonathan and Hollie I'd rather hang out with Dan.

He smiles at me now, that full wattage beam. "Don't worry about it. I'll figure something out." He walks to the door and grins over his shoulder as he pulls it open. "This was fun. Thanks."

And before I have a chance to do more than nod, he's disappeared, leaving the door to swing shut behind him.

CHAPTER 5

Dan

I CANNOT STOP TOUCHING the place on my wrist where Luke's fingers rested. I can't do it. I tried. I failed.

It's been forty-eight hours since it happened and still, it's all I can think about. That, and the way Luke lay there and watched me attempt to play drums while he ate square after square of chocolate. He sat on the chair next to me for a few minutes, then moved to his bed, where he sprawled against the ginormous stack of pillows and watched.

I saw him yesterday, when we all had dinner together at a little Italian restaurant, then played more PlayStation in Jonathan's downstairs rumpus room.

I'm probably being paranoid, but I'm pretty sure Luke spent the entire time avoiding being anywhere close to me. He seemed distracted and almost nervous, and while the hopeful part of me wants to think he's nervous around me because he might like me back, the realistic part keeps denying those thoughts.

It's more likely I was too forward and now he doesn't know

how to tell me to piss off without causing conflict with Hollie and Jonathan.

But still, when I casually asked him what he was doing this afternoon he didn't say he was too busy to hang out.

So here I am, about to see Luke again.

I'm picking him up, we're grabbing dinner somewhere and hanging out for a while. In my head I know it's not a date. But it feels like one. It feels like my one chance to impress him, even though I have no idea what it would mean if I managed it.

I stand in Jonathan's bathroom, staring at my reflection. What is going on with my hair? Maybe I should borrow Hollie's straighteners.

I take a deep breath, bracing my hands against the sink. Hair straighteners are taking it too far. I've never straightened my hair; why the hell would I do it now? I fiddle with it some more, but it's really as good as it's going to get.

I study my wrist again, brushing my fingers over the place I can feel Luke's touch branded into my skin.

I knew the moment I laid eyes on him that he was something special. I can't explain how or why I knew that, but I did. I do. He's something else. Seeing him again has confirmed it as fact.

I need to get a grip or I'm never going to be able to leave the house tonight.

I manage to drag myself away from the mirror and head back to the room Hollie's staying in. She gets the honour of the guest room. I get Jonathan's bedroom floor. It's kind of ironic how all the parents in this situation are playing into archaic gender roles. Considering how desperate I am right now to touch another boy.

I open my mouth to say something witty (which will actually probably be utterly ridiculous) as I cross the threshold into the room, but catch myself just in time.

Jonathan is helping Hollie with the clasp thing on the back of her dress. It's a job I've been required to do a number of times in the past, but it's never been this intimate when it was me, which is probably a good thing.

Jonathan finishes doing up the dress then traces his finger along her skin, right at the edge of the strap, as he reaches up to slide a loose lock of hair into place. He presses a kiss to the side of her head, and something twists inside me.

I'm overcome with a blinding flash of envy.

That was … unexpected.

I'm not bitter about Hollie finding someone, especially someone who makes her as happy as Jonathan does, or someone who understands her and supports her in all the right ways, despite his own struggles. But for a second I'm so jealous of everyone in the world who has someone loving them.

Hollie turns and catches sight of me, standing there awkwardly in the doorway.

"You two are so cute it's sickening," I say, trying to snap out of whatever dramatic moment I'm having.

"I know," Hollie says with a grin. "We're revolting." It's so good to see her happy.

Jonathan grins down at her, tucking her into his side as she leans towards him.

"You look rather nice," Hollie says, fighting a smile. Does she know? That I'm completely obsessed with her boyfriend's best friend? How would she? I'm sure I'm more subtle than that. God, I really hope I'm more subtle than that.

I catch myself, stop the thoughts and force out a grin.

"What? Uh, not really," I mutter. "I'm heading out now. I'll catch you guys later."

CHAPTER 6
Dan

LUKE DIRECTS me through the city. I try very hard to concentrate on not crashing my parent's ridiculously fancy car and not the way Luke's hand rests against the denim of his jeans.

Because jeans make me think of legs and other things that are generally kept in jeans, and I neglect to check my blind spot as I merge or completely forget give way rules.

I pulled into Luke's driveway to find him already waiting for me, leaning against the exterior wall of his garage room wearing the world's greatest jeans, a blue t-shirt with an adventure sports logo on it and a grey hoodie hanging over his crutches.

The sight of him made my breath catch, and I spent the time it took for Luke to walk to the car and climb inside taking several long, slow breaths.

It was all for nothing though, because as soon as he was sitting beside me I was struck by the scent of him – coffee and chocolate – and when he settled himself and his crutches he turned to smile at me. My heart nearly gave up entirely.

This crush I have is all-consuming. It's almost too much.

I take some more deep breaths now and steady my hands on the steering wheel.

I don't know where we're going, but glimpses of ocean become more and more frequent, and I can't help but get excited. I love the ocean but living in a land-locked rural town I don't get to see it nearly enough.

I park the car, grateful there's plenty of empty spaces because city parks are *small* and parking too close to other vehicles makes me stress an excessive amount.

I meet Luke at the passenger side door before he has a chance to climb out.

"It's okay," he says, "I've managed to improve my vehicle exiting since we met."

I laugh, then realise it might not have been a joke. Whyyy am I no good at talking to him? Why do I never have the right thing to say? I can talk fine to everyone else, even about horrible, sad things, but with Luke I turn into a fool.

I shove the thoughts away – one of my greatest talents: smothering the emotions with a smile – and head for the beach. I'm so excited, even the smell of the ocean has me happy.

I stop abruptly as the beach comes into view.

"Well, this is different," I say, more than a little disappointed.

Luke arrives at my side. "It's a city beach, man, what were you expecting? They're all better down your way."

"Yeah," I say, studying the strip of white, almost grey sand dotted with the occasional person and the gloomy looking water as it gently brushes the shore. No waves here. No crashing *boom* as they break and tumble up the sand. Only a couple of sad-looking seagulls.

"I mostly brought you here for the food," Luke says, indicating a building set back a little way from the beach. We wander towards it, because every walk with Luke is a wander, or an amble. Not that I mind, because it's more time at his side. It's almost a relief to be forced to slow down.

We order insanely huge, delicious looking burgers, fries and milkshakes to take away, then head for a seat outside to wait for our food.

"Luke!" A girl's voice calls across the grass and a blur of red and blue comes hurtling towards us. Luke winces, sighs and turns towards her. She reaches us and immediately leans into Luke, wrapping her arms around him. She's wearing a turquoise bikini with a denim skirt and her red hair is pulled up high on her head. She looks gorgeous and she knows it.

"Hey, Stacey," he says. A couple of other people have followed Stacey over and he greets them too. "This is Dan," he says, indicating me. I give them a little wave. I try to enable the "comfortable around people" part of my persona, which in Luke's presence is apparently faulty.

They make small talk for a minute or two with Stacey fussing over Luke, asking him every question under the sun, including demanding to know why he hasn't been hanging around with them lately. I can feel anger building in me. Anger on Luke's behalf. Because it's up to him what he wants to do and this girl is being super pushy.

I realise I might be angry because there's a chance she's flirting with him.

Maybe my feelings towards this girl are completely misplaced and she's simply trying to be a good friend to Luke. I shouldn't jump to conclusions about her just because she's gorgeous and confident and friends with Luke.

Our order number is called and I gesture for Luke to stay where he is while I go to collect our food. Stacey's moved onto quizzing him about when he's going back to school. By the time I get back she'll probably be asking him what kind of underwear he prefers. And just like that, I'm thinking about Luke's pants again.

He's standing when I return, though, and Stacey is urging him to head down onto the sand to eat with them. I try to steady my breath and calm down. I'd love to spit out some snappy line that will mean I get Luke all to myself, but it's really his choice. Who am I to stop him hanging out with his actual friends?

"Not today, Stace," he says. "Sorry. I've got something to show Dan. But I'll see you soon. I promise."

He watches as she and a tall blond guy make their way across the grass and jump down the bank to the beach where there's a collection of towels laid out.

Wordlessly, he turns, tilts his head and heads for the car. He's setting quite a pace on those crutches and I walk beside him, also silent. We've almost reached the car when I blurt out, "You can stay and hang out with them if you want. I don't mind."

Luke turns to me. "I thought I might show you a better beach," he says, gaze flicking back to his friends.

"But if you want to stay here, it's okay. I promise," I say. "They're your friends. You should hang out with them." I don't want to be saying the words. I want to keep Luke all to myself. But he doesn't need that, and I'm always going to put what he needs first.

He reaches out and grasps my wrist, covering the place he dragged his thumb across two days ago. He holds tight, leans towards me and holds a serious amount of eye contact. "I don't want to hang out with *them*," he says, voice low and serious. "I want to hang out with *you*." He finishes speaking but maintains the eye contact and the firm grasp on my wrist.

I have this extreme urge to say something flippant, to crack a joke and bounce away from him. But I don't. I swallow the urge and clear my throat.

"Okay," I whisper.

He grins, a full, wide smile. It's to die for. "Let's go find a real beach, then."

He's got his wicked smile and a flash of adventure in his eyes and I wonder if this is who Luke really is, behind the crutches and pain and injury.

I really hope I get the chance to find out.

CHAPTER 7
Luke

DAN DRIVES. And drives. This is a stupid idea. But he was so visibly disappointed with that crap beach I took him to. And fair enough. It was rubbish. Especially with my friends there.

I don't even know at this point if I can still call them my friends. I've not been a very good one over the past few months. There's a small group, Stacey and Tyler included, who do keep me in the loop, though. They always invite me to hang out. They just don't always understand the logistics. I took one look at the group sitting on the ground and knew I couldn't stay there. It's not that I can't sit on the ground, but it's always uncomfortable and getting up and down is an exercise in itself.

Plus, I didn't want to waste the small amount of time I get with Dan around other people.

"It's a bit of a way," I say. "Sorry, I didn't really think it through."

"It's all good," Dan says, tossing a hot chip into his mouth. "Driving these roads is much nicer than in the city, and Mum gave me her card for fuel expenses, since the main reason for this trip is to pick up stuff for her." He pauses, eats another chip. "Plus, I miss driving people around now Hollie and Jonathan usually go everywhere together." He flashes that grin at me.

"It's so weird," I say. "Johnnie, I mean. Seeing him with a girlfriend. It's … different."

Dan huffs a laugh. "It's the same for me with Hollie. And you don't even have to see them together *all the time*." He pauses. "I'm very happy for them. Hopefully that much is obvious. They're so perfect together, it's sickening. Despite everything they went through they're so damn happy, and it kind of makes me want to throw things." He glances my way, his grin turned sheepish. "I hope that doesn't sound awful."

I laugh and shake my head. Laughing. I haven't done much of that lately. "I know what you mean. Sometimes I wonder how you're ever supposed to find someone, and when you do, how do you know that they're the right one?"

Dan smiles a little wistfully as he focuses on the road, a series of sweeping bends that mean we've nearly arrived. "Hollie said she just knew with Jonathan that he would be special somehow. She found being around him was easy. Well, not always easy, like when she tried to run him over, or one of the times—" He cuts off and I'm not sure if I want to know what he was going to say. He chews his lip.

"She tried to run him over?" I say, in an attempt to smooth the awkward moment.

Dan smiles again, a full-on grin, and I release a breath in relief.

"Yep," he says. "It was the first time they met. She was running late and he walked out in front of her in the school carpark. She didn't hit him or anything, but he did fall over."

I snort a laugh and Dan joins in. "They talk about it fondly now," he says.

We round the final bend and the coast opens up before us. We're high up in the hills so we get a bird's eye view of the crashing waves sweeping into shore, the rugged rocks jutting out at each end of the tousled sand. Dan pulls into a lookout area without me even suggesting it. He puts the car in park and leans forward over the steering wheel, resting his arms across it, taking in the sight.

I try not to take in too much of the sight of him, the way the muscles of his arms flex as he moves. Or at least, I try to do it covertly. All I can think about is the way I touched his arms the other day, and the back of my neck flares with heat.

He turns to me, and of course catches me watching him. "Now this is more like it," he grins. "I can hear the waves from here." He swings his door wide and climbs out. Before I've even grabbed my crutches he's at my door, pulling it open and helping me out. His smile is wide and infectious, and I grin back at him. I'm out of the car faster than I have been since the accident happened, and it's because of Dan's help, but it doesn't really *feel* like Dan's doing much. He is, but for once I don't feel like I'm a burden.

It's been a problem since the accident, my constant reliance on other people to help me with simple things. People either expect me to be the same person I was before, or completely incapable of doing anything and they vastly overcompensate, but with Dan it doesn't feel like that. He doesn't look at me with pity, or regret for the things I've lost. To him, I've always been this way. He makes allowances for me without ever making me feel like that's what he's doing.

Dan rushes ahead of me and climbs onto the railing fence

separating the lookout parking lot from the farmland that's between us and the actual beach. He opens his arms to the wind and whoops into nothingness. He suits this place – the wild freedom, the ruggedness, the chaos and the power.

He turns and sits on the railings, facing me, as I slowly make my way over to him.

"You're missing the whole point of the lookout," I say. "The great view is that way." I indicate the coast with a wave of one crutch. It's an interesting way to gesture but I've pretty much got the hang of it by now.

"Is it?"

I glance up, right into Dan's face, and catch my breath. He's closer than I realised and he's staring down at me from his seat, where he's perched in a way I'd never be able to manage now. Normally I'd be jealous, a little ball of toxicity boiling in my gut, but not with the way he's looking at me.

Looking at me like *I'm* the great view.

I lean against the railing, right next to him. Sitting on the fence has him a head taller than me, which is kind of nice, because I'm usually the tallest one in the room.

I try to take in the view. It's one of my favourites, and I haven't been here since before the accident. I used to be out this way all the time because the mountain bike trails I rode the most are a few minutes further up the coast. The thought of those trails, my bike, the things I used to be able to do, rushes towards me. I push it away. That was then and this is now. There's no point in dwelling on what was.

I refocus on the view, the way the sea wind is blowing through my hair, but it can't hold my attention. I can feel Dan's eyes on me and they're pulling my gaze up to meet his.

He stares at me for a moment – the barest moment – then

leans down and brushes his lips against mine. He pulls back briefly, giving me a chance to object, but I'm frozen. Dan takes a breath, and when I still don't move, he presses our mouths firmly together.

It's all over in a second, but it's the greatest second of my life.

CHAPTER 8

Dan

A SECOND PASSES, two, then I pull my lips away from Luke's soft, soft mouth and turn to look out over the view again.

I grip the railing, trying to quell the shaking in my hands as I give Luke time to process me throwing myself at him.

God, that might have been the stupidest thing I've ever done. But I can't bring myself to regret it. Not yet.

I count my breaths, the number creeping higher and higher before I finally break and glance down to where Luke is standing beside me. There's the tiniest smile playing across his lips. At the sight of it my lungs expel all the air in them at once.

I feel winded, like I can't draw breath again. I'm so utterly awash with relief.

At my dramatic expulsion of breath, I feel the slightest brush against my knuckles and glance down again, ready to brush some kind of insect off my hand where it's still clenched around the railings.

But it's not a random creepy crawly.

It's Luke, trailing the tip of his pinky finger across my skin.

"You should eat," he says, his voice deliciously low and raspy. "I'm sorry I made you drive so far before you could. I didn't think about how long it would take to get here."

"It's okay," I say, twisting my hand to trap his finger under mine and giving a light squeeze. "The wait was worth it." I want to capture the look on his face in a photograph. His soft smile, the brightness in his eyes, the way his face changes ever so slightly when his gaze lands on me.

So, I finish eating my dinner sitting on the railing at the lookout.

Waiting really was worth it.

Every bite, every time food touches my lips, it reminds me of that kiss. When I finish eating we head back to the car, not speaking but in comfortable silence. He climbs in slowly as I stash his crutches beside him, then drive down the twisting road to the actual beach.

It's wild and rugged out here, surf crashing loudly and rolling up the sand and the wind charging along the length of the exposed coastline. It thrums in my bones. I taste the salt in the air and feel the vibrations of the tumbling surf through the soles of my feet.

Out of the car again, Luke stands at the edge of the dunes we have to cross to get to the ocean. He studies them, a crease between his brows, and I'm about to suggest we head back rather than make him say it, when he opens his mouth. "You coming?" Then, one foot in front of the other, with his crutches sinking into the soft sand, he starts towards the sea.

Luke makes it. It's a slow trek and he looks tired by the time we arrive at the edge of the waves. He stumbled twice but reached out for me, and we managed to keep him on his feet. I'm worried how much he'll hurt later – or perhaps he's hurting now and won't admit it. But maybe it'll be worth it, judging by the blissed-out expression on his face.

I kick my shoes off and follow him as he sets off down the beach towards a huge driftwood log. The sand, sea, salt and wind graze across my skin, across my senses, and I realise this is how Hollie feels when she's on horseback. It doesn't matter what else is going on, how muddled my mind feels, a wild beach always brings me back to what's really important.

I climb onto the log, perching next to Luke as he balances himself carefully. He kicks his shoes off too and slides his bare feet through the sand. He tips his head back and sighs. "I've missed sand," he says quietly. There's a long pause, because I have absolutely no response to that. "Thanks for bringing me here," he says to me.

He reaches out and slides his hand along mine, pressing our palms together and interlacing his fingers with mine.

We're holding hands. He gives me a tentative smile, and I send him one right back.

"It was you who brought me here," I say, trying to keep the mood light, trying to stop the emotions roiling around inside me from spilling over. "I was just the driver."

He smiles again. "Regardless, thank you. It's been so long since I've been here."

"Did you come here a lot?" I ask, desperate to know another tiny kernel of information about him. "Or beaches in general?"

"I came here a bit," he says, turning away from me and staring out at the waves. "There's a…" His words trail off, but I don't say anything, waiting for him to find the right words or the courage to say whatever it is he needs to say. "There's a mountain bike park near here," he says at last in a heavy exhalation. "I rode there at least a couple of times a week, more if I could. I'd come here afterwards, for a swim if it was hot, or to walk on the beach. Sometimes I was with Johnnie, a lot of times by myself. It was my place to chill out, especially if the ride was intense and the adrenaline was still kicking." He stops talking and looks over at me, ducking his head with something like embarrassment. "Sorry, didn't realise all that was coming out," he says a little sheepishly.

I shake my head. "Don't apologise." I try to figure out how to best phrase my next question, without it sounding pitying or condescending or plain rude. "Do you have anything to do with mountain biking now? Like, do you even talk about it with anyone?" I tack on the last question as I see him tensing, preparing to respond to the first part of the question.

It's obvious he can't ride at the moment, and I don't know if that's going to be a forever thing. I'm assuming that even if he can get on a bike again someday, it's likely he won't be able to ride like he did. I don't know a lot about mountain biking. I'm not even sure my family owns a bike. But I do know, based on things Jonathan has said and on the trophies lining the shelves of his bedroom, that he was really, really good at it.

I've seen Hollie struggle with a broken leg after a car accident a few weeks ago, and she's going to fully recover from her injury. I can't comprehend what it must be like facing such a life-changing one. But I also don't want to press him for information he isn't ready to give me, and I don't want to be rude or careless about it either.

Luke's low voice pulls me back to our conversation. "No," he says. "I suppose I don't really talk about it with anyone. All my friends ... they don't understand. They don't understand that I'm not the same person I was, that I physically can't be, that I can't sit with them on the beach and have a picnic, because sitting on the ground is too hard. They either don't realise I can't do something and behave like I should be able to, or they treat me like I'm a total invalid who can't do anything for myself." He takes a deep breath. "Most of my friends from school or anywhere else were a different crowd to the mountain bike lot anyway. Johnnie was really the only one who'd ever get on a bike and come with me, and while I appreciated that, he didn't want to compete like I did. So, the biking friends were different, and when I had the accident I dropped off their radars pretty quickly." Another breath whooshes out of him. "I'm not upset by it. I wasn't really close with any of them. I had a few messages or calls from some of them, but I wasn't great at replying and they carried on with their lives."

I squeeze his hand and shift slightly closer, so our shoulders brush. His heat brands along the side of my arm. "Please tell me if I'm ever being ignorant or overbearing," I say. "I can be both, but never intentionally, and I *really* don't want to be either with you." My voice is low and breathy and sounds so odd for a moment I wonder if it's even me speaking.

He leans into my shoulder, tightening his grip on my fingers. "So far you've been perfect," he says.

We sit there holding hands, shoulders brushing, until the sun dips below the horizon and dusk is upon us. We've barely talked. I know so little about him except for how his warm palm feels against mine.

As the darkness steals over us, Luke exhales heavily then whispers into the dusk. "Did Johnnie tell you about me?" He tilts his head, pressing his face into my shoulder, like he can't bear for me to see him.

"Did he tell me what?" I whisper back.

He takes a shuddering breath and I hold his hand tighter, pulling it into my lap so I can trace his knuckles with my free hand.

"That I'm gay."

Oh.

"No. He didn't tell me. He wouldn't do that."

Luke sighs again and I lean back so I can look at him better. He lifts his chin at my movement and meets my gaze.

"You know he wouldn't do that, right?"

"Yeah, I do know that." He shakes his head, like he's dislodging a thought. "How'd you know then?"

I shrug. "It was more like a hopeful hypothesis than actually knowing." I laugh then, when Luke gapes at me like I've lost my mind. Which I have, I guess.

"I had no idea about you," he says. "I was hopeful, but there was no hypothesis. I can't believe you just went for it."

My insides fizz at his words. He was hopeful. "Honestly, I had no idea about me either," I say with a laugh. "Not until I met you."

He almost chokes on his breath but doesn't reply. He rests his head against my shoulder and we spend several long moments watching the moonlit waves roll in.

Eventually Luke sighs and pushes off the log, his hand slipping from mine. I'm reluctant to let it go, but he can't hold my hand and operate crutches at the same time. My body feels his absence keenly, like a little piece of me has been taken with him.

We make it back to the car unscathed, and as we pull back onto the road Luke slips his hand back into mine, resting them entwined between our seats. He may have taken a little piece of me, but he's given me a little piece of him, too.

CHAPTER 9

Luke

AS DAN SHUTS my bedroom door I'm trying to calculate how much time we have before Jonathan and Hollie are finished at the fundraiser they went to tonight.

Dan and I were mostly quiet on the drive back from the beach, my hand in his. Most of our trip was spent in silence actually, aside from my emotional dump about riding.

I spent the whole time we were together running through potential conversations in my head, but was incapable of putting any of them into actual words. I didn't want to risk ruining the perfect moment of sitting on that beach feeling his fingers wrapped around mine.

I turn back to face Dan. He's staring at me with an intensity that's startling. My stomach turns over.

The flying sensation I felt in the brief seconds he kissed me has faded away now, especially since he hasn't tried to do it again. Maybe it was an experiment. But he held my hand, on the beach and in the car.

My breath is caught in my throat and my heart is pounding. I want to lose myself in him, but I don't know where we stand. I don't know what any of this means. I barely remember my one interaction with a guy; I was drunk and I suffered a head injury immediately afterwards.

All I know now is that this is likely my last chance to ever kiss Dan again. I'm not ready for that chance to slip away from me.

So, I meet his intense gaze and step slowly towards him. One step away from him, I drop the crutches and let them clatter to the floor. I wince at the noise and silently hope my parents don't hear and panic, thinking I've fallen.

I take the final step unaided, reaching for his hands. I slide my fingers through his, grasping one hand and letting my other hand slide up his wrist, up his arm. His head tilts up as his gaze follows my hand until he can't see it anymore where I rest it against his neck. He swallows and I feel it.

A warm weight rests on my side and I suck in a breath. His hand. He's put his hand against my waist. The last few moments have played out in slow motion, but that hand on my body snaps me out of it and I close the distant between us, pulling him in.

Our lips meet and the flying sensation sweeps me away again.

The kiss at the beach was quick, simple, sweet.

This is not.

This is open mouths and exploring tongues and heavy breaths.

My previous experience has nothing on this. We'd barely got started before Jonathan literally stumbled in and interrupted us. I'd panicked and there was that long, long flight of stairs I'd fallen down, leaving me broken at the bottom.

The kisses with that guy, they weren't like kissing Dan. All of my senses have narrowed in on him. Panic rushes through me at regular intervals. Panic that this is a terrible, disastrous idea that's going to ruin me in more ways than one.

But those panicky feelings – the racing heart, the stuttering breath, the feeling that I'm going to explode or crumble or melt or do all three at exactly the same time – could be because I'm standing in my bedroom kissing a heart-stompingly gorgeous boy.

I break the kiss, breathing heavily, my fingers tangled in the golden curls at the back of his head, my other hand still entwined with his, and tug him with me as I take a step backwards, then another.

His stare is heavy on me and I almost stumble, but this time it's nothing to do with my injury.

Dan flicks his gaze over my shoulder, then back to my face. I tug at his hand again. His gaze travels over my shoulder again, to my bed, then to my face. My breath catches and he traps his lower lip between his teeth. I might not make it to the bed before I want to kiss him again.

We stop moving when I feel the press of the mattress behind my legs. Dan stretches up and kisses me again. His hand is somehow against my neck, his thumb dragging along my jawline. My knees go weak. He breaks away, thumb still tracing along my skin. Then it brushes against my lips.

As I exhale against his thumb, the haze of desire clears enough for me to realise that while his presence is making my knees weak, it isn't all him. My body is exhausted. I need to sit.

I sink onto the mattress, pulling away from him.

"Sorry," I whisper. "Too much standing."

I expect him to be disappointed, to move away, go back to the drum set he was so into last time he was here, to pull his phone out and text Hollie. What I don't expect is for the mattress to dip under his weight as he lowers himself gently beside me.

He's left a tiny space between us, giving me that little bit of room if I need it.

I've never hated one inch of space so much in my life.

"You never have to apologise," he whispers into my hair as he presses a kiss against my temple. If I hadn't already been sitting that would have been the fatal blow to my knees. He may as well have taken them out with a baseball bat. Did I just swoon? Is this what it feels like? "What do you want to do?" he asks as he reaches over and tangles our hands again. Who'd have thought holding hands could be such an amazing experience?

I feel the blush hit my cheeks before I even look over at him, before I even say the words. I suck in a deep breath. "I'd really like to kiss you some more." I lift my gaze from where I've been studying the way our hands fit together in time to catch the flash of a grin. A grin I'm already obsessed with.

"Good, because I'd really like to kiss you some more, too." That grin again, then it slips away and his face grows serious. "I'm going to ask you if you're more comfortable lying down, not because I want to get you on your back or anything, but purely because I'd like you to not be in pain." He pauses, tilting his head in thought. "Or in as little pain as possible, I suppose."

I breathe a sigh of relief. This was going to be my next tricky stepping stone. How to explain to him that I really do need to lie down without him thinking I'm trying to lure him into my bed. But once again, Dan has the solution before I've even got to the problem.

"Lying down is best," I say, my voice low and raspy, "but for back-related things. I'm not trying to seduce you under false pretences."

He grins, the full wattage smile that releases his dimples, and again I'm glad I'm sitting down already. "When you do try to seduce me, no false pretences are needed." Then he shifts away and kicks off his shoes and I blush – *hard* – as I move myself up the bed.

Once I'm settled he slides onto the bed beside me, resting on his elbow looking down at me. "You good?" A softer smile this time, gentle, caring. There are a lot of feelings in that smile. Some of my earlier bravery returns. It's a steady confidence that this is right.

I reach up and pull Dan to me, kissing that smile right off his face.

We start slow, soft, easy. But as Dan runs his tongue along my bottom lip, the gentle pace and unspoken lines we've drawn disintegrate. I bury my hand into those glorious curls and pull him to me hard. His leg slips over mine and his weight presses down along my side.

I break the kiss, tearing my mouth of his and gasp. "I – I need…"

Dan pulls back immediately, his weight across my leg lessening as he leans back on an elbow. His hand remains resting on my chest, a heavy reassurance.

"I've not done this before," I say between haggard breaths, my face burning.

"Neither have I," Dan murmurs. "I'm not going to push you, Luke. We can stop this any time you want. And just so you know, for now I'm happy doing exactly what we're doing."

I exhale all the panic – again. Of course he's not going to

push me. With everything I've come to learn about him, I should know this already. He always puts everyone else first. Always.

I nod. "Exactly what we're doing sounds good."

Dan smiles then slides closer, his lips brushing across my cheek and his leg slipping over mine once more.

He's not on top of me – I don't think I could handle having his full weight on me while knowing this is going no further than kissing – but the pressure is pure bliss. My body hasn't felt this good in months. Not since before the accident.

Dan inhales a sharp breath as my hand, which has been roaming down his back, slips under the hem of his t-shirt. Hot skin meets my fingertips, but he doesn't pull away, he doesn't stop kissing me, so I press my palm against him and slide it higher, slide it around to his side to fit perfectly into the space where his waist dips in between his ribs and hip bone. A concave curve that perfectly fits the shape of my hand, like it was made for me. He kisses me harder. My fingers trail across his stomach and I feel his muscles flex as he sucks in a breath.

Dan pulls away, pushing upright, and the absence of heat and weight is startling. He kneels on the bed beside me, his eyes finding mine. He's breathing hard, his eyes and hair chaotic. He holds eye contact and raises the hem of his shirt an inch or so, then stops. My gaze flicks from his face to the strip of exposed skin and back as I nod. He pulls the shirt off and where it goes I have no idea, because he's back against me and now both my hands are running across the bare skin of his back, his chest, his stomach.

His hands run along my neck, down my arms, across the span of my stomach. He slips his hand under the hem of my shirt, the slightest brush of fingertips.

But he knows about the brace; he can't help but have felt it by now. The brace that keeps him from spreading his palm against my skin, that keeps us to only light brushes of skin against skin between the metal components that help keep me upright, that help keep me safe from re-injury.

"I'm—" I start to say as we break our kissing to breathe.

"Don't say you're sorry," he cuts me off, his voice gentle but firm and a little hoarse at the same time. "It's not your fault and I'm happy with whatever you want to give me. Don't be sorry." He rests his head against my shoulder, simultaneously curled into me and sprawled beside me. This moment is perfection.

"What are we even doing?" I whisper, terrified of the realities of this.

"Having fun, enjoying some great kissing," he says, like this is no big deal.

"Well, yeah, obviously." Well, at least I hope it's obviously great kissing. "But we live hours apart; it's not like this can go anywhere."

He shifts back onto his elbow so he's looking down at me again. He gives as much of a shrug as he can in that position. "Things change. There's technology. I have a car." I inhale, ready to cut him off, but he carries on talking, right over my objections. He trails his fingers across my cheek, along my hairline, and nestles them into my hair. "I'm not asking for anything, Luke, but I did mean it when I said I was happy with whatever you can give me. Even if I never see you in real life again, or kiss you again, or whatever – the thought of which makes me quite sad by the way – I'd like to hope that we can be friends." He gives me that little smile again, the gentle one. The one with all the feelings behind it. "But for now, even if it never goes anywhere, I'd really like to keep kissing you."

My head is full of objections about while he might be happy with whatever scraps of myself I can give him now, things change. But I'd really like to keep kissing him too, so I shove those thoughts aside.

We kiss until my face hurts from smiling and thoughts of that conversation are swept from my mind.

We kiss until the doorknob rattles and a fist bangs on the door.

"Luke," Jonathan calls. "Let us in."

Dan jerks away, stumbles backwards off the bed and grabs for his shirt. I hastily pull mine back into position and make a poor attempt at smoothing the duvet as I drag myself to sit with my back against the headboard. Dan pulls on the shirt, glances once at me to make sure I'm ready, and when I give an unsteady nod, unlocks the door.

"Hey," he says, opening the door wide to Hollie and Jonathan. "Sorry, I must have flicked the lock when I shut it before." He fires a smirk over his shoulder at me.

There's a weird feeling in my gut that something is wrong, but I can't quite put my finger on it.

I feel like I should be panicking and stressed and anxious that Jonathan will take one look at me and know *everything*, but somehow, I can't find it in myself to care. Maybe that's what my weird feeling is – that I'm actually relaxed in this situation. That I'm *happy*.

Hollie steps into the doorway ahead of Jonathan and studies Dan for a second before glancing my way. Her eyes trail down Dan again before she steps backwards.

"Oh!" She says, her voice weirdly high. "I think I left my

phone in the car." She spins around and heads right back out the door, grabbing Jonathan's hand. "Come with me to get it." She drags him away as he throws a confused glance back at us, trying to protest before she pulls him back down the driveway.

Dan turns to face me. "What was that about?"

I grin, attempt to hold in my laugh and fail. "Dude, that is *not* your shirt."

He glances down at himself, takes in the huge fluoro-green sports logo on his chest and flashes a sheepish grin at me.

"Ah, oops."

CHAPTER 10

Dan

THERE'S no answer when I knock on Luke's door. I knock again, step back, walk in a little circle. He's not here.

But he told me last night, when Hollie, Jonathan and I finally left his place, that he'd be home all morning.

We all said our goodbyes then, after the four of us had hung out in Luke's room for a couple of hours until Hollie was falling asleep with her head in Jonathan's lap. I spent most of that time sitting behind Luke's drums, needing a physical barrier between us so I didn't try to climb his body again. I know he doesn't want to tell our friends about what happened between us – not yet, anyway – so touching him while they're around is a definite no-no.

I played off me wearing his shirt by telling Hollie I'd spilled food on mine. She seemed to buy it. In fact, it was almost too easy to convince her. I'm not sure if I should be offended that she thinks I'm that messy an eater.

Conveniently, the whole debacle has given me the perfect excuse to come by this morning and return Luke's shirt and have a private goodbye, one that doesn't have our best friends bearing witness. It also gave Hollie and Jonathan time to say goodbye to his family without me lurking in the background.

I stare at the door to Luke's room, willing it to open. He told me he'd be here this morning. Then it hits me that he has more house than what I've seen. Obviously. This boy has scattered my brain so thoroughly, it took me this long to realise he might be home and not in his room. Or he's pretending he isn't here at all because he doesn't want to see me, which is a sobering and depressing thought.

My hands are shaking as I reach up to knock on the front door. It's only a moment before a beautiful woman answers the door. She's got Luke's eyes; the shape, the colour, even the fringe of thick, dark lashes framing them. They're identical. His mum, without a doubt.

"Hi there," she says with a smile, her voice warm.

"Hi," I say, my voice coming out as shaky as my hands. "Is Luke here?"

"He sure is. Come on through." She leads me through the entry hall and takes a sharp turn at the bottom of a staircase into the kitchen. Most of the back wall is windows, letting in the morning sun and looking out onto a flat green lawn bordered by flower gardens.

Luke is in the corner of the room, sitting on the floor, executing some form of exercise that I can only assume is good for his injury. I can't explain what exactly he's doing for two reasons: The first is that I know nothing about any form of exercise, and the second is that Luke is shirtless.

S-h-i-r-t-l-e-s-s.

Not even the brace he's always wearing under his shirt. Only a pair of dark shorts, and there's a sheen of sweat on his brow when he glances up at me, giving a little start of shock.

"Uh, hey," he says.

"Hi." I give a wave like I always seem to be doing these days because I'm some kind of socially inept person. I'm staring and I really need to stop, but also I'm overcome with a desire to press my hand to his chest and feel his heart beating.

"Do you boys need anything?" Luke's mum interrupts the long silence following our greetings and I'm quite tempted to lean over and kiss her. Or at least hug her. Kissing her might be even more awkward considering the kissing I did with her son yesterday.

"No, we're good, Mum, thanks," Luke says, his eyes not leaving me.

"All right, I'll be in my office. Shout if you need me." She picks up a bottle of water and a stack of notebooks and leaves the room, giving me a curious look as she does so. I throw a weak smile in her direction.

"Sorry," Luke says once she's gone. "I'm having a bit of a slow morning." He dips his head a little, tugs at his hair. "I, uh, might have overdone it a bit yesterday." He blushes.

Yesterday. The kissing. Does he regret it?

"Sand is apparently not my friend," he says.

Sand. The beach. Our walk and sitting on the log until the sun set. Not the kissing. He's not saying he overdid the kissing.

"Are you okay?" I ask, and he nods. "I can't stay for long. We're about to head off and I needed to give Jonathan some time with his mum. She was getting a bit emotional, I think."

Luke laughs a little and it's only small, but it lights up the world. Or me, at the very least. The sound of it fizzes through my blood. "Yeah, Kristen said she misses him a lot, though she's happy he's happy…" He trails off, rearranges himself to lean against the wall and stares out the window for a minute. "Is he happy?"

I gesture to the space beside him, and when Luke nods again, I slide down the wall so we're sitting shoulder to shoulder.

"I think so, yeah," I say. "I don't know for sure. We're not at that stage where we talk about all the things, and Hollie isn't going to tell me his secrets. But since he and Hollie sorted themselves out and opened up to each other, he seems way more settled – since whatever happened between you two was resolved, too."

"Do you know what happened? With me and Johnnie, I mean?" he asks, avoiding eye contact and fiddling with what looks like a giant rubber band.

I shake my head, and realise he's still not looking at me. "No, I don't know."

He looks up then, surprise on his face. "I assumed he'd have told you, or told Hollie and she'd have told you."

I shake my head again. "Hollie and I share a lot, almost everything, but only things that are ours. This isn't our business. I'm pretty sure she knows, but she hasn't told me. Your secrets are safe with them … with me, too." I brush my fingers against his hand where it rests on his thigh, just a brief touch before I return my hand to my own lap, but it's enough to electrify my entire body. I do not want to be leaving this boy.

Luke nods. "I told Johnnie he could tell her if it would help sort out their fight, or whatever." He laughs lightly again. "Whatever he was doing before that clearly wasn't working."

I laugh too. "I mean, it was, but also … he needed you back. I didn't know him before, obviously. But since you visited, he's more settled. He's happier. It's Hollie, but it's also you."

He frowns at that, a sad smile flickering across his face. "So you know, he wasn't actually ever without me." He looks at me for a long time and it feels like he isn't done speaking, so I meet his gaze and wait. He sighs. "Maybe one day I'll tell you about it." It's a question and it makes me smile.

"I'd really like that. But only if you want to."

He nods, and the silence between us suddenly feels too much.

"I tried to find you online. But you don't exist," I blurt out. "Well, except for quite a few articles about bike stuff. But no social media."

The corner of Luke's mouth lifts into half a grin. "I'm not on any social media." He shrugs like it's no big deal.

"What? How? Why?"

"It's a long story. Maybe I'll tell you one day … when I tell you all the other long stories."

I laugh at that. "Deal."

My phone vibrates before we fall into another extended silence. A text from Hollie. They've said their goodbyes. Which means it's time for me to leave Luke.

"They're ready to go," I say, pushing myself up from the floor and placing the t-shirt over the back of a chair.

There's a notepad on the table, a list of exercises written out. It must be Luke's rehab plan. On a whim, I flick to a blank page and scrawl my email address across it.

"You have email at least?" When Luke nods I continue. "Email me sometime then, okay? If you want."

Luke nods again, still sitting on the floor, not moving to get up.

I don't want to leave, but I have to. And he's not giving me anything. He doesn't look upset that I'm leaving, he doesn't look happy that I was ever here. So maybe I'm kidding myself that there's something more to this than a random bit of fun.

Then he gives me a shaky smile and I realise it isn't that he doesn't care. He probably cares too much and doesn't know how to deal with that. I can handle that.

I sink down beside him so I'm crouching. I slide my hand into his, gripping his warm fingers in my own. "I've had a great time with you. Whatever you want to do from here, somehow I'll make it work."

Luke is staring down at our hands and I study them too, wondering if he's noticing the same details as I am, like how they fit together perfectly and how utterly glorious his hands are, all warm and big and wrapped in mine.

"I don't know what I want to do," he whispers, barely audible.

I push the hair back from his forehead, the edges damp with sweat from his workout, and he lifts his gaze to finally meet mine.

"That's okay too," I whisper.

"I really like you," he breathes, and I might come undone altogether. I might refuse to go home. "But I don't know what to do." He pulls in a shaky breath. "Can you – can you not tell Jonathan or Hollie about this? Or anyone else?"

I take his face in my hands, enjoying way too much how well it fits between my palms. "I won't say a thing," I say. "All of this … it's only ours. When – if – you want to tell people, it'll still be only ours. Nobody else gets an opinion."

He tilts his chin up, looking me right in the eyes. He's trying to hold everything together but I can see the fear, the worry, the uncertainty.

He gives me a wobbly smile and I lean in to kiss him one

last time while the sun streams in on us, making his brown skin glow and his grey eyes sparkle like quartz. We break apart and he runs his fingers through my hair, staring at it like he's trying to memorise it, or maybe I'm wishful thinking again. He runs his fingers along my jaw, brushes them against my cheek and slides them down the centre of my nose before finally dragging his fingertips across my lips.

"I might not be able to give you anything," he murmurs, voice still shaky.

"Luke." I will him to meet my gaze again, and after a long moment he does. "There's no hurry, there's no rush, there's not any expectation. My email address," I push the paper into his palm and he wraps his fingers around it. "For when you're ready. If you want."

He nods. "Thank you, for all of this."

I nod too, and I really need to get out of here because people are waiting for me and also because I might be about to cry and that is not at all a no-pressure look. I'm saying all these words to comfort him, to make him feel okay with it all, and for the first time ever I wish I wasn't saying something to make someone feel better. I want to tell him how much I want this, how I want to know every single little thing about him, from how his accident happened to what he likes on his toast.

But I can't.

I can't say those things, not when I know it'll only make everything harder for him. The pain it's causing me is worth it for the relief I see in his eyes when I don't push him.

"I need to go." I start to stand but Luke is still holding tight to my hand. He squeezes hard, opens his mouth to speak, but no words come. We stay there, me half standing, him with words frozen on his tongue, until finally: "Say goodbye to Johnnie and Hollie for me."

I squeeze his fingers tight, then untangle them from his.

"I will. Email me, yeah?"

Luke doesn't reply. I glance back as I leave the kitchen to grab one last memory of him. He's staring down at the piece of paper, running his finger over the address.

I can only hope he'll use it.

CHAPTER 11
Luke

IT'S BEEN a week since Dan pressed that piece of paper into my hands and asked me to email him.

I haven't done it yet. I don't know if I even want to.

Well, I want to. But I don't know how to deal with everything as it is, let alone adding that to my list of issues.

Having his hand in mine or his arm around me as he pressed kisses to my skin felt completely natural, but also like a fantasy. Like you've been sucked into a really good book. Then the book ends and you're dropped abruptly back into real life and all the painful reality involved.

The few days I spent with Dan felt like that. Now they're gone and he's back in his real life with Jonathan and Hollie and I'm here, with my own stuff to deal with. Number one being starting school again.

I skipped a term, unable to even comprehend going back to school a mere two months after the accident, but now the time has come.

Kristen drives me to school. I refused to let Mum do it. I need things to be as normal as possible and she never drove me to school before. I caught the bus until Jonathan got his license. After that we always drove together.

Since Jonathan left, Kristen has pretty much been my best friend. I'm not sure if it's cool, or exceedingly lame. But Kris is undeniably awesome, like her brother, so I'm relying on some of that to get me through today.

We climb out of her car and I stare up at the school, wondering how many of my classes will be in the second-floor rooms – how many sets of stairs I'll have to navigate today. I'm only doing four classes this term instead of the usual six. I'm carrying on my pitiful attempts at correspondence for the others to limit the time I have to traipse around school. But my physical therapist, my parents and my counsellor all deemed it time for me to start venturing out into the world again.

I can't help but feel that if Dan were here this would be much, much easier.

But he's not, so I take a deep breath, shoulder my backpack and settle my crutches. Kristen keeps pace beside me as I make my way in, heading for the administration office to collect my schedule and no doubt receive some motivational platitudes that I really don't need.

It feels like eyes are following me as I pass groups of students milling around waiting for the bell to ring. I don't know if it's real, but it feels like whispers are trailing behind me like echoes. Surely everyone knows what happened to me already and is well past the gossiping stage.

"Luke, man!" A voice calls out and I turn to see Tyler and Matt coming towards me with grins on their faces. Tyler's holding a rugby ball under one arm, his pale blond hair gleaming in the overcast morning light. I resist the flinch when

I think about how I'd usually be on the rugby team with them this year. I wonder who's replaced me.

"Hey," I say.

"We didn't know you were coming back today," Tyler says.

I shrug. I haven't been great at keeping in touch with anyone, and I deleted all my social media after receiving way, way too many posts, comments and DMs about my accident, mostly from people I barely knew and as a result barely cared about. The one I did care about was Jonathan, and by then he was already out of my life. I also didn't want to succumb to the temptation of watching his life through my phone screen, so I deleted it all.

"It's been all up in the air," I say, brushing it off, trying to make out like this isn't a huge deal.

Kristen edges away from us, watching me closely for confirmation that I'm okay. I give her a small nod and she waves her phone at me, telling me to text her if I need anything.

I turn back to my old friends. I don't even know if I can call them friends anymore. They did try. It was me who didn't.

"I'll catch up with you later, okay? Gotta go get my timetable and stuff."

"Yeah, sure," Matt says. "Find us for lunch or something, yeah?"

I nod and move away. They stand and watch me go, their heads leaning in to each other, no doubt to start talking about me. I sigh. I'm well used to it but it doesn't mean it's pleasant.

I get my sparse timetable from the dean in charge of my year, then get my several lame motivational platitudes as expected. Every teacher I pass has something inspiring to say to me. I grin and bear it.

When I finally escape the office, Tyler is waiting for me

outside, leaning casually against a post and tossing his rugby ball repeatedly. He spots me and tucks it under his arm.

"Got everything sorted?" he asks as he falls into step beside me.

"Yep. Got a year's worth of pep talks, too," I say, rolling my eyes.

He laughs. "Ah, yes. Because somehow they think it'll make a difference when they actually have no idea what any of us are going through."

I wonder what he means by that. Tyler started at our school this time last year. He was new to the city, but I don't know much more about him than that. He started right as rugby trials were running, and after seeing him play for five minutes it was obvious he was on the team. He didn't even need to try making friends. They came built in with the sport.

I played, but not particularly seriously. It was mostly for the compulsory fitness training that benefitting my biking. It was easier to do it with a team than motivate myself to do it alone.

"What's your schedule like?" Tyler asks after a few moments. He's realised I'm not going to respond, but only because I don't know how.

I hand over the slip of paper, already crumpled from being shoved into my pocket. "I'll be doing correspondence stuff in all the study breaks," I say, before he has a chance to comment on my empty timetable.

"Cool," he says, handing back the paper. "We have no crossovers. Shame. I won't be able to get you to help me with English. You always know exactly what to write. I'll catch you at lunch, all right?"

I nod, staring dumbly after him as he strides across the

courtyard, heading for the science block, leaving me to head for my math class.

I know he was talking about knowing what to write in essays, but all I can think about is the email address tucked inside a notebook beside my bed, and how I wish Tyler's comment included knowing what to write to Dan.

Because I have absolutely zero clue.

CHAPTER 12

Dan

I CHECK MY EMAILS AGAIN.

It's only been fifteen minutes since the last time I looked and they automatically update.

I know this, but I check them anyway.

In the past week my email app has had the workout of its life, but there's still no email from Luke. No messages, phone calls, social media contacts, morse code or smoke signals.

It's like nothing ever happened with him. Like I didn't spend hours hanging out with him, extensive periods of time with my body draped over his, my lips on his.

I sometimes think the entire thing was a dream. Like a really, really vivid dream. Some elaborate concept my brain came up with to let me know I'm queer.

I'd believe that were true if it wasn't for Hollie and Jonathan talking about the trip and Luke like it all actually happened.

I was hoping for a distraction during this utterly tedious math class, but no such luck, not unless an email notifying me of a camera sale is going to do it.

Which actually could be quite a good distraction – usually.

I can spend hours comparing different camera models online – not that I'm going to buy one, but because the options are endless and the prices high and the indecision crippling. So I'll continue using my iPhone camera to try and capture little moments of joy for people in my life. I don't know where the desire to take photos came from, but I started doing it years ago and realised how important capturing moments could be for someone. A vivid recollection of a moment of happiness. A reminder that joy exists.

I glance to my left and watch Hollie for a moment, head down, carefully copying equations into her book. I sigh softly and turn my focus to the board at the front of the classroom, making like my friend and attempting to actually learn something this period.

It's been over a week now and it's time for me to let it go. This is what happens when you leave the ball in the other person's court. Sometimes they don't want to return it. Or maybe they can't, and I need to be okay with that.

Luke's so mysterious. Not in a purposefully mysterious way; it's more that I really didn't want to push him with questions all the time. Because boy oh boy, do I have some questions for him. I could have quizzed him for three days straight until I knew every little detail about him, from how he drinks coffee to his dating history. I am very interested in his dating history. I'd like to know a lot about that. Except maybe I don't, because even the thought of his hands on someone else in the way they were on me makes me both a little sad and a lot jealous.

I force myself to focus on the board again. Thinking about Luke's hands is not conducive to learning about algebra equations. Sadly.

The teacher has barely started speaking again, to explain the next concept, when the classroom door swings open, banging loudly as it hits the wall. I jump out of my skin, then sigh heavily as I see the person strolling through, not a care in the world.

Jake Daly. Arch nemesis.

Or really, no nemesis. Just someone who used to be my friend. My best friend, until we got to high school and I suddenly wasn't cool enough for him to speak to me. I'm not that cut up about it because his refusal to acknowledge me led me to the group of friends that includes Hollie, and now Jonathan, as well as several others who dip in and out depending on their extracurriculars. Since Hollie, Jonathan and I have none of those, we've ended up the core, which is fine by me.

I love Hollie to pieces and Jonathan is growing on me since he stopped being such a moody mess and admitted how great my best friend is. Now he's completely smitten with her and worships the very ground she walks upon. As he should.

So, I'm not exactly upset about Jake ghosting me. It's just that sometimes when I look at him, like right now, I get all these little stabby pains in my chest, which I don't understand because I'm not sad.

He's also turned into a bit of a moron in the past few years, so I miss his friendship even less. He's the one at the party encouraging people to do stupid, reckless things, or making jokes at someone else's expense that are always more hurtful than funny. I really don't understand what happened, because he was a pretty nice guy when I was friends with him. Otherwise I wouldn't have been friends with him in the first place.

Jake saunters into the room and drops into an empty desk

right near me. I pull my gaze away from his hands resting on top of the desk before I have a chance to analyse whether his hands make me feel like Luke's did.

It's something I've started doing over the past week, studying people as they come near me, seeing if it's guys or girls; or only some guys or girls; or if it's only Luke that gives me that weird dizzy feeling you get when you're into someone. So far it's only been Luke, and I absolutely refuse to let Jake Daly be the second.

He smirks at me and I don't know why. I immediately look away, not acknowledging his presence at all, but as I tear my gaze away I realise it's not his usual smug expression. There's something missing in it. I only notice because I once knew him so well, and despite my brain telling me not to, I immediately wonder why the missing piece has been replaced with something like sadness.

No new emails.

What a surprise. Not only did I not manage to figure out what χ equals, I still haven't got an email from Luke.

The final bell of the day has rung and I'm heading for my car to go home and spend another exciting afternoon doing homework, or maybe I'll go down to Mum's work and see if she's got some chairs I can stack or something, maybe some tablecloths to wash. She runs an event management company and has a whole warehouse full of things people can hire for their events, from weddings to business dinners and kids' birthday parties.

I have got to get myself a life. Maybe it's time for the

camera purchase and for me to actually learn how to take decent photos. Or I could get Hollie to hang out with me for a while. We could go and do something ridiculous like we used to. Maybe bumper cars this time; something that'll make her forget herself and laugh until she hiccups and her mascara smudges.

I pull up the app to text her when a loud whack startles me. I whirl around and see Jake leaning with his head against the nearby building, his hand resting above his head where he must have hit the building. His other hand holds his phone to his ear.

"Well, what am I supposed to do, then?" His voice growls across the space between us. "Where am I supposed to go?"

A pause, while whomever he's talking to answers.

"Whatever. I'll figure it out myself." He ends the call and turns. I'm not fast enough and he catches me watching him. I wish he hadn't.

"What do you want, Danny?" He says my nickname with a sneer. The little stabby pains in my chest strike. He always called me Danny, but it used to be with a smile, not the glare he's giving me now.

I try not to care. I really, really try. I want to walk away, leave him to whatever is going on. But I can't. I can't leave him standing there, distraught, and simply walk away. My body won't allow it. It's something I usually pride myself on, this ability to be able to help people, make them feel better, solve their problems, but when it comes to Jake I want to be able to walk away. I want to not care.

"Are you okay? Is everything all right?" I ask. I fail to not care. Typical.

"Just peachy." Jake glowers at me. "You don't need to fix

everything you know. It's not like we're even friends anymore." He almost sounds like he regrets it, but I'm pretty sure that's just the reminiscent part of my brain.

Jake strides past me, a dark look on his face, and disappears into the carpark.

I end up helping Hollie at her job. Which isn't so bad because she works with horses, including this little pony, who has more attitude than size.

Jonathan's Aunt Beth gave Hollie the job helping with her horses after Hollie's depression diagnosis. She'd given up riding herself in the months prior, feeling overwhelmed and worn out by it all. But Beth needed an extra set of hands that knew how to handle horses, so it worked out perfectly for them both.

Then Jonathan showed up and it got even more perfect for all of them. My own thoughts sound really bitter at times, but I'm sure I'm not. I'm really, genuinely happy for them.

I spend the afternoon doing all the running around for Hollie since she's still wearing a moon boot from her recent car accident.

Hollie's at her happiest around the horses – even when Harley, the cheeky little one, tries to eat her ponytail as she's grooming him, and I love watching her complete confidence with them.

By the time I get home I smell like horse and something I can't exactly identify, that gets mixed in their feed. Mum's car is in the driveway, which isn't totally unheard of, but it isn't common either. It makes me a little wary.

Which, as it turns out, is justified. I slide open the kitchen door and stop dead.

Jake Daly is sitting at our kitchen counter.

What the fuck.

Mum is nowhere to be seen.

Jake looks my way at the sound of the door and grimaces when he sees me, though to give him credit, he tries to hide it. I have no words, so I stand in the doorway staring back at him. He looks away, unable to hold my gaze.

"Why are you here?" I ask eventually.

He sighs and rubs a hand over his jaw, staring down at the bench before him. "I'm staying here for a few days."

I open my mouth to ask why the hell he'd be staying with us when he cuts me off. "It is *not* my choice." His voice is bitter.

I try to respond again, but this time it's my own traitorous mother who interrupts me. "Oh, Danny, good. You're home," she says, bustling into the room. "Jake's going to stay with us for a while." She hands him a couple of towels. "Here you go, love."

"Thanks," he mutters, pushing away from the bench and leaving the room. He doesn't glance my way again.

"Mum?" I turn to her.

She exhales a long breath. She knows Jake and I aren't friends anymore. I can't even comprehend how we've got to this point. "I know you and Jake don't really hang out much anymore, but April called and asked if he could stay for a little while."

April. Jake's mum. I'd forgotten that while Jake and I aren't friends anymore, Mum and April have stayed in touch – as much as they could after April moved to Australia, at least. Jake stayed behind when she moved, to live with his dad.

"But why?"

"He just needs to. His dad has some stuff going on and Jake needs somewhere to stay. Are you okay with that?"

It's the vaguest, most useless answer ever, but Mum is standing there, asking me to put aside my issues with him because her friend asked her for a favour. And what am I going to do? Throw a tantrum and refuse to let him stay here? Where's he going to go then? It'll only cause Mum pain.

I take a deep breath and let it out slowly, like I've seen Hollie do in times of stress. Then I plaster my brightest smile across my face. "Sure," I say. "Of course."

Because of course I'm not going to say no to her, even when I really, really want to.

CHAPTER 13

Luke

I SHRUG my backpack on then finish zipping up my jacket, sighing as I watch the rain falling outside the building. The hallway is deserted, everyone else having already made their escape. I've been caught up in a fantasy novel in the back corner of the library, not realising the end of the day was even approaching until the bell rang and the few students near me charged for the door.

I'm impressed how quickly the school has emptied out. No one's willing to linger in this rain.

I stare at the torrent of water falling from the sky through the glass panel in the door. The weather matches my mood. I didn't want to come to school today, especially with the rain looming. It's only Thursday of my first week back and this morning I was ready to chuck it all in and refuse to finish school at all.

But I know I have to keep moving, even when I'm tired in every conceivable way.

My body is tired from being constantly on the go. It's sore

and achy from having to sit in the most uncomfortable seats known to humankind for hours at a time. There's no place I get to lie down, stretch out and simply rest for the hours I'm at school.

My brain is tired too. I only missed a term of school but I'm so far behind. It's exhausting trying to figure out what I missed, learn it, and try to keep up with everything that's going on.

On top of all that, my social limit has been reached. It exceeded the limit two days ago, but somehow I keep pushing through and finding more reserves.

So far, returning to school has been about as I expected it would be.

After a day or so of extra attention, the teachers have mostly returned to their strange aloofness, barely acknowledging me, even when I struggle into classes late. It's for the best, really, because I don't need extra attention or allowances from them when I'm getting all of that from other students.

The whispers of people in my classes (and complete strangers) have followed me all week, but they seem to be dying out as my novelty value wears off and the outrageous stories of my injury die out.

My old friends are either completely oblivious to the changes in me, both physically and mentally, or they're totally overbearing and therefore totally oblivious also. But they're trying, and I have to admit I wouldn't know what to say to or how to act around someone in this kind of situation. Sometimes I wish they'd ask, but when they do it usually irritates me.

I'm essentially impossible to be around.

Kristen is the only one who doesn't seem to bother me. It

could be because she's been with me through it all from the day of the accident, through every tiny improvement. She knows everything about my injury and has come to terms with it alongside me. Or maybe she just gets me on another level.

Thinking of her reminds me I need to leave this deserted hallway, because she'll be waiting for me so she can drive me home.

I take a deep breath and push the door open, feeling the first drops of cool rain hit my face.

"Let me help," a voice says, and the heaviness of the door is pulled away from me. I glance up and my eyes meet Tyler's. I give him a little smile.

"Thanks," I say. "You don't need to walk with me," I continue as he falls into step beside me. "No one else needs to be out in this."

"I don't mind," he says. "I love being in the rain. It's weird, I know."

I feel a drop slide down the inside of my collar and shiver, wondering why anyone would ever love being in the rain. Then I'm struck by a memory from last winter, when I managed to convince Jonathan to leave the house and come for a ride with me, poor weather and all. The rain wasn't heavy but it was enough to make the trails slippery, so we took it pretty easy. Jonathan is a fair-weather rider, so any hint of a wet trail makes him nervous, and he was being entirely dramatic about the whole thing.

But there was a moment, as I swooped down a hill, hitting a jump at exactly the right speed and angle, when everything came together perfectly and the rain fell around me as I flew through the air. I skidded to a stop just down the trail, turning back and laughing as Jonathan took the hill at a sensible pace, neatly swerving around the jump while swearing at me about my recklessness.

Moments like that are the reason I loved biking, that feeling of everything being right in the world and the utter weightlessness of flying.

It was the second to last ride I ever went on with Jonathan, though I push that thought away, returning to my conversation with Tyler as we walk through the rain towards the carpark.

"I was going to agree that you're completely weird, but I actually really like the rain too," I say. "It's been a while since I've been out in it, though."

Tyler falls quiet beside me and I wrack my brain for something to say to him. I don't know what he wants from me. He's been popping up all week – between classes and at lunchtime, when he coerces me into sitting with him and his friends.

Before the silence manages to turn awkward, another person falls into step beside me, this one sensible enough to be carrying an umbrella.

"Hey, Lukey," Kristen says. "Want some umbrella or are you enjoying being soaked?" She grins at me, her glossy red lips stretched into a smile, dark hair braided into a crown across her head. Even in her stiff, boring school uniform this girl is the epitome of cool.

"Actually enjoying the rain," I say to her. "I can't remember the last time I was outside in it."

"Fair call," she says, and lowers her umbrella. It folds down into a miniature thing that she clips to her bag before skipping out and twirling in the rain in front me and Tyler.

A laugh bursts out of me, the sound so light and carefree it startles me. She turns to face me, walking backwards, her mascara already smudged and running. Her grin is wide and for a moment I wish I could also twirl in the rain.

"Who is that?" Tyler asks. "And is Lukey a thing?"

"No, it is not a thing. Not for anyone but her, anyway." It's one of the perils of being friends with someone in high school that knew you when you were six. They retain all the cringey bits, including the nickname she called you when you first met.

Tyler laughs but nods. "So, who is she? I've seen her around, but…"

"That's Kristen. Jonathan's sister."

He nods slowly, processing the new information. "I can see the resemblance. But I never saw you guys with her last year."

"Nah, she kept to herself, mostly. I don't think we were cool enough for her. But she's taken pity on me now I don't have anyone else. Plus she's my ride to and from school."

An odd look crosses Tyler's face, but it's gone in a flash and he smiles again, water dripping off the tip of his nose. "Better keep on her good side then, huh?"

"Yeah. Without her I'd be totally alone."

Tyler's face twists again, then he glances at his watch. "Man, I've gotta go or I'll be late for training. But you're not on your own, all right?" He spins on his heel and strides off into the rain towards the school gym.

I stand and watch him go, too exhausted to realise the significance of the moment, but knowing it means *something*.

Kristen skips back to me as I start walking again. She's utterly soaked and dishevelled but somehow still looking beautiful, as usual. Objectively I know when girls are attractive, but they don't make me feel the way I do when I find a guy gorgeous.

"Who's that?" she asks, and it almost makes me laugh. I

should have just introduced them to each other and saved myself from being the middle man.

"Tyler. He's on the rugby team."

"He's cute," she says, staring into the rain as if she can still see him.

"Ah, yeah. I guess. Not really my type."

"Oh yeah? Who, pray tell, is your type, Lukey?" She grins up at me, mischief on her face. "I've noticed you spending some time with Stacey this week."

I snort. "You're reading way too much into that," I say. "She's in a couple of my classes and it's like her mission to involve me in as much as possible."

"Still, she's really pretty, and from what I know of her, really nice."

"Yeah, she is," I say. I don't know how I've got myself into this conversation and I certainly don't know how to get myself out of it.

I know exactly who my type is. He's got curly blond hair and the biggest heart of anyone I've ever met. Just the thought of him makes me a little dizzy.

Kristen is studying me as we stand in the rain, which has thankfully eased somewhat. "What I'd give to know who you were just thinking about," she says with a smirk.

"Why? Why does this feel like it's important to you?" A thought occurs to me and my mind goes blank for a second. "Are you hoping it's you?" I whisper.

She laughs right in my face. "God, no!" I breathe a sigh of relief and she continues. "Maybe when I was, like, fourteen. But not now." She pulls a face and I wonder if I should be offended, but I'm mostly relieved.

"Then why is this so important to you?"

"Because, my dear Luke, you deserve to be happy and to have some fun, and if Stacey or someone else is into it then I think you should at least entertain the idea of like, hanging out with someone." She catches a glimpse of my expression which, based on my current emotional state, is probably somewhere in the vicinity of terrified. "I'm not suggesting you propose marriage. But just enjoy it. A bit of flirting, a few dates maybe, some making out, whatever's fun."

"Fun?"

"Yeah, you know, that thing you used to have?"

I give her a gentle shove. "Oi. Low blow."

"Anyway. Stacey?"

She looks so hopeful. Like she really wants this for me.

"Not Stacey," I say with a sigh. "She's less my type than Tyler."

Kristen stares up at me with mascara-smudged eyes, blinking raindrops from her lashes. She's waiting for me to say more. My head suddenly feels like it's filled with cottonwool. It's pure fluff. My hands are shaking and despite the chill of the rain on my skin I feel like I'm overheating.

I've never had to come out to anyone. I didn't have to specifically tell Jonathan and Dan. But in this moment I know it's the perfect time to tell Kristen. Our conversation has led us exactly to this. Somehow she's opened the door for me without even knowing what she was doing.

"I'm gay, Kris," I whisper.

She blinks. Once. Twice. "So, definitely not Stacey, then."

I laugh, and the sound startles me. I don't know how I was expecting her to respond, but it definitely wasn't like that.

She turns and starts walking towards her car, loosely

looping her arm through mine as I traipse along with my crutches.

"You are so loved, Luke."

She says the words softly, barely audible above the rain around us, but the words travel straight to my heart and nestle there.

CHAPTER 14

Dan

BECAUSE I LIKE TORTURING MYSELF, I check my emails again.

It's a fun little game I like to play with myself.

No new message.

I curse and slam my laptop closed.

I rest my head on my desk and think back to those few days with Luke. I think about the way we made out on his bed for ages and how good the kissing was, lying stretched out beside him, his hands on my skin. Big hands with rough callouses and blunt fingernails. Hands that haunt my dreams.

I think about the way we sat on the log on the beach and Luke told me about the way mountain biking feels, when you sweep around bends, fly over jumps, when it all comes together and it's smooth and flying and free. I always imagined that's what Hollie feels when she's on horseback. The freedom of it.

I think about the look on Luke's face as he tells me about this thing he clearly loves and has lost. He didn't say it, but I think he was pretty good. A sneaky Google search pretty much confirmed it: he was going places in the sport. And now he is not. But that look, the longing for that feeling again, when even walking down a beach hand in hand with someone is impossible.

I think about how hard he laughed after Hollie and Jonathan interrupted us and I unlocked the door wearing his shirt. He laughed himself hoarse while I found my own shirt. We'd tossed it so far across the room, it was no wonder I'd picked up one of his. He was still lying flat on his bed, chuckling to himself, when Jonathan and Hollie came back. By that time I'd come up with my cover story and was sitting behind the drums again, watching the grin on Luke's face widen every time he glanced in my direction. I loved every glance more than the last. Every time I wanted to pull out my phone and snap a picture that I could gaze at later to memorise every detail.

I think about all the little moments when I caught him looking at me, the way he trailed those fingers across my skin, how *he* kissed *me*, over and over.

It wasn't all in my head.

It wasn't all one-sided.

But I have to let it go, because clearly he's not interested, or he would have emailed by now.

Unless I didn't write my email address clearly enough…

I shut those thoughts down. No. I'm not going there. I'm not going to sit here and pine away over a guy who clearly isn't interested, or doesn't have the follow-through or whatever he needs to be friends with someone through email. I won't do it.

Besides, I have a bigger problem to deal with right now. Namely Jake Daly.

A throat clears behind me and I jerk my head off the desk. Think of the devil. I've bloody summoned him.

"So you know," he says, looming in my bedroom doorway, "this isn't my idea. I wouldn't have chosen to stay here if I had anywhere else to stay." He bites at the side of his thumb, and from that tiny gesture alone I know how uncomfortable he is. The benefits of knowing your nemesis as a friend first.

"It's fine," I say, because sure, whatever, it'll have to be. It's out of my hands and I'm not going to make anyone feel bad about it. I'll grin and bear it, for my mum at least. "No big deal." I kind of hate that I'm here making him feel better about it. I wish I could make him feel bad. But that'll only turn around on my parents, and they don't deserve that.

Jake smirks, a ghost of his usual version, but with a little more effort than he gave earlier in class. "You slam laptops and bang your head on the desk for fun, then?"

I glower back at him and wonder how the hell we got to antagonising each other. We'd been friends, good friends, especially when our mums became friends too. They'd hang out and we'd hang out. Everyone wins. Then, right as we started high school, things started to shift.

We both got busier with school and sports. Well, sports for Jake. No sports for me. I tried to play football once and ended up face planting after tripping over *my own foot*. The ball wasn't even near me. Physical endeavours are not for me.

Things were crazy at home too at that time, though I try very hard not to think about that period in our lives.

But despite the gradual shift from friends to whatever this is now, we simply avoided each other rather than stooping to sneering at each other. Jake smirks at everyone by default, so giving me that same look wasn't in any way antagonistic.

"This may shock you, but not everything in the world revolves around you. Especially not things in my life."

He huffs a laugh, regaining a little more of that spark that makes him an insufferable prat. "Whatever you say, Danny." He turns to leave.

"Are you seriously being an ass to me while you're staying in my house? This isn't ideal for either of us, but maybe you can try to be less of a dick for once."

The aggression in my voice stops him and he turns back to me. The severity is unusual for me, and I can tell I've surprised him. I've surprised myself.

"I wasn't trying to be an ass." His voice is quiet, the arrogance gone. "I do appreciate being able to stay here … so, thanks."

He's down the hall before I process that he's just been somewhere close to apologetic. Normal. Maybe nice. There's a slim chance he was even being genuine.

I shake my head and turn back to my desk, laying my head down again.

My phone bleats its email alert and I almost throw it across the room in my attempt to grab for it.

From: Nicole.lawler@ezmail.com
To: Daniel.lawler@ezmail.com

No email body, only a subject line: *ring me dork.*

I don't know why she does this. She could just text me or call me herself. I think she sends the email because it makes her feel less intrusive. It's a throwback to before I had access to email on my phone 24/7. It's also hilarious that she'd be concerned about being intrusive when she's my big sister and has been intruding on my life since the day I was born.

I sigh, disappointment flooding me again, then hit the button to video call her.

"Dannnnnny!" she yells down the phone as she answers. The room behind her is dark and noisy.

"Are you at the pub?" I ask her.

"Yes," she says, the phone jerking and jolting as she heads outside. "I didn't realise you would receive my email and call quite so promptly."

"Apologies for my promptness," I reply, promptly. We grin at each other for a few seconds and it's the most ridiculous thing. I love it. "What's up?"

"Just wanted to see how you were doing." Her voice drops to a whisper. "I heard you've got a house guest."

"Ugh, yes." I scrunch up my face in disgust. Nicole giggles. She knows bits and pieces of what happened with Jake. Well, bits and pieces of what I know of what happened with Jake. I don't know his side of the story, and by this point I don't care to.

It was around the time we finally became close; more like friends than older sister and annoying little brother. She'd always ask me to tell her stories about my days at school. I loved having my big sister take an interest in me, and loved telling her slightly embellished stories about everyone in my class.

She asked about Jake one day, when I'd been mentioning other friends but never him. I never let her know quite how much it hurt, though. She doesn't know about those stabby heart pains. We didn't need more drama or sadness at the time. It was my job to make her feel better, to cheer her up along with Mum and Dad, so I told her some funny, extravagant story and brushed off our friendship breakdown as though it didn't bother me at all. As though I was glad I wasn't friends with someone so feckless.

"How's it going?" Nicole's wandering down the street now, giving me a shaky, somewhat useless tour of her route home. There's a breeze throwing her hair into her face, hair that used to be an identical colour to mine until she lightened it up to a real blonde. She's even tamed her curls down. She's looking all respectable and proper, not wild and a little like she's been through a bush backwards, which is what my hair currently looks like.

"Well, I've seen him for a grand total of about five minutes since he's been here, so not too bad, to be honest. Dinner soon though, that might be a different story. How'd you even hear? *I've* barely heard."

"Dad told me. I was texting him."

"Is everything okay?" I ask, suddenly nervous.

Nicole rolls her eyes, brushing her hair out of her face with her free hand. "Yes, Danny, everything is fine. We were just chatting. I can do that with our dad sometimes without you having a freak out, okay?"

"Yes, okay, sorry," I say, a little embarrassed. She's right. She's a grown adult. He's our dad. They actually have things in common occasionally. I mean, not often, but occasionally. Dad is so reserved, sometimes it's hard to get him to have a conversation. Mum makes up for it all, though. Sometimes we can't get her to stop talking.

Again, my thinking about someone summons them, and Mum appears in the doorway to my room. "Dinner's up," she says.

"Hi, Mum!" Nicole calls from my phone.

"Hey, Nic. We'll chat soon, okay? Better feed these boys before they get hangry."

Nicole laughs. I roll my eyes and groan. Parents.

"Bye, Dan." Nicole ends the call and Mum tells me again that dinner is ready.

I don't move from where I'm sitting, because there's a new email alert on my screen.

CHAPTER 15
Luke

KRISTEN TAKES me out for coffee after my grand coming out, which really wasn't that grand, but apparently it's worth celebrating. I wasn't going to refuse a cookie almost the size of my face.

We go to a little cafe in the back of a bookshop. It's warm and cozy back here, despite the fact that I'm still wearing my wet school clothes. Kristen orders for me while I find a table as close to the bookshop section as possible. It's our favourite spot, where we can drink coffee and check out new books. Then we argue about who's going to buy them.

We've been here a lot in the past few months, once I was allowed out of hospital but very quickly getting sick of the four walls of my bedroom. I've also been reading a lot since then.

As I think about how many times Kristen and I have been here together, she sits down opposite me and sends a huge smile in my direction.

"I'm so happy for you," she says.

"Why?" I ask. "This isn't news for me."

She shrugs. "I know. Maybe I'm happy for me because you

told me." She gives a little frown. "I'm assuming it's not public knowledge yet." I shake my head and she continues. "Does Johnnie know?"

"Yeah, he does." I tug at the ends of my hair, which is harder to do now its short. Before the accident it brushed my shoulders and my nervous habit was much less noticeable and awkward, but they had to shave half of it for the stitches I needed in my head, and it looked ridiculous with only part of it short.

"But? Don't tell me he was an ass about it. God, I'll kill him." She pauses as the waitress deposits our order on the table between us. Kristen picks up her cup but doesn't drink. Her eyes widen as they fix on me. "Do not tell me his total personality transplant and disappearing act was because of this. I really will bloody kill him."

I laugh, but it's short-lived and fizzles out quickly. "He wasn't an ass. He found out by accident, though. And I freaked out because I wasn't quite ready for him to know, and that was maybe three minutes before I fell down those stairs." I tug at my hair again as Kristen covers her mouth with her hands, her purple nail polish vivid against her pale skin and bright red lips, smudges of mascara still under her lashes.

"No," she breathes. I continue.

"He ... he thought it was his fault. That I fell. I didn't handle it very well and avoided him once or twice when he came to see me, so he thought I was angry with him. He spent all that time thinking he was entirely to blame." My voice cracks several times as I speak, but I manage to hold it together.

I've told no one this story. As far as I know it's only ever been between me and Jonathan, and maybe by now he's told

Hollie, though I don't know how much detail he'd have told her. Even now, telling Kristen, I can't tell her all of it. I don't want to tell her all of it.

I don't want to admit to her how stupid I was, sneaking out to go to a club I wasn't old enough to be in. How I lied to her and Jonathan. How I told no one where I was going. I don't want to tell her that I went there planning to admit my feelings to one person, but after seeing him with someone else I ended up making out with someone else entirely. Someone I tried to go home with.

Until Jonathan happened to walk past and caught me in the act.

There are parts I still don't remember, like Jonathan refusing to let me go home with a random stranger. How I was angry at him for that, and shoved him, how he pushed me away and how my foot slipped off the edge of the step.

I push away the memories of Jonathan telling me the parts of that night my concussion made me forget, the anguish on his face as he placed the blame squarely on his own shoulders.

I couldn't blame him. I never did and haven't for one second since I heard the full story. I don't even blame him for running from my life, from his own life. Sometimes I try to be angry, but the reality is I just really miss him.

I think Kristen misses him, too. They were always close siblings, and even before he physically left he withdrew emotionally from her. She used to come and sit with me in the hospital, watching movies or playing card games, but we never directly spoke about him. I didn't want to know what he thought of me and she didn't know what was wrong – only that our tight-knit trio was no more.

When Jonathan and I sorted everything out I saw the relief

on her face, the joy. And the disappointment when Jonathan announced he was planning to stay where he was and not come home.

I was disappointed too, but once he admitted to Hollie how he felt, and she reciprocated those feelings, I knew he wasn't coming back.

Not with the way he looked at her, the way his whole face changed when he talked about her.

Plus, a clean slate was really working for him. He was moving forward without the ties of his guilt-ridden past holding him down. I did envy him that.

I've only met one new person since the accident that hasn't somehow been related to the injury. I've met other patients, other guys who've been through similar things, or I've met therapists for the physical and mental healing I've needed, but only one person separate from all that.

Dan.

He's the only new person who's been more than a one-off meeting, a passing acquaintance.

Kristen reaches across the table, grasping my hand. "I'm so happy you guys figured all that stuff out."

"Me too," I say, my voice settling back to normal.

"So, is there someone special?" She pulls her hand back and sits there watching me, a teasing smile tugging at her mouth.

"No," I say, hoping to sound convincing.

"Liar." Her mouth curves up into a full, smug smile. My face burns. "Is it Tyler?"

I laugh. "No, it isn't Tyler."

She leans back in her seat, studying me, trying to figure it out. "You don't know anyone I don't," she says slowly. "Is it someone from rehab?"

I shake my head, taking a sip of my coffee in a lame attempt to hide the blush. "It's nothing," I say. "No one. Why do you think there is?"

She shrugs, eyeing me speculatively over the top of her mug. I'm worried she isn't going to drop it, but she takes a drink, places her cup carefully on its saucer and indicates the nearby bookshelves. "What's next on your list?"

I let go of the tension that's been creeping up my neck, and the blush fades with it as we settle into a conversation about books. We bicker over the pros and cons of each of the new titles for a few minutes. Then Kristen locks eyes with me, drops the piece of muffin that's halfway to her mouth and points an accusing finger at me. "It's that Dan guy!"

"What?" I freeze, my cookie in midair.

"Your someone special. It's that Dan guy that's friends with Hollie."

"Uh, no." I shake my head. The blush is back, flaming across my cheeks. "I told you, it's no one."

She picks up the dropped muffin and pops it into her mouth. She even chews smugly. "But you spent time together when Johnnie and Hollie were here."

"Uh, yeah," I mutter. "He had nowhere else to go while you guys were doing family stuff."

"Whatever you say." Her eyes are twinkling. She knows I'm lying.

"Johnnie found out because he saw me kissing a random guy outside a club." And why the heck did I say that? This conversation topic is even worse than talking about Dan.

Unfortunately Kristen is now holding her cup again, and it

crashes loudly into the saucer as she slams it down. "What?" Her voice is several octaves higher than normal.

I sigh. There's no way out of this one. Even if I tried to change the subject back to Dan, there's no way Kristen will let this one drop. "I snuck out and went to a club. Jonathan happened to walk past when I was outside with someone and that's how he found out. I freaked out and…" I gesture at myself, taking in the crutches leaning against the table.

Her hands are covering her mouth again. "No wonder you freaked out," she breathes. "Bet you weren't expecting that."

"No, no I was not," I say with a laugh.

"What happened to the guy?"

I shrug. "Don't know. I can't even remember his name."

Kristen smirks at me. "Yeah, 'cause you've replaced all those memories with ones of Dan, right? You must be into him if you'd rather tell me about kissing some random guy than let Dan come into the conversation."

Ah, crap.

I drop my head onto the table with a groan and Kristen laughs. She pats me gently on the head. "It's all right, I totally get it, because he's gorgeous. Like that hair of his. And he's very nice. Almost too nice. It's kind of suspicious."

I lift my head again, automatically opening my mouth to defend him. She's sitting there so smug and I manage to catch myself before saying anything. I shake my head at her and she laughs.

I want to shut this conversation down, but also, she's been with me through everything and it seems ridiculous not to talk about it. It's not like I've got anyone else to talk about it with.

"It's not only the hair. It's the eyes, and the way he smiles.

He played my drums and I don't think I've ever seen anyone happier."

"He played your drums, huh? That's a euphemism I haven't heard before." She laughs. "But you're right. He's like a giant puppy. He bounded around the house all weekend, being helpful and charming. If he wasn't so likeable it'd be revolting." She pauses to take another sip of coffee, but it doesn't feel like she's finished talking, so I wait for her to continue. "Where did you guys leave things? Did anything happen?"

I blush again, harder than before, harder than when I came out to her. I tug at my hair again. "There was some kissing and he left me his email address." I throw the words out in a single breath, like it's some kind of confession.

Kristen squeals, claps her hands and sits up in her chair. "Please, please, please tell me you've emailed him."

I take a drink and realise my cup is empty. I place it carefully back on the table. Kristen knows my answer without me even having to speak the words. She reaches across the table and lightly whacks me across the head. "Luke." Her voice is low, eyes locked with mine, serious and intense. "Email the poor guy. He's a delight and you clearly like him."

I shake my head. "I don't even know what to say to him. I've waited so long now. I have no idea how any of it would work. He's so far away and it isn't like I can even drive down to see him. He said he doesn't have any expectations and that he's happy to just be friends, but honestly, Kris, sometimes I think I've forgotten how to be friends with someone." I take a deep breath.

She takes my hand, squeezing it tight, still holding that intense eye contact. "All you can do is see how it goes. If it turns out he's a jerk, there's a block button. Let it play out. I struggle to see how you could end up regretting it. But I can see how you'd regret not getting in touch." She pauses, mulling over her next words. "As for knowing how to be friends with someone: yeah, you do, Luke, because despite everything that happened with you and my brother, you never gave up on him. Despite what happened to you, you've always been the greatest friend to me, so don't worry about that part. Send Dan an email and deal with whatever happens when it happens. You deserve to be happy. Don't limit yourself before you even give it a chance."

I hold her hand and look into her green eyes, so much like her brother's, and give a small nod. Too many emotions are swirling around my chest, but the one floating to the top, the tiniest glimmer in the raging chaos, is hope.

Kristen is right. What do I have to lose? The second I get home I'm going to email him.

CHAPTER 16
Dan

From: Luke.ashwell@ezmail.com
To: Daniel.lawler@ezmail.com
Subject: Freak outs and apologies

Hey Dan,

I know it's been a while and sorry I didn't email sooner. I'm not sure why I didn't.

That's a total lie. I know why I didn't.

I didn't email before now because I'm a coward. It was easier to pretend those few days never happened and to hope I'd forget about you.

Because it all feels like too much.

Liking you felt like too much. It still does. So, I had a total freak out.

Even before my accident, dealing with all the stuff involved in a relationship seemed like it would be impossible. I used to watch my friends do it — have a crush on someone, find the nerve to ask them out, go on dates or whatever. I always wondered how they found the emotional energy to do it, you know?

Right before the accident I was just starting to understand it. Then, well, the accident happened, and I've had other things on my mind.

No one else knows about me, aside from you and Jonathan and I guess Hollie, but I'm not exactly sure about her. I've never actually told anyone.

But that changed today.

Today I came out to Kristen, Jonathan's sister (I say that as if you won't remember her, but she's pretty unforgettable).

I didn't plan it, but it came out (ha!) while we were hanging out after school today. I've known for a long time, but coming out felt like a whole "thing" and I honestly didn't know how to deal with it.

Jonathan found out by accident, and this sounds way worse than it is, and please don't hold it against him, but that's part of the reason we didn't talk for so long. (I don't know how much you know about any of that, but maybe one day I'll tell you about it.)

Anyway, Kristen put me through an interrogation (in the nicest way, she was amazing) after my coming out and somehow she figured out that there's a person I quite like. (She figured it out because I'm a terrible liar, okay?) Then she kicked my ass for not getting in touch.

That sounds a lot like I'm only emailing you to keep her off my case, which is part of it. But mostly, I'm emailing to say sorry I haven't emailed before now and it doesn't mean I regret anything that happened.

If you're still into it, I'd really like to be friends.

Luke

I CATCH MY BREATH. This email. From Luke. There's an email from Luke right here in front of my face.

He spells it out clear as day that he likes me.

I drop my phone, covering my face with my hands and

actually kicking my legs, trying to expel some of the excess energy suddenly coursing through my body. Thankfully I draw the line before I start squealing, because I realise Jake is in my house and my bedroom door is wide open.

I read the email again. And again.

"Dan!" Mum shouts down the hallway at me.

I forgot I was supposed to be having dinner. I go to slip my phone into my pocket, holding the email close. But as I leave the room I change my mind. If it's with me I'm going to want to reread it fifteen times during the first five minutes of the meal, and my parents only have so much tolerance of phones at the table. I toss it onto my bed instead, immediately longing to read his words again, and head for the kitchen.

Jake's arrogance has returned by the time I reach the table. I try to avoid looking in his direction. I can't be bothered with him. I really, really hope he isn't here for long. I slide into my seat and mumble an apology for my lateness.

Unfortunately I don't come across as particularly sincere when I cannot stop smiling. My face is beginning to ache with the constant effort of trying to smother the grin that wants to devour my face.

Dad raises an eyebrow at me from across the table. "Had some good news, have you?"

I shake my head, but the movement distracts me from the battle with the smile and it sneaks out for a second. "Nope. Just got an email from a friend I haven't heard from in a while."

"Oh, someone we know?" he asks.

I shake my head again and begin shovelling food into my mouth. Dad gives me a look and I slow it down a bit. I can barely sit still, though. I need to go and read Luke's email again, on repeat, until I've committed every word to memory.

He didn't even skirt around the fact that he likes me. He likes me and he wants to be friends. Even though I'd really, really like for us to be more than that and spend hours kissing like we did that one time, I'm happy to be friends, and maybe something else will work out later. At this point it's pretty much my life goal to kiss him again.

I eat my dinner using my table manners, but ignore the conversation Jake is having with my parents. They're asking him a million questions about his life, catching up on everything they've missed since we stopped being friends. Like they are with my actual friends, they're easy-going and fun, so everyone thinks they're cool. Usually I don't mind. Usually I appreciate how laid-back my parents are, how approachable they are. Except Jake isn't my friend. He's oozing pleasantries, behaving the exact opposite of how he behaves around me at school, and it makes me want to gag.

But for some reason him being here means a lot to Mum, and I refuse to let her down so I suck it up and bear it.

Having the email to think about helps, a lot. I'm intrigued by the comments about Jonathan and I'd love to ask all the questions about that story right now. But I'll bide my time. I spend most of the meal mentally composing what I'm going to say back.

I finish dinner, clear the table, load the dishwasher and finally, *finally* make it back to my room. I close the door behind me, grab my laptop and sit down to write my reply.

CHAPTER 17

Luke

I CAN'T BELIEVE I did this to Dan.

It's been half an hour since I sent my email. A measly thirty minutes and I'm losing my mind waiting for a reply.

I made Dan wait days.

I check my email app again, making sure I typed his email address correctly. I did.

I know I did because I've checked approximately once per minute since I hit send. That's after checking multiple times before sending.

Kristen delivered me home, still damp from our moment in the rain, after realising there was no way I could concentrate on holding a conversation with her while simultaneously drafting an email to Dan in my head.

I sat on the edge of my bed with my head in my hands and my laptop open beside me for an undetermined amount of time before I managed to put down enough words.

The second the email whooshed away I started regretting it, rereading it over and over, realising how stupid I sounded.

I can't believe I asked if we could be friends.

But it's too late to take it back.

I head for the kitchen right as Mum is plonking a pizza box down on the bench.

"Dad's working late and I'm about six years behind on paperwork," she says, catching sight of me. "Sorry, not much of a family dinner tonight."

"It's all good, Mum." I grab us plates from the cupboard. "I've got heaps of homework to catch up on."

She purses her lips in a little worried frown. "How's it all going?" She sighs and runs a hand through her hair. "I feel like I've barely seen you this week."

I swipe my thumb across her forehead, smoothing out the creases. "That's because I haven't been here. I've been learning about statistics."

She pulls a face. "Gross."

"Exactly. But it's going okay. I'm just tired."

"Sore?"

I nod. "Yeah, but I'll get there. Physically, anyway. Jury's still out on stats."

She laughs and cups my cheek for a brief moment. I lean into the touch. "Right, well, eat pizza. Do homework. Sleep."

"Sounds like a plan. Love you." I take my plate, now fully loaded, and head back to my room.

"Love you too, my baby," Mum says as I leave the kitchen.

Sliding my plate onto my desk, I glance at my laptop screen still open to my emails, and nearly knock the food straight to the floor.

What's that saying? A watched pot never boils. Something like that. It must be true. Because in the few minutes I was in the kitchen with Mum, Dan has emailed me back.

From: Daniel.lawler@ezmail.com

To: Luke.ashwell@ezmail.com

Subject: Re: Freak outs and apologies

Luke! Hey.

It's good to hear from you. I'll admit I was starting to give up hope that you'd email. But I'm glad you did, and I understand the delay. I don't think you're a coward at all. The total opposite, actually.

Congratulations on coming out to Kristen. (Is this the kind of thing you say congratulations for?) It's not something I've ever done either, though I didn't realise until recently that it's something I might need to do.

Next time I see that girl I'm going to have to buy her some cake. Thank her for me for now though.

You mentioned school. Have you started again? I think I remember Jonathan saying you weren't at school last term. How's it all going?

From: Luke.ashwell@ezmail.com

To: Daniel.lawler@ezmail.com

Subject: Re: Freak outs and apologies

First of all.

I'M SO SORRY.

I waited less than an hour for you to reply to me and I made you wait an eternity in comparison. You really should have made me sweat more. Why did you go with email as our form of communication?

School is fine. Well, it's shitty, to be honest. I'm exhausted, constantly sore and I have literally no idea what's going on in any of my classes. It's weird being there without J. I keep expecting to see him come round the corner or sit down next to me and start bitching about some teacher. I guess now you get that pleasure. I might be a little jealous. But don't ever tell him that. The world couldn't handle his ego any bigger than it is.

From: Daniel.lawler@ezmail.com
To: Luke.ashwell@ezmail.com
Subject: Re: Freak outs and apologies

I can promise you, I'll never tell Jonathan what you said. About you missing him, or the size of his ego (you're not wrong though).

As for emails … Well, it seemed like the least confrontational form of communication (besides snail mail, but that's expensive and I'm technically unemployed) and I thought that might be easier for you.

I'm not too proud to admit that I really, really wanted you to get in touch, so I'd have done just about anything to help you to reach out. We can go to snail mail if you want. I'll beg my mum to actually pay me for helping her out. I'm doing her a favour right now so maybe it's a good time to ask.

I'm sorry school sucks.

Is there anything I can do to help?

I lean back in my chair and read through the email again.

Dan. He's a revelation. I don't think I've ever met anyone

who is so conscious of the people around him and the best ways to help someone, regardless of the situation.

Jonathan's told me a bit about him, the ways he's helped Hollie and him, even though Jonathan's pretty sure Dan doesn't like him, or at least he didn't at first. I disagree. I think Dan was probably just looking out for Hollie, because that's what he's always doing.

My homework sits completely abandoned next to me. I need to focus on that for a while. I also don't know how to respond to his question. Is there anything he can do to help?

The logical answer is to stop emailing so I can focus, but the little thrill I get when I see a new email pop up has been the best part of this entire week, and I don't want to give that tiny glimmer of joy away.

I decide to send one more email tonight, then I'll do my homework and sleep and maybe tomorrow I'll understand something that happens in class.

Maybe it'll feel worth it.

From: Luke.ashwell@ezmail.com
To: Daniel.lawler@ezmail.com
Subject: Re: Freak outs and apologies

Is there anything you can do to help school suck less? I don't know.

Maybe you could tell me something about you. What's the favour you're doing for your mum?

I really have to try and study now, but write to me, yeah?

CHAPTER 18

Luke

EMAILING Dan swiftly becomes a regular part of my day.

That first night, while I studied, he wrote to me and told me all about how his old friend is staying with him. He told me he's not exactly thrilled with the development, since they've barely interacted since they started high school. He doesn't want his mum to worry though, so he's shutting up and enduring it. He didn't tell me why they aren't friends anymore though, and I wonder if there's more to the story. He kind of glossed over the whole thing, like it's all fine, when it obviously isn't.

At first our emails are short, but as the days pass they're gradually getting longer.

Most of the time we talk about nothing in particular, just random things like the music we like or TV shows we're watching, what classes we're taking at school. Dan talks about Hollie often and the horses she's getting back into working with now her broken leg is healing. He tells me plenty of stories about Jonathan trying to learn to ride, which never fail to make me laugh, sometimes so hard I end up with tears in my eyes.

I reply, telling him about my readjustment to school, which is still slow and exhausting. I'm being a lot more physical than normal, having to move between classes, not being able to lie down for several hours a day. But it's good. It's nice to be out in the world again.

My friends are the same as they've always been. We hang out at lunchtimes, there's always someone to sit with in class and we have a good time, but there's always a little bit of distance there now. I don't think it's anyone's fault; it's just what happens when someone goes through something like I have. The things that seemed big to me before don't seem so big anymore, yet to my friends those fears, dreams, feelings … they're all still a big deal.

Being around other people again is great. My classes, on the other hand, are a different story. I knew I'd missed a bit. A whole term out of school is a lot of learning and on top of that, I don't think I can even remember what I learned last year. I'm not sure I can blame the head injury I suffered, but regardless, I need to figure something out before I fall even further behind.

Which is why I find myself climbing the stairs of my house for the first time since the accident happened. I'm heading for my old room, hoping to track down some of last year's textbooks. At least my inability to go riding means I have way more time to study.

I pause at the top of the stairs. I'm not sure if I'm physically tired because I haven't been up these stairs in months, or if it's emotional strain because I haven't been up these stairs in months.

I readjust and start making my way down the hallway past

the bathroom, past my parents' room, and I pause outside the last door on the right, which is slightly ajar.

Before I have a chance to think about it – to change my mind – I push the door wide with the end of my crutch and walk into my old bedroom.

It's eerie in here. It's like a half-decimated time capsule of my old life. Some of my stuff got moved down when my parents converted the old garage into my new bedroom, but there's a lot still up here that I didn't care to ask for, that Mum or Dad or Kirsten didn't think to bring down or that I specifically said I didn't want or need, like the books I'm currently looking for.

I take in my old room. My bed is still here, stripped bare of sheets but the duvet folded neatly on top of it. Spinal injuries qualify for fancy new mattresses, which I'm extremely grateful for. I can't imagine getting comfortable in my old single bed.

There's dust in places I've never seen it before, on the desk and the bedside table. A few books are stacked on the desk, and there's a pile in the corner that I realise is my biking gear, shoes and gloves and helmet, and next to that…

I freeze, my breath catching in my chest as I take in the shape tucked away in the corner under an old sheet. I catch a glimpse of tyre and my hand shakes as I reach out to pull back the fabric, exposing my mountain bike, gleaming in the afternoon sunlight streaming through the window.

I stare down at it, unable to pry my gaze away as I sink down onto the bed.

The bike I told my parents to sell. The bike that is of absolutely no use or value to me or them anymore.

It's spotless. Not a speck of dirt or dust on the charcoal

frame. Even the tyres have been cleaned. I run my fingers over the handle bar grips, trail them along the seat.

My eyes are burning and I realise my cheeks are wet. I'm crying over my bike.

I stand, move closer, and place my hands over the grips, feeling the curve of brake levers and gear shifters under my fingers. They're a perfect fit, moulded to my hands like I never stopped riding. It's so familiar I never want to let go.

A hole has been ripped through my chest. I haven't touched this bike since three days before the accident, when I went for a quick ride. I've never thought much about it, especially not at the time. I never considered it would be my last time on my bike. I wish my last ride was something more memorable.

I miss the feeling of being on a bike more than anything else I've lost because of this injury.

I sink down onto the bed again, lying down because there's no way I can be upright anymore. The stairs and the emotions combined have drained me completely. I lie on my back but turn my head to stare at the frame.

I think back to sitting on that beach with Dan and talking about what riding had meant to me. How it felt to say the words out loud. No one else seems to have realised what I've lost.

People know I can't ride anymore, and Mum and Dad obviously know. They've known all along; it's why I told them to sell my bike. But they didn't, so either they haven't accepted my injury and my new body limitations, or … I can't think of an alternative. They can't really believe I'm going to be able to ride again. Maybe I'll get on a bike again one day, but I'll never ride to a level that requires a bike like that.

My mind flickers to Dan again. The way he sat and absorbed every word I said as his palm pressed flush against mine. The way he asked if I had anyone to talk to about riding.

I don't. Not anymore. Not since I neglected all those friends and they drifted away and carried on with their lives. Though I suspect the only thing I had in common with most of them was the bikes.

But Dan asked. He wanted to know. He's never judged me harshly for a single thing I've ever said to him, or for acting like a complete fool when he gave me his email address.

There's no one else I can talk to about this; no one else who will understand, so I pull out my phone and lie there on my old bed, in my dusty old room, staring at the bike, and write him an email.

CHAPTER 19

Dan

THERE'S a little brick wall that runs along the front side of the school, and that's where I wait for Mum to pick me up after school.

I read over Luke's last email and start planning my reply in my head while I wait, trying to ignore the fact that I'm surrounded by other kids waiting for their parents to pick them up. Kids who seem way too tiny to even be at high school.

It's kind of mortifying, because Mum hasn't taken me to school or picked me up in years. Nicole drove me until she left for university and I caught the bus in the short time between her leaving and me getting my own licence.

I should feel less awful about sitting here though, because there's a reason Mum's picking me up today and it's a pretty cool one.

She's taking me to buy a camera. Like a fancy proper one.

I love creating images, capturing the perfect moment, preserving the emotion and joy of a moment forever. It's something I've considered trying to do when I finish school, but it's hard to learn the skills needed when all you have is a phone.

I've been doing a heap of research and printed several sheets of information regarding different camera models. I left them sitting on the kitchen table last night after I emptied out my bag looking for a worksheet I was supposed to complete for biology. I found the sheet, then got an email from Luke and left my mess behind as I vanished to my room to read and reply.

Mum found the pages and quizzed me relentlessly about them until I caved and told her I loved it.

I've been thinking about it more and more, especially since Luke found his bike and told me more about his accident. One moment, one clumsy step, and his life was changed, the two things he loved the most out of reach.

It seems wasteful to not follow through on something I've been wanting to do for a very long time.

So, Mum offered to come with me, to buy the camera for me, and now here I am, perching on a little wall surrounded by Year Nine kids.

Hollie wanders over and sits down beside me. Her long blonde hair is in a high ponytail that spills down over her shoulders, and she's wearing this super-cute pink hoodie with her jeans. She looks one hundred percent like a wholesome country girl and it's adorable.

"Hey, gorgeous," I say to her. I don't know when I started calling her such things – gorgeous, my love, babe – but they make her smile, and that always makes me smile. "What you got there?" I indicate the tattered green notebook in her hands. It's had a life, I can tell that much from here.

"It's Jonathan's," she says as I take it from her hands. "I found it in my car. Beth's picking him up here today so I figured I'd try and find him to return it."

I flick through the book. It's crammed with scrawled words,

sentences that aren't quite sentences. "Are these ... lyrics?" I ask, a little dumbstruck. Neither Jonathan nor Luke has ever mentioned Jonathan's a songwriter. Hollie's never mentioned it either.

Pages and pages of notes, some carefully written, some scribbled. The pages are tattered and worn and there's more than a few places where the ink has smudged, so it's hard to read the words.

Hollie peers over my shoulder. "Maybe," she says. "He's always scribbling things down, but he's never said anything to me about songs. I thought he just played covers."

Jonathan is a guitarist. He was in a band with Luke and Kristen before everything fell apart for them. When he came here he tried to block out as much of that as he could.

I do know Luke brought Jonathan's guitar with him when he came down to resolve their falling-out. But I've never seen Jonathan play it, or even mention it.

I snap the book closed after my quick skim and glance up as worn grey sneakers stop on the edge of my vision.

"What are you doing with that?" Jonathan's voice is tight.

I glance up at him. His jaw is tense, his green eyes sharp and angry.

"Oh, I found it in my car. It's yours, right?" Hollie says beside me, her voice casual, but she stiffens as she takes in Jonathan's posture.

"Yes, it is," he says though clenched teeth. He reaches towards me and snatches the book away as I hold it out to him. "But why do you have it?"

"I was coming to give it back to you," she says, standing up and taking a step towards him. She reaches out a hand and brushes it against his wrist, but he shifts away. His hand slides into his hair, and while sometimes he smiles when he does this (after Hollie once pointed it out as his nervous habit), he doesn't smile this time.

"But you read it? And you gave it to him?" His voice is furious. It's an anger we haven't seen from him in a while.

The thing with Jonathan is, he blamed himself for everything that went wrong with Luke, and after hearing some of Luke's side of the story I can sort of understand why.

Not that I think it was Jonathan's fault, but I can see why he would feel the guilt for his friend's accident.

When he first arrived and anyone got too close to him, he'd lash out like this. He didn't think he deserved friends, or for people to even care about him. He didn't believe he was allowed to be happy.

His guilt and emotions really put him through the wringer – Hollie, too – but over the past few months as they've worked through most of those issues and Jonathan's started seeing a counsellor, he's been way, way better.

He's mostly happy. He's generous and funny and totally devoted to Hollie, his Aunt Beth and baby cousin, Thea.

But this notebook. It's obviously tangled too tightly with those times. The times before the accident, when things were always easy for him and he was surrounded by love and could give it freely. Then the aftermath, which I assume are the pages in the book that are written in an angry scrawl.

"She didn't give it to me," I say, keeping my voice as calm as possible, trying hard not to be angry at him for taking this out on Hollie. "And I didn't read it."

"I saw you." He glowers down at me, then turns to my best friend. "Just because you're my girlfriend, it doesn't give you the right to go through my things," he says, his voice rising with each word.

Hollie's mouth drops open and she takes a step away. Her cheeks are going red and blotchy. The tears are coming. "I – I didn't," she whispers. She's trying to stay strong, to stay calm, but she's never been good against an angry tirade.

"I saw it," he says, towering over her.

"Hey, man," I say, standing up, shoulder to shoulder with Hollie. "We didn't read it, I swear."

"It's none of your business," he shouts at me. "None, so stay out of it, would you?" He spins around, taking a few steps.

"Jonathan," Hollie breathes, fighting to making her voice heard. I'm so proud of her.

"I don't want to talk right now," he snarls over his shoulder, then storms away.

We watch him approach Beth's car and climb in, and as she pulls out into the road and he disappears from view, Hollie wilts. She leans into me, taking shaky breaths.

I turn to her, my arm automatically wrapping around her shoulder, pulling her in against me. "It's gonna be okay, Holls," I murmur into her ponytail.

She buries her face in my chest and my heart implodes as I feel the wetness of her tears seeping through my shirt.

As much as I really don't want to, I cancel on my mum. The camera can wait. Hollie's pain cannot.

CHAPTER 20

Luke

"HEY."

Someone falls into step beside me. I glance up and catch sight of Tyler's blond hair. Not blond like Dan; Tyler's is lighter. Everything about him physically is lighter. His hair, his skin, his eyes, which are a sky blue.

He's got his bag over one shoulder and his rugby ball under the other arm. I'm beginning to wonder if he goes anywhere without it.

"Hey," I say, lacklustre. I'm not doing so well with all the peopling. I'm so damn tired. God, all the time, I'm tired.

I'm into my third week of school. The drudgery is even worse than I remember. I don't know why I was even remotely excited about coming back to school. Maybe I should give up on it altogether. Except I have absolutely no idea what I would do instead.

I always imagined I'd leave school and go riding for a while, try and get into competing in the United States or Europe and see a whole lot of the world. Not being able to do that never crossed my mind.

Tyler's studying me while I'm tangled up in my own thoughts. "Rough day?"

"Huh?" I glance up at him and realise how far away I've been. "Oh, yeah, a bit. Still adjusting."

"Yeah, I can only imagine," he says, and for some reason, coming from him it doesn't bother me. "How's it been going?"

I look over at Tyler and wonder why he cares. We knew each other before. We played rugby together last year and while he was much, much better at it than me, he wasn't arrogant about it and wasn't a jerk in other discernible ways, so we hung out a bit.

I didn't think we were particularly friendly though, and he was silent in the post-accident social media apocalypse, except for one text that said something like he was thinking of me and to get in touch if I needed anything.

I ignored it. Like I did the flurry of other messages and comments I received. At least Tyler's was a private message, so I know he wasn't doing it for everyone else to see how kind and caring he is.

"It's fine," I say, finally reaching the picnic table I've been heading for. I step over the bench awkwardly and can't suppress a small groan as I sit down.

Tyler gestures to the opposite seat, asking if it's okay to sit. I nod my agreement, still wondering what he's doing.

"You're looking at me like I'm going to murder you," he says, dumping his bag and pulling out a sandwich. He unwraps it and takes a huge bite.

"I, uh…" I have no response.

Tyler swallows. "I'm not, in case that's really a concern of yours." Another bite. Half the sandwich is gone already.

"I'm surprised, I guess," I say, tapping my fingers against the edge of the table.

"Why? Because I'm eating lunch with you? I eat lunch with you most days."

"But usually with your friends."

He stops chewing and studies me over the fragment of sandwich that's left. "Are you not my friend?"

Oh. Am I? I don't know. I really wasn't lying when I told Kristen I didn't know how to be a friend anymore.

I shrug, then drop my head into my hands, groaning. "I'm unfit for human consumption."

"Can't imagine you'd be that tasty anyway," Tyler says, deadpan. "But seriously," his voice resumes its normal candour, "do you think we aren't friends?"

"It appears I've forgotten how to be friends with someone," I mutter.

Tyler laughs, but not meanly. Because I made a joke, or at least I think I did. It's been a while; I can't remember how to do that either.

"We've been hanging out pretty much every lunchtime since you came back to school. I like you. I'd consider us friends."

Was it really that simple?

I've never really been a loner, because I always had Jonathan by my side. But it was him who tended to bring in the rest of our friend group. It wasn't my charm and charisma, that's for sure. Without him I probably wouldn't have had any friends. It's a painful thought.

"I know you've had a really tough time; not only the injury, but Jonathan leaving, and I can't begin to imagine what it's been like for you. I don't want this to be condescending so I apologise in advance if it is, but I do sort of know parts of what you're going through. I guess." He pauses and gives a little shrug.

I cut him off before he can continue. "You thought we could bond over it?" Oh, ouch. That was harsh.

Tyler shakes his head, unaffected by my outburst. "I don't know how to say it. But I've had to go back to school after an extended absence that was caused by awful circumstances and I've had to start a new school with exactly zero friends in it. I figured that if you came back with at least two friends, it'd help."

"Two friends?" I glare at him even though he's being generous. I came back to school thinking I had one friend. Maybe I was wrong.

"Kristen and me," he says, holding my gaze, still unflinching against my outburst.

I sigh and rest my chin on my hand, elbow propped on the table. I pick at the peeling green paint that every school picnic table I've ever laid eyes on has. "Sorry," I mutter. "I'm being super cranky." Which probably means it's time I eat and take some pills. I don't say that part out loud though.

Tyler huffs a little laugh again.

"Thank you," I say.

"No worries, but next time I behave in a friend-like way, don't be so suspicious."

I laugh this time, and the sound startles me.

"I'll try. It's been hard, adjusting to the injury, having everyone staring at me, hearing the rumours. Doing it without Jonathan makes it even harder."

Tyler nods. "You guys were pretty tight. How's he doing? He came up for a few days in the holidays?"

"Yeah, he did. He's doing real good. Never thought I'd see the day he became a farm boy, but there he is."

Tyler laughs, no doubt remembering Jonathan and his penchant for nice shoes and hair products. "Farming?"

"Yeah. He went to help his aunt out." I pause at Tyler's questioning look. I wonder what everyone thinks happened to Jonathan to make him leave. I wave my free hand in the air. "He was dealing with some shit and decided it was a good idea to have a fresh start."

Tyler nods. "I understand a fresh start," he says. I file that away with the other questions this conversation has raised.

"Anyway, this girl was working for his aunt, riding and looking after the horses. The rest, as they say, is history. Now even Johnnie rides."

Another laugh bursts out of Tyler and I can't help but grin at him. Maybe being friends isn't so bad. I'm like seventy-three percent convinced I can do this.

"What did you mean before," I ask, "when you said you had to have an extended absence?"

"Oh, um…" Tyler fidgets in his seat. It's the most uncomfortable I've ever seen him. "My mum died." He says it in such a rush I think I misheard him. Then it really hits that no, I didn't mishear him.

"I'm sorry," I say automatically, knowing as I say it how pointless and weak the words sound. "We don't have to talk about it if you don't want to."

"No, no, it's okay. I'm usually fine talking about it unless I'm caught off-guard." He shoots me a little smile. He takes a deep breath. "She was in a car accident. She spent some time in intensive care. But she never woke up."

Oh god. This is awful. At least no one died in my situation.

I don't know what to say, because I'm awful with people. I start hunting in my bag for my painkillers.

"I had some time off school. And eventually, when I went back, everyone was different. Or they were the same and I was different. They were all caught up in the latest drama of who was into who, or whatever the latest scandal was, and I'd seen this whole other side to the world."

I nod. I know exactly what he means, and he knows I know.

"Eventually it settled down, but then my dad needed more support so we moved here, closer to the rest of the family. I had to start over anyway."

"Does anyone here know about your mum?"

He shakes his head. "Not really. Some people know she died; most don't know anything. Those who do know, I don't think they know how she died, or how recently."

"Man, that sucks," I say. That's really all I can say.

"Yup," he says. "But going through that made me more aware of other people who might be in the same spot."

"Thanks," I say, truly meaning it. "For telling me. And for being my friend, even when I didn't realise it."

"No worries." He flashes me a grin, then his eyes flick up to something over my shoulder.

"Hey, Luke." Kristen leans over that shoulder, dropping a plastic container onto the table in front of me. "You must have dropped this in my car." Oh, thank God. It's the painkillers I've been searching for. The dull ache in my back has settled in and the thought of going the afternoon without them would likely bring me to tears.

I tilt my head and briefly rest it against her arm. "Thanks, Kris. You're a lifesaver."

"I know," she chirps, then presses a kiss to the top of my head and trots off to do whatever it is Kristen does during lunchtime.

I turn back to Tyler, snapping open the container as I do so. I could be imagining things, but I'd swear that as he watches Kristen walk away his cheeks are pinker than they were a moment ago.

CHAPTER 21
Dan

I **TEXT** Mum to tell her I need to help Hollie with something, which is technically true.

I'm sure she won't mind, not if Hollie needs me right now. I'm sure she'll understand.

But that doesn't mean I want to tell her face to face that I'm cancelling on her. I don't want to see her face fall, then watch her trying to cover up her disappointment.

Things have been weird since Jake moved in and I think Mum might feel guilty about it, especially after telling me this morning that he's staying even longer.

She was making the effort with the camera thing, and I've blown her off.

It's easy to bury those thoughts under all the others though. Hollie sniffles beside me as I drive her to work, which *of course* has to be at Jonathan's freaking house. At least we know he isn't here right now, because he's gone somewhere with his aunt, but I have no idea when he'll be back.

I park Hollie's car and she wipes at her eyes again. I rub a hand across her shoulder as she leans back in the seat.

"You know this isn't about you, whatever your head is telling you," I say. Hollie's been through emotional ups and downs over the past year and it all came to a head late last year when she was finally diagnosed with depression. She started therapy and is taking medication, and she's been much, much better. She still has rough times when something upsets her or she gets worn out – the usual ups and downs everyone experiences, but hers tend to drop her lower than most, or she can't bounce back as easily.

I'm horrified to realise I have no idea how she's doing at this moment. Not the thing to do with Jonathan, because I know she's feeling distressed about it and that she's going to blame herself for it, but her general mood lately.

With her dating Jonathan and working, plus school, and me being caught up in my own head about Luke, we haven't seen each other as often as we used to. Even when we do catch up it's been surface stuff, so I don't know where she's sitting and I don't know how hard it's going to be for her to bounce back from this blip.

But it's not something I can ask her outright – not right now, anyway.

"I should have known that stupid book was a thing for him," she says, her voice thick with tears. "He's always scribbling in it, but he's never shown me and I should have known."

"You can't know all the things that are going to upset him. It's not your job, Holls."

"But I should have known about that one. For a start, the picture of him and Luke is stuck inside the front cover. He loves that picture. The first time I ever saw him lose it was over that picture." She sniffles some more, then moves to push herself out of the car. "He's been so happy lately, I'd kind of forgotten he can get upset like that."

"I know." I climb out of the car as well. He has been happy, and I'm sure Hollie has too, the more I think about all the times I've seen her recently. But she can disguise her depression well. I know she can. "What's the plan today? Put me to work, boss," I say, trying to snap us both out of this gloomy mood.

It does the trick, and a smile plays at her mouth. "Up for a ride?"

I groan, dramatic and over the top. Hollie's smile widens.

"For you my dear, anything."

We tack up the horses and are wandering through the first paddock when Hollie returns to our conversation. "I'm always worried about him," she says out of the blue.

"Jonathan?"

"Yeah, like, I know he's doing better than he was. Having Luke back and everything between them cleared up, he's doing so much better. But I still really worry about him. I don't think he's even told me all of it, but it must have been pretty awful for him up there, after the accident." She pauses, chewing her lip. "It had to have been pretty awful for him to leave. To walk out one day and not come back. You saw the photos on Luke's wall. He had all those friends, that whole life."

I nod. "He's doing okay though, Holls," I say. I don't tell her that this is my feeling. This is how I always feel. I'm always worried about everyone – about her, about Nicole and my parents and Luke. Even stupid Jake Daly. I push it all down and pretend it's not there, because I don't want them to have to worry about me, but the fear for them is always there.

"I know he is." She takes a deep breath and her exhalation

is shaky. "But," her voice drops to a whisper, "what if he wants all that back?"

My heart fractures for her. Her wide grey eyes land on mine, her bottom lip quivers and she tangles her fingers in her horse's mane.

"I'm always scared for that," she breathes, then tips her head back, face to the sky, which I know is a trick of hers to fight back tears.

I nudge my horse close to hers until our knees are bumping. I pull my horse to a stop and hers stops beside us. I rest my hand on her shoulder, pressing my thumb against her jaw to make her look at me.

"I know he's angry right now," I say, looking her dead in the eye, "but I don't think he's going to give this up, Hollie. I really don't. He's sorting things out. He learned to ride for you, he chose to stay here. He chose you. I don't think he's giving that up, so don't give up on him yet, okay?"

She leans into my hand, then tilts forward so she's leaning her head against my shoulder. I wrap an arm around her in an awkward hug.

"Okay," she mumbles into my shirt. "Thank you." She pushes back, wiping her tears on the shoulder of my sweatshirt as she does.

"Anytime, my love. I'm always here for you."

We finish our ride with no more tears, and when we get back Jonathan is sitting on the railing fence beside Hollie's car. We dismount and I silently take both sets of reins, leading the horses away as Jonathan climbs down and meets her halfway. She folds her arms and stares him down, waiting for him to explain. I lead the horses around the corner and begin to untack them.

Jonathan joins me a few minutes later.

"I'm sorry," he says without preamble or deliberating. I pause in removing Alaska's saddle and face him while he continues speaking. He gets straight to the point. "I write a lot in that notebook, things I'm thinking and feeling. Not all of it is stuff I'm proud of. I was surprised to see you with it and I reacted badly."

"You think?" I'm not annoyed for my benefit. Hollie didn't deserve it.

"I know. I'm sorry. I'm working on it, you know that, right?"

"Yeah, I know. I appreciate your apology, but how is Hollie?"

He smiles, but before he can answer me she appears around the corner, holding Jonathan's baby cousin Thea on her hip. "I'm all good, Danny," she says.

When she drops me home later, Hollie is tired. The emotional upheaval of the afternoon has worn her out, but she's happy again. Her fears from earlier are drifting away, or at least being pushed to the side for now. Jonathan's sincere, emotional apology has helped.

She pulls out of my driveway with a cheery wave, but still, that worrying feeling I have, that ingrained need to make everything better for everyone – it never quite goes away.

CHAPTER 22

Luke

TWO DAYS after my heart to heart with Tyler we're heading to the carpark after the final bell. He's in his training gear and tossing his rugby ball from hand to hand and I'm trying not to be too jealous of his ability to do so, while *walking*.

I've mostly stopped using two crutches around home and for short excursions, but I still use them both for school days, just in case.

We reach the carpark and approach Kristen, who's sitting on the bonnet of her little hatchback. I don't mean she's leaning on it; she's fully sitting up there, cross-legged. She's talking on her phone, waving her free hand in the air. Hot pink nail polish today. Wisps of her dark hair are flying free from a messy knot on the top of her head.

"Thank you so much," she says to whoever's on the other end of the call, then hangs up right as we reach her.

Tyler is still right beside me. He's stopped tossing the ball.

"Oh, Luke," Kristen says, "I'm so sorry. My car's dead."

"Dead?" I say. "What kind of dead? It's the battery, isn't

it?" I've warned her about it before. If Jonathan were here he'd have already fixed it for her.

She hangs her head. "Yes," she grumbles. I crack a smile at her sulking. "But it means I can't get you to the gym."

"Oh, right," I say. I've momentarily forgotten my session this afternoon with my personal trainer. She specialises in injury rehabilitation and I see her every week. Then she gives me exercises and workouts to do at home to regain strength and mobility.

"Do you have jumper leads?" Tyler asks. "I could jump it for you?"

Kristen shakes her head. "I don't. It's okay, I've called Luke's dad. One of the minions is on the way."

"The minions?" Tyler looks at me confused.

I laugh. "My dad has a panel beating business. He'll send over one of the guys to jump start it. Then Kris can go buy a new battery."

She pouts, but I can see the amusement in her eyes. "It still doesn't solve your problem though," she says.

She's right, of course. I don't have time to wait for someone to turn up, jump start her car and make it to the gym on time for my session.

"I can drive you," Tyler says. "If you're all right here?" He turns to Kristen.

"Sure," she says. "Thank you so much. Haley will kick his ass if he's late."

"You sure it's all right?" I ask Tyler, already heading around to the boot of Kristen's car to dump my school stuff and grab my gym bag. Because we all know Tyler is going to insist.

"Of course. I insist."

Tyler drives this slightly beaten-up SUV that's old but comfortable. There's nothing flashy about it, which sort of sums up Tyler, too. Not flashy, but genuine.

Old school rock is playing through the speakers as we manoeuvre through the streets. My fingers start tapping without my consent. I let the rhythm of familiar beats carry me away.

Until I catch sight of Tyler staring at me as we wait at an intersection. I stop abruptly, heat creeping up my neck.

"You're really into music, huh?"

"Um, yeah, I suppose," I say, trying to rub away the heat on the back of my neck. I sigh. "I used to play the drums … before." I gesture at my legs.

"Oh," he says. He concentrates on the intersection, pulling into the traffic before speaking again. "I think I saw you play once. I was really new here and you guys played at an assembly or something? But I think that's the only time."

"Yeah, it was probably us. But we weren't playing much towards the end of last year," I say. "Jonathan and I got caught up in trying to pass exams, and when I wasn't studying I was riding." The words fall out, casual and easy, because that's how everything feels with Tyler. Then I realise what I've said. I want to talk about riding even less than music.

"Riding? Mountain bikes, right?" Ugh. He noticed.

"Yeah. Mountain biking." I turn my head away and watch out the window.

"Shit, man," Tyler says, as he pulls into the gym parking lot. "Can you still do either? Riding or drums, I mean?" When I shake my head, he continues. "That's rough. I'm sorry."

I shrug. There's not much I can do about it.

Except … I keep thinking about my bike, tucked away in my old bedroom under that sheet. I keep thinking about the feeling of wind on my face, that swooping sensation when you hit a berm just right. I keep thinking about what Dan said after I told him I'd found it.

"Thanks for the ride," I mutter to Tyler, trying and failing not to sound like a cranky child.

"No worries," he smiles, dropping the touchy subject and letting me know he's not bothered by my mood. "How long's your session? I'll drive you home after."

"You don't have to do that," I say. "I can call my parents, or Kristen."

"I don't mind," he says. "I'll go for a run while I'm waiting for you. There's a good park a few streets over."

Running. The jealousy again. I shove it away, because it's not fair and it won't do me any good.

"If you're sure," I say, sliding out of the SUV, taking only one crutch. I grab my bag and slip it over my other shoulder. Dropping one crutch has made such everything so much easier. "I'll be about an hour."

"Of course. Have fun."

I pull a face at him, showing how much fun personal training rehab sessions are. He laughs as he locks the car and turns to jog off down the street.

My session is, as always, a bitch. I assume most personal training sessions are the same. The reality, though, is that I always feel a million times better after the exercise. These sessions, and the workouts I force myself into doing at home, are the only things that keep my mental state under control most days.

Haley is a feisty little woman. There's really no other way to describe her. She's short and fierce. She has no time for excuses. But she's not brutal, and will take into account any pain or niggles I'm having. But she knows how to motivate me and doesn't tolerate my general whininess. In short, she's really, really good at her job.

She puts me through my paces with a variety of strength work.

"Right, onto the bike," she says as I finish my final set of lunges. The fact I can even do lunges now is amazing, and if my legs didn't feel like they were going to fall off I'd appreciate the moment a little more.

I head for the stationary bike, the same oily feeling settling in my gut as every other time I've been near this machine. I've used it a lot in the past few months because it's such a good low-impact exercise that doesn't stress any of my joints.

I hesitate when I reach it, resting my hand on the seat and imagining for a moment that it's my own bike.

"You all good?" Haley says, striding up beside me.

I turn to her. "Will I be able to ride a real bike again?"

She doesn't look surprised at my question. She studies me thoughtfully for a moment. "Like I say every time you ask me what your abilities are going to be going forward, every injury is unique and I can't say for sure."

I deflate. I don't know why I was expecting her to tell me I could do it. That I'd be able to ride again.

She continues. "In saying that, you've made amazing progress and if it's something you really want to do, I don't see why you can't. It's really going to have to be a matter of carefully testing it, though. You might be ready now or you might not be ready for six months, a year.

"But." Her voice takes on a warning tone. "Do not expect to be able to ride like you did a year ago."

Oh, so she knows. I suppose I should have expected that she would. Of course she would want to know who she was dealing with, and it wouldn't take any more than dropping my name in a Google search to find out that I was doing pretty well.

Haley is still talking, the warning becoming sterner. "You might be able to ride again, you might be able to ride trails again, but I don't want you to get your expectations up that you'll ride like that again."

I nod, solemn. I know I'll never ride like that again. I think I've come to terms with that. Apparently I haven't come to terms with not riding at all though, which is a surprise to me. I thought I was done with it, for good. It's why I told my parents to sell the bike.

But ever since I found it, I've been thinking about how it would feel to ride it again. Dan's words from an email he sent me after I poured my emotions out to him come to mind.

Whatever your parents' reason for not selling it, I'll bet it comes from love. Maybe they simply didn't want to get rid of something you love. Yeah, you'll probably never win a world championship on it, but maybe one day you'll be able to enjoy it again, and they didn't want to take that option away from you. Maybe it's less that they haven't accepted your injury, and more that they know you're stronger than you give yourself credit for.

I'm stronger than I give myself credit for. I grip the seat on the stationary bike and turn my attention back to Haley.

"But I can try?" It comes out a whisper, like I'm too scared to hope.

She nods, gives me a small smile. "You can try, mate. Take it easy and be careful. But for now: this bike." She pats the seat, then my shoulder.

I climb on and begin to pedal.

***

Tyler is nowhere to be seen when I emerge from the gym, sweat-soaked and exhausted. I lean against his car and pull out my phone.

There's an email waiting for me.

Dan.

Of course.

I smile when I see his name. His emails are always the highlight of my day. I'm about to open it when Tyler runs up beside me, coming to a stop and panting hard.

"Sorry," he says between breaths. "Lost track of time."

"All good," I say, sliding my phone back into my pocket. I'll read Dan's email later, when I'm alone and can savour every word of it.

We climb into the vehicle, my movements already becoming slow and clumsy as fatigue sets in.

"Good workout?"

"Yeah," I say. A little bubble of excitement, of hope, is building in my stomach. "She said I can try riding again." I didn't mean to blurt it out like that, but I'm too excited to actually care right now. I'll have time for regrets later.

Tyler glances over at me, his brow creased. I don't know

him well enough yet to know if it's confusion or concern, or something else.

"I might not be able to yet, and she said I'll probably never be able to ride like I did. But maybe one day I can ride trails again."

The crease in his brow clears and Tyler grins at me. "That's awesome, man."

I nod, the little bubbling feeling spreading through me. "I might try this weekend," I say, the idea running away with me.

I can't do it on my own though, and for some reason I don't want my parents to know. Not yet. In case I can't do it. I don't want to get their hopes up as well as mine.

I glance at Tyler. My friend, according to him. "I don't suppose you'd be able to help me get my bike out?"

I explain where it is, and he grins. "Sure thing. I'm so there when you actually get on it too. Saturday morning?"

I grin back at him. "Sounds like a plan."

CHAPTER 23

Dan

FRIDAY AFTERNOONS USED to bring me such joy.

Really, they did.

Once school was out for the week and I could go home and do whatever I wanted for the entire weekend, even if that meant lying on the couch and binge-watching Netflix.

I could sleep all day, or lie on the lawn attempting to take interesting photos of leaves. I could eat whatever I wanted, whenever I wanted.

A lot of the time I'd be on my own, which I relished after a week of hanging out with stinky teenagers and their terrible jokes. Most people would assume I'm one hundred percent social, one hundred percent of the time. But I don't think they realise that even I need time out now and again. That being "on" all the time can be exhausting. Sometimes I want to be left alone to do whatever it is I want to do.

Not every weekend. Some weekends I'll help Mum at work, or hang out with Hollie, or go to parties and be around people. But every so often I really enjoy being left to my own devices.

This Friday afternoon, though, I am not looking forward to my blissfully peaceful weekend at all.

Oh no, I'm dreading every moment of the next two days.

Because Jake Daly is still in my house. There's no sign of him going anywhere. In fact, yesterday he arrived with another bag of his stuff.

Last weekend I forced myself on Hollie. She was very good about it. Jonathan was even better, considering they were supposed to be doing all these romantic things together and I totally crashed their date. Then on Sunday, when Hollie was with her best friend of the girl variety, I actually turned up to Jonathan's to help him fix a fence. Me, with a hammer in my hand, building a fence.

The things Jake being in my house is forcing me to do.

I pull into the driveway and head inside. I don't notice anything is amiss until I put my key in the back door and find it already unlocked.

How did Jake beat me home? I left school before him and came straight here. Also, I'm sure his car wasn't parked out the front, otherwise I'd have spent at least fifty percent of my walk between my car and the house throwing murderous glares at it. I'm sure neither of my parents' vehicles were in the driveway either.

I slide the door open and step inside, listening intently. I close the door silently behind me, slip my backpack off my shoulder and place it carefully on the floor.

My phone is in my hand, ready to dial the police, or my parents, or someone, if I need to. It's a ridiculous notion, because if I've caught someone burglarising my house I'm pretty sure they'll simply bowl me over on their way out.

I step carefully across the tiled kitchen floor and peer into the lounge.

The TV is on. I'm pretty sure it's an episode of *Queer Eye*. There's a box of tissues on the coffee table, used ones scrunched up and tossed on the table.

"What the…" I don't finish speaking as I realise there's a person curled up on the couch, a worn grey hoodie covering her hair.

At my words she lifts her head, red-rimmed eyes peering at me. "Danny," she croaks, and I hurry across the room, tumbling onto the couch beside Nicole.

"Nic," I say, wrapping my arms around her in a giant hug, pulling her upright. "What are you doing here?"

I fight with the feelings of panic and fear writhing under my skin. I'm not going to let them take over, not now.

This is not the first time I've walked in to find Nicole curled into this couch, this same hoodie cocooning her.

I hate this hoodie with every fibre of my being, but she insists it's a favourite. It obviously still is for her. I used to like it, once upon a time, about five years ago, before it became the depression hoodie.

No one else calls it that. I'm not sure anyone else even relates it to that. But for me, every time I see the damned thing I want to tear it to shreds. Because it reminds me. It reminds me of those long days sitting beside her as she slept, her face pale, heavy purple circles under her eyes.

On a good day, she refers to them as Prada, her designer bags.

When she's wearing the depression hoodie, there are no jokes.

Nicole wipes her eyes with the cuff of her sleeve, sniffling away her tears.

"What's wrong?" I ask, squeezing her even tighter to me.

"*Queer Eye*," she says, gesturing to the TV with a hiccup of a laugh. "It gets me every damn time."

I study her, trying to figure out if she's telling me the truth, if it's the show making her cry, or if it's something else. She's selected the perfect show as her cover, because I really can't tell what's causing the tears. I know when I watched the episode that she's paused I bawled like a baby too.

"Honestly, Danny, I'm fine," she says, pushing me away and sitting straighter. She faces me, sitting cross-legged. She pushes the hoodie back and I'm weirdly relieved to see her hair has recently been washed. It eases some of the weight on my chest. "Am I not allowed to come and visit my favourite brother without him worrying about me?" She smiles, and maybe my conviction that there are no jokes in the depression hoodie is slightly off.

"I was surprised to see you," I say, giving a little shrug and slumping into the couch, feigning nonchalance. I pick up the remote. "What episode are you watching?"

Two episodes later Jake crosses the room, heading straight to the guest room where he's sleeping. I manage to hide my tears as he passes.

On the fourth episode Mum arrives home, containers of Chinese food in hand. Jake finally emerges from his room to grab a plate.

"Ooh, yay," Mum says, eyeing the TV while handing plates to Nicole and me before settling down on my sister's other side. I eat until I think I'm going to explode.

Once Nicole is finished with her food she slides her plate

onto the coffee table and curls into me, her head resting against my shoulder.

Barely ten minutes later she's fast asleep. I wrap my arm around her and try to focus on the show even though I've seen it before, but my thoughts keep wandering to my sister.

I worry about her constantly.

I worry about her being away from home where I can't keep an eye on her.

I worry about how often she wears this hideous hoodie.

I worry about why she's suddenly here on our couch, even though she swears she's simply visiting because she wants to see us.

Most of all, I worry that there's nothing I can do to help.

CHAPTER 24

Luke

I BARELY SLEPT.

I really tried, but every time I closed my eyes I imagined how this morning is going to go.

Most of the scenarios didn't go well. Most of them had me sprawled on the ground, tangled in my bike, the deep ache of broken bones radiating through my body.

My teachers always said I have an overactive imagination.

I must have passed out somewhere around 3 am and scraped in a few hours of unrestful sleep, so hopefully I'll be awake enough to actually do this.

Tyler is arriving any minute.

Dad's at his workshop, like most Saturday mornings. Mum is probably there too, catching up on paperwork. I figure we've got at least three hours until she's back.

A vehicle outside. He's here. I take a deep breath and push myself off my bed, where I've been sitting and fidgeting. I would have been pacing but it's frustratingly hard these days, and not nearly as dramatic.

"Ready to do this?" Tyler grins at me as I swing open the door.

"Yep," I say, pushing the words out past the lump in my throat.

He strolls into my room, eyes darting around, taking it all in.

His gaze lands on the drum set and his eyes light up. "You been playing?"

I shake my head. "No, a friend was. I haven't got around to covering them up again." There's a funny feeling in my chest when I say the word friend in relation to Dan. I don't know if it's because I love that he's my friend, or because it's not enough.

Tyler nods, then wanders over to the wall of photos. He's probably in a couple of the group shots. I don't even know what's up there. A bunch of Jonathan for sure, but Kristen put them all up for me. I haven't paid that much attention.

The only addition I've made is one photo taken the night Hollie and Jonathan interrupted Dan and me making out. The four of us are tucked in a tight huddle, grinning up at the camera. You can only see our faces. You can't see where Dan's hand slid inside the sleeve of my t-shirt and caressed my bicep right as Jonathan took the photo.

That moment is the happiest I've been since the accident. I can't recall a happier memory, even from before it.

I tear myself back to the present moment and gesture towards the main part of the house. "Shall we?"

Tyler grins and follows me. He makes no comment about my slow progress on the stairs, and when I pull the sheet off the bike he lets out a low whistle. "Dude, this is some serious bike."

I give an awkward laugh and stoop to grab my helmet as Tyler easily lifts the frame and heads for the stairs.

He gets the bike down the stairs with more ease than I would have before the spinal injury. He pushes it through the front door and stops so abruptly I almost crash into him.

I manoeuvre around him and find Kristen standing in the driveway, applying lipstick in the wing mirror of Tyler's car. She's wearing loose ripped jeans and a tight purple sweater made from some fuzzy kind of fabric. For a girl – and my best mate's sister – she looks pretty damn hot.

But shit.

I haven't told Kristen about this potentially disastrous attempt to ride. It seemed easier not to tell anyone. I didn't even tell Dan in any of the three emails I've sent him since I decided to do this.

Kristen snaps her lipstick closed and studies us for a moment, eyes narrowed, before they widen and those deep red lips curve into a wicked smile when she catches sight of the helmet I hold in my hands.

"You're going to ride?" She bounds over to me, hope and joy and glee radiating from her.

"I'm going to try," I say, trying to take slow, deep breaths.

She grins, then turns to Tyler, still standing frozen with the bike. "I didn't know you still had it," she breathes, trailing her fingers over the handle bars. "I'm so coming with you." She glances at Tyler. "Hi, I'm Kris," she says, and holds out her hand to him.

"Ty-Tyler," he stammers. I could be way off base here, but I'm pretty convinced he's into her.

She grins up at him and says simply, "I know. Nice to officially meet you." Then she turns to me as if she didn't make all his Christmases come at once and asks where we're going to ride.

I sigh. "I don't really want to do it in public, but it's got to be in the park round the corner."

Like I really, really, don't want to do it in public, where people who don't know me, who don't know what happened, can judge me if this goes horribly wrong.

But I can't do it in our short little driveway, and we have about a metre of grass behind the house, so the park it is.

Tyler finally snaps out of his daze and the three of us make our way down the street, Tyler wheeling my bike between us.

We arrive at the park and I'm grateful when I realise it's pretty quiet. It must be too early for all the kids to be at the playground. There's a couple of people walking dogs and a lone toddler and parent pair over by the swings.

We find the largest expanse of flat grass we can, and I run out of ways to stall.

It's time.

I pull my helmet on, revelling in the simple but oh-so-familiar motions. I push the seat down as low as I can without adjusting the actual post, grateful for the automatic seat dropper that is going to make this so much easier and swing my leg over. Well, "swing" might be taking it too far. It's awkward and clumsy, but I manage to stand astride the bike while Tyler holds it in place. Kristen wordlessly takes my crutches. Neither of them laugh at my attempt at just getting on the bike.

I run my hands over the grips and settle them into position. I adjust the pedals, bracing my left foot against one. All that's left to do now is push down and ride.

"Luke," Kristen says, covering my hand with hers. I glance up into those green eyes that for a second make me catch my breath. They're so much like Jonathan's. "Regardless of how this goes, know that we're all super proud of you, and think you're completely badass." Her mouth tilts up.

I twist my hand, turning it so I can hold onto hers. I squeeze it tight. "Thanks, Kris."

She slides her hand from mine, stepping back. "Now, ride," she calls out, like she's announcing some massive event. She spreads her arm out, pointing directly ahead of me.

I flash Tyler a grin, but his gaze is on Kristen.

Then, I push down on that pedal, using the movement to push myself up onto the seat.

I push down with my other foot. The bike wobbles. I push again. Not enough power. The bike wobbles more; it's tilting and I'm going down.

I urge my foot to move, to get off the pedal and onto the ground to stop myself from going over. But it's not moving fast enough.

"Oof. Got you." Tyler is there. He's caught the bike, and too late, my foot moves. I settle it onto solid ground and lean over the handlebars, heart hammering in my chest. I rest my head on my arms, breathing slowly, trying to kill the adrenaline surging through my veins.

A hand on my shoulder. It's small. Kristen. I take a deep breath and let it out slowly as I raise my head to meet her gaze again. She gives me a small, determined nod and I return it.

I adjust my pedals again, and push.

On the sixth attempt, I do it. I ride a loop around Tyler and Kristen, who stand in the middle and whoop like this is the greatest day of their lives.

It might be the greatest day of mine. I ride another loop then come to a stop before my two friends, my own smile as wide as theirs. I slide my phone out of my pocket and toss it to Kristen. "Photo, yeah? For Johnnie," I add, lying to us both. We both know this picture is going directly to Dan.

CHAPTER 25

Dan

I'M SITTING at a cafe table waiting for Hollie when the picture arrives.

Luke is standing astride a gleaming charcoal-coloured mountain bike, his smile taking up his entire face. I wonder for a moment why he's sending me an old picture. Then I realise his hair is short under the helmet. Before the accident he had long hair.

The photo is quickly followed by a video of Luke riding the bike in a big sweeping loop around what looks like a park. There's a kids' playground in the background.

Two voices are shouting, a girl's and a guy's, whooping and hollering at him as he slowly pushes the bike forward, his legs pumping in steady rhythm.

He's doing it. He's riding his bike again. When he talked to me about it he gave me the impression he wouldn't ride again. He hasn't mentioned it since.

He talked about his bike though, telling me about finding it stashed in his old room while he was searching for school books. He told me how it had felt, to see it again and know it was useless to him. He wondered why his parents had kept it. The shock of the discovery, the pain of the memories: it was all evident in his words.

And now here he was, riding it again. His rare jewel of a smile is spread across his face, grey eyes gleaming with wicked delight.

I'm overcome with the desire to touch him. It happens now and again, my body craving the feel of him. Sometimes it comes on so violently it makes my head spin and my knees weak.

Hollie's voice cuts into my swooning. "What are you looking at?" she says, dropping into the seat across from me, leaning over trying to get a better view of my phone.

"Nothing," I say, locking the screen with a click. "Just a stupid video of clumsy penguins."

She grins. I know how much she enjoys clumsy animal videos. I suddenly worry she's going to ask to see it, and I won't have anything on my screen except a photo of Luke.

I don't know if I can tell her. Luke doesn't say anything in his message, but I get the feeling he's going to want Jonathan to find out directly from the source.

I want to tell her, though. I have to catch myself a million times a day.

I want to tell her about Luke and about all the *feelings* I have buzzing around my chest when I think of him.

I want to tell her how shitty I feel having Jake living in my house and having to pretend like our lack of friendship doesn't hurt me still.

I want to tell her about Nicole and how her history of mental health has left me constantly worrying for her, even when she's doing really well.

But Hollie doesn't need more stuff to worry about – not when she's just getting herself back on her feet.

"Danny," Hollie says, her voice soft. "You okay?"

I realise I've been lost in my thoughts, and I drag my focus back to our conversation. "Yeah, of course. I'm all good."

She looks like she doesn't believe me, like she's going to argue with me about it, but Jonathan arrives and saves the day.

He tilts his chin up at me – the universal guy greeting – then drops a light kiss on Hollie's head. The ease and comfort in it makes me want to throw things. Because I'm super envious, not bitter that they're together. Just jealous I'm alone.

Jonathan's green eyes are sparkling and he's grinning ear to ear. "Check this out." He slides into the seat beside Hollie and pulls his phone out of his jeans. Hollie leans into him and that envy sweeps me again.

I hear the sound before I see what's on his phone screen. But by the sound alone, of those two voices cheering and whooping, I know what Jonathan is showing Hollie. It's the video of Luke riding.

My breath catches in my throat. How am I going to handle this? Luke asked me not to say anything and I promised I wouldn't. I said it was only between us; no one else needed to know. Luke hasn't told them – not as far as I'm aware, anyway. I assume if he did tell them they'd have brought it up with me one way or another.

"Oh my gosh," Hollie exclaims, excitement bubbling over as she realises what she's watching. "He can still do it!"

I'm not sure if that was a question or a statement, but yeah, either way she's right. I try to look blank, confused about what they're looking at.

"He looks so happy," Hollie says, grinning up at Jonathan.

Jonathan is gazing down at the phone, also looking so very happy. He gives a small nod but doesn't look away from the screen. I know Jonathan thinks the accident was his fault. I also know that since he and Luke reconnected, Jonathan has mostly processed that he isn't to blame. But the way he's looking at that video, I can tell he still feels some of that pain, that guilt.

Hollie glances at me and I do my best to look like I don't understand what's going on. "Oh, Danny, look," she says, guiding Jonathan's hand towards me, turning it slightly so I can see.

There he is. I widen my eyes, let my mouth fall open.

"Is this the first time?" I say, hoping my voice sounds breathless and excited. I mean, it should, because I *am* breathless and excited. Riding was the thing Luke loved most in the world, even more than that drum set.

I drag back the feelings I had a moment ago, when I opened my own email containing the same video.

Jonathan nods. "I didn't even know he was going to try it. This is awesome."

I didn't know he was going to try either, and it makes me feel slightly better that Jonathan's in the same boat.

Then I feel like a brat for it. I told Luke he didn't owe me anything, and I meant it.

The fact that the tall blond guy caught in the tail-end of the video clearly knew about it doesn't hit me like a punch to the gut at all.

"That's so cool," I say, pushing away that bitter bile. I told him I was happy with friendship, and I am. I'd be happier if the friendship involved kissing and hand holding and that comfortable couple-ease Hollie and Jonathan share, but I meant what I said. I'll take whatever he wants – or is able – to give me.

For all I know, the tall blond guy is Kristen's boyfriend. It's clearly her filming; I can tell by her cheering.

"Who's that?" Hollie asks, and I don't know if I should hug her or hate her for it.

Jonathan studies the clip again, then rewatches the last few seconds. "It's Tyler, I think," he says eventually. "Nice guy. He's on the rugby team. Plays really well. I don't know him that well, he only started at our school last year."

A waitress arrives then, loading our food onto the table. She looks exhausted, harried and completely done with today. I can relate.

"Thanks." I grin up at her, forcing away all the tortured feelings that have been spinning through my head in the past few minutes. The waitress glares at me for a moment, but I keep grinning. "Appreciate it," I say, and finally the glare cracks, showing the tiniest glimmer of a smile.

Breaking that stare, getting that twitch of a lip: it does it for me. It pushes the roiling bitterness away. I use that tiny moment of making someone's day fractionally better to smother the negativity and turn to my friends. "So, Hollie, my love, what's the plan for the day?"

She beams at me across the table, and whatever bad feelings were lingering vanish. Because making someone else happy – that's all that matters.

CHAPTER 26

Luke

I'VE JUST RIDDEN three laps of the park. Every time I get on my bike it's slightly easier, though I'm definitely not up for long rides yet despite the amount of time I've spent on that stationary bike in the gym. The balance required is still too much for my back and core to handle.

I even told my parents last night, after Mum came into my room in the garage and stopped dead at the sight of my bike leaning against the wall.

She stood there, mouth opening and closing like a fish as she took it in, including the helmet hanging from the handle bars.

I called out for Dad, asking him to come in before Mum completely malfunctioned. He wandered in, a curious look on his face, then he too stopped dead, staring at the bike.

They both turned to me as I sat on my bed, grinning at them. "So, uh, I started riding again," I said. "Surprise."

They laughed, and Mum cried a little bit and I promised to show them sometime soon.

Now, Tyler and I are sitting at our usual picnic table,

working on the stupid math homework I'm still struggling with. We've taken to studying here after school on the days we're both free and the weather isn't bad, squeezing in assignments between my laps of the park. We've been working in silence for a few moments when he scowls at his textbook and drops his pen.

"So, before the ball everyone's meeting at my place. A bunch are staying there afterwards, too," he says.

The ball. The school's biggest social occasion. People plan for this for years in advance. This year is supposed to be my last one. It doesn't quite have the same hysteria around it as an American prom seems to, but it's still a pretty significant thing for most senior students.

I haven't paid much attention to everyone at school getting excited about it. Tickets are on sale; they have been for weeks. Dates are being asked. Dresses bought and suits hired.

I realise I'm sitting here staring at Tyler not saying anything.

"You are coming, right?" he asks, breaking my suspended silence.

"Uh, no," I say.

I decided ages ago I'm not going.

But that was before Tyler and feeling like I have friends again.

Tyler hesitates and I know he's going to ask me a touchy question, one he's worried I'll react poorly to. "Is there a particular reason you're not?" he asks eventually and I have to hand it to him, that was very diplomatic.

I sigh and shut my math book, chewing on the end of my pen. "Various reasons," I say eventually, weighing up what ones I want to share, then deciding to hell with it and letting them all roll out. I check them off on my fingers as I go. "My body's half broken and I don't know if I can handle it. I couldn't dance before, so I definitely can't now. It feels crap going without Johnnie, and even if it didn't feel crap going without him, I don't think there's anyone I can go with because I've been a social hermit for months. And that's only thinking about friends. An actual date is so far from being a consideration…" I trail off as an image passes through my mind.

What would Dan look like in a suit? I've only ever seen him in shorts and t-shirts, and once in a pair of jeans that made me want to write thank you letters to whatever company had made them.

"Dude." Tyler interrupts my thoughts, and it really is for the best considering where they were headed. "For a start, there's seats. You can rest if you need to. Nobody can dance, so that concern seems irrelevant. You know that everyone shuffles around and does the occasional headbang. You'll be fine. As far as people to go with—" he says, breaking off to gesture to himself with raised eyebrows and a sardonic grin. "You have me. Matt's coming, Stacey, all of them. Some have dates. Some do not." He shrugs. "It's no drama, but I suspect the way your eyes went all fuzzy just then you've thought of someone to ask." He rests his elbows on the table and watches me, waiting for me to spill the beans.

"Uh, actually, maybe I have," I stammer. Could I? Could I ask Dan to come with me? Would he even want to? It's a long way for him to come, but maybe. And how could I not have a good time with him by my side?

It would mean something major. Coming out. I'd have to go through with it. Everyone would know.

Can I do it?

"I don't know, though. This person." I sigh and run a hand over my hair. "It's so complicated. I don't want to mess things up with them."

"What makes you think you'll mess things up?" Tyler asks, closing his textbook. He's clearly more interested in this conversation than math.

"Because I'm a total disaster. As my friend, you will have noticed that I'm a shit one. Seventy percent of the time I forget I have friends, and the rest of the time I don't believe it's actually real." I give him a knowing look and he laughs. He knows I'm right. I continue, my voice getting more frenzied with every word out of my mouth. "So if I can't be friends with people, how am I supposed to be in a relationship with someone? If I invite this person then that's where it'll end up. That, or it'll all burn to the ground in a fiery inferno."

"Dude," Tyler says, lifting his hands in a placating gesture. "First, chill. Second, you're doing fine with the whole friend thing. Yeah, you've got a lot going on, but the right person will get it. You sound like you already know this person pretty well?" I nod at his question. "So have they ever given you any indication they're not going to be supportive of you?"

He has a point.

"It's still terrifying."

"Damn straight it is. But you'll never know how it's going to turn out if you don't even try." He gives my bike a knowing look and I sigh. His point stands, reinforced.

I glance at the bike sitting beside me. The thing I thought I could never do again. I can still feel the power in my legs as I pushed down on those pedals and made the wheels go round. It's such a tiny thing to most people. But I thought I'd *never* be able to do it again. And I did.

So surely I must be able to come out, to show people who I am. Especially for Dan, even if it's only for a single night with him.

I look up at Tyler, still watching me.

"Yeah," I say, a smile spreading across my face. "Okay. I'll ask tonight. Even if they say no, then yeah, I'll come anyway."

Tyler raises his hands in the air in celebration, face open wide in a grin. "Yes!" He exclaims. "And don't worry, man, there's no way they'll say no. Not to you."

My face flushes. He has no idea, but here's hoping he's right.

CHAPTER 27

Dan

I HIT send and fall back onto my bed, holding my phone against my chest.

I'm completely lovesick and it's revolting. I do not care.

Luke and I have been emailing daily, sometimes more than once a day, for weeks now.

I've told no one. Not Hollie, not Jonathan – not even Nicole. I want to. I want to be able to talk to my best friends about him, but I don't want the drama. I don't think there'll be any; at least, not from Hollie and Nicole. I have no idea how Jonathan will process this fledgling relationship I have with his best friend. I'm not sure I'm willing to risk it.

None of them will have an issue with Luke's gender, although as far as I know it'll be news to them, like it was news to me. His gender feels irrelevant in the bigger picture. He's Luke and it doesn't matter. I want to know more about him, be near him, feel his touch on my skin again.

For Jonathan, it'll be less about gender and more about the fact that it's his best friend.

Jonathan's a good guy. I know he is. Hollie wouldn't love him like she does if he wasn't. Neither would Luke.

Once he started dealing with his problems and fears, he went from a cranky brat who lashed out at everyone trying to help him to a really sweet guy who's also a lot of fun to be around. He makes Hollie laugh so hard, he cracks bad jokes and dances – badly – with zero shame. He'll go riding with Hollie, or when she couldn't ride with her injured leg he rode the horses for her; again, fairly poorly, but he had a great teacher.

Things with Jonathan and Luke are still rebuilding though, the scars fresh, the wounds barely healed. I won't come between them, like I won't come between Hollie and Jonathan.

But I'm bursting with the truth. I want to scream from the rooftops that Luke emails me every day, that he tells me lovely, swoony things, that he's opened up to me.

The day he found his bike and emailed me from the very spot he was when he found it, my heart broke for him, but also, selfishly, it felt amazing. He wanted to share that with me.

I wish sometimes, though, that he wanted to share our relationship – or whatever this is – with someone else.

I want to be able to tell my friends and family about him.

I want more. I want more of him.

I want to see him again. Touch him again. Kiss him again.

I want to be able to text and call him instead of only emailing, but we've never broached the subject of communicating any other way. Luke hasn't suggested it, and as much as I want to, I don't want to push him too far.

I sometimes wonder how long I can wait. I wonder what will happen if one day I ask him if I can tell Hollie about us.

Will I be okay with it if he says no?

The reality is, of course I will. Any part of Luke, in any part of my life is enough. I told him I'll have whatever he can give me, and I meant it.

My phone bleeps the email alert. That was a quick turnaround. He's barely had time to read my last one, let alone reply.

I tap the app icon then open his latest message. This email isn't at all related to the one I just sent. This is something else entirely. My breath catches in my throat as I read the first lines.

From: Luke.ashwell@ezmail.com
To: Daniel.lawler@ezmail.com
Subject: A question for you

Hey Dan

I have something I want to ask you. But I don't want you to feel like there's any pressure or anything. You can absolutely say no and I'll understand.

God, I don't even know where to start…

My school ball is next Friday.

I never thought I'd go, because, well, because of everything, and I wasn't sure if I'd have any fun at all. But I heard yesterday that there's a few tickets left.

I realised that there is one person I would have a good time with, no matter what. And it's my last year, the last chance for me to go.

So … will you go with me?

I know it's a huge drama and you'd need to take a day off school and it's ages to drive and you might not even want to go, and that's totally okay too.

It would mean people would know about us and I have no idea how you feel about that. We'd have to tell Jonathan.

I'm not even sure I should send this – my hands won't stop shaking – but I've been honest with you all the way through and it doesn't seem right to be a coward now.

Let me know what you think?

L

My heart dips and soars and the urge to vomit strikes me again, but this time it's a feeling of utter joy making me nauseated.

He wants me to go with him to his school ball. We'd have to tell people. I'd be able to tell Hollie. I'd get to see him again – touch him. Maybe even kiss him. He's not asking for a relationship, for anything serious, for anything more than hanging out together for one single night. But I don't care.

Yes, yes, yes.

There's only one thing that might get in the way.

I drop the phone on my bed and head straight for the kitchen, where Mum is cooking dinner. Jake is nowhere to be seen. Thank God.

"How's the homework going?" Mum asks, smiling up at me as she pulls a tray out of the oven.

That's right. Homework. That's what I'm supposed to be doing. "Uh, yeah, good," I mumble.

I slide onto a stool at the bar and she slides a lettuce in front of me. I start pulling the leaves off automatically. "I wanted to ask you something."

She looks at me more closely, setting the tray onto a board. "What's up?"

"A friend of mine, they've asked if I wanted to go with them to their school ball. It's next Friday."

Mum nods, waiting for more, because I've made this a thing by asking if I could ask her, instead of throwing it out casually in normal conversation.

"Well, they're in Auckland. I'll need a day off school, and to drive up there. And stay, for the weekend."

"Who is this friend?" She puts two tomatoes, a knife and a chopping board in front of me. "I didn't know you had any friends in Auckland."

"I met them when I was up there with Hollie. They're friends with Jonathan."

Mum studies me, her clear brown eyes assessing. "Where will you stay? With your friend? Are their parents okay with it?"

"Uh, I haven't got that far. They only just asked."

She grates some cheese then sets the block down, leaning on the bench across from me. I try not to squirm under her gaze and attempt to remain cool, as if her decision is not going to be life changing for me.

"You can go," she says. My heart soars. My face breaks into a smile.

"Thank you so, so much," I yelp. God, that was embarrassing.

"But," she warns, "I want to speak to their parents and you need to have a pretty good plan about where you're staying and what you're doing."

I groan. "Mum."

She cuts me off before I can go further. "You know I trust

you, and I know you make good decisions – most of the time." She flashes me a sly grin and I poke my tongue out at her, begrudgingly warming to her bad, bad joke. "But you'll be a long way from home and you don't know anyone else up there."

I nod. "All right. You're right … I suppose."

She laughs. "Occasionally I do know what I'm talking about."

"If it helps, Beth's sister lives around the corner. Maybe I could stay with her again … Or she could vouch for him."

The corner of her mouth twitches.

"Him?"

Oh. I hadn't meant to say that. But I suppose it had to happen at some point, especially if she's going to be talking to his parents. "His name is Luke. He's Jonathan's friend."

"Is he – is he your boyfriend?" Her face remains neutral.

I snort. "God, I wish." I slap a hand over my mouth in horror as I realise I've said the words out loud. My face burns and my mother absolutely loses her shit.

Tears are streaming down her face as she laughs so hard she needs the bench to hold her upright. "Oh honey, your face."

I lie my head down on the cool stone bench top and groan, loudly.

Eventually her laughter dies down, reduced to a few sniggers every few breaths.

"Are you quite done?" I say.

She grins and nods. "I think so, yes." She giggles again. "So not your boyfriend?"

I shake my head. "Just friends," I say, trying not to sound like a brat.

She smirks. "Maybe this ball will change all that?"

I doubt it, but I don't say it. I climb down from the stool, already planning how I'll respond to Luke's email for maximum dramatic effect.

"Danny," Mum says, before I can leave the room, "if he is your boyfriend, we'll only be happy for you." She reaches over and squeezes my forearm, holding eye contact.

"Thanks, Mum," I say, barely managing to hold my voice together. I give her fingers a brief squeeze and head back to my room.

CHAPTER 28

Luke

"KRIS, ARE YOU STAYING FOR DINNER?" Mum sticks her head round my bedroom door.

"Yes please," Kristen replies, smiling up at Mum from where she's sprawled across my floor, math books spread before her.

"All right. Ten minutes, okay?"

We nod our agreement and Mum disappears back to the kitchen.

"There's something I need to tell you before dinner," I say, hauling myself upright. I've been lying on my back, staring at my ceiling, running through Dan's last email in my head.

It's not only Jonathan we need to tell. Not if Dan is coming here, to be my date to the ball. My date.

I can't believe he said yes. I can't believe his mum said yes. I can't believe I sent the email in the first place.

"Oh yeah? What's up?" Kristen closes her textbook with a thump and shoves it away, pushing herself to sitting. I watch with envy as she wraps her legs easily underneath herself, sitting cross-legged on the floor.

I take a deep breath. Then another one, for good measure. "I invited Dan to the ball." The words flow from me in one long exhale.

Her fingertips fly to her lips and muffle a small squeal. Her nails are turquoise today, her lips a bright, glittery pink. The tips of her winged eyeliner sparkle with more pink. "Ohmigosh, I'm so proud of you," she squeaks. In one swift, fluid movement she's on her feet, skipping across the room to me. She falls onto the bed and claims my hands. "What did he say?"

My stomach swoops at the thought of his words. "He's coming."

Kristen squeals again, squeezing my hands so tight her nails start digging in.

"I have to tell Mum and Dad."

She stops squealing. "Oh. How are you feeling about that?"

I sigh, and the breath leaving me is heavy. "I'm terrified," I whisper. "I think they'll be okay, but I didn't really consider it all before I asked him. But I want people to know."

Her grip tightens again. "You want me here?"

I nod. "It's a good thing you're staying for dinner … because that's when I'm doing it."

"You got this, Luke. I promise. And truly, I'm so proud of you for inviting Dan. God, I'm so jealous, he's so gorgeous."

I laugh and give her a nudge with my shoulder. "You could get a date of your own, you know."

Her cheeks tint pink and she glances away, laughing softly. I want to tell her to ask Tyler. It'd make his year. But I have no idea how either of them really feel about the other, and I do *not* want to mess up my only two friendships here.

Kristen gets up from the bed and whirls to face me, realisation on her face. "You're going to have to tell Johnnie."

I nod grimly. "Or Dan's got to tell him. He said he'll do it, but maybe it's better coming from me?"

"Well, you know him best, but Dan knows him now too." She gives a little shrug. "Either way, he's not going to care, is he? Like, he's not going to be a dick, because you're his best friend and Dan is his girlfriend's best friend and they get along, so it'll be fine."

"I hope so, but I've still got to get through this one first." I slide off the bed, standing slowly, and reach for my crutch. Only one crutch these days.

Kristen nods and opens the door.

I take slow careful breaths as I trek through the laundry room to get to the kitchen, then the dining room. I slide into my seat as Kristen brings our plates over.

"Having any luck with that math homework yet?" Dad asks.

"Getting there," I say.

He nods. "I know I'm not much help, but I can try if you like."

I give him a small smile. He tries so hard, but I know he's struggled since the accident, since I had to give up riding. He never rode himself, but the mechanics of the bikes were always his interest. Crutches don't really need mechanics.

I can't drive for the moment either, so the car we were working on together for me seems irrelevant. I'm sure we'll get back to that common ground eventually, and in the meantime, he always tries.

Mum finally sits in her seat after fussing over Kristen like a mother hen. Jonathan and Kristen have been raised by my parents as much as I was raised by theirs, so I don't really understand why Mum still fusses over Kristen like she doesn't know she can get herself a drink when she wants.

I fiddle with my fork. I clear my throat. I open my mouth but the words stick in my throat. I don't know why this is hard. A son of one of Dad's workmates came out last year and neither of my parents even blinked. They shrugged, said something along the lines of good on him and carried on with their lives. But maybe it's different when it's their own child.

Kristen kicks me under the table. I kick her back and she scowls at me. She tilts her head and mouths something at me. She's asking if I want her to start the conversation. I tug at my hair.

"What's up with you two?" Mum asks, watching us suspiciously.

"Luke needs to talk to you about the ball next week." Kris drops the words like a bomb. I cringe, but I know I needed the push.

Mum turns her gaze on me, an eyebrow quirked in question. "I didn't think you wanted to go."

"I didn't. But I do now," I say, my words trailing off. "I, uh, I found someone to go with, who won't make it be awful."

Kris coughs. "Excuse me," she says with a laugh. It takes the tension off.

"Oh, hush," I tell her, and she laughs.

Mum and Dad share indulgent smiles at our sibling-like behaviour. Maybe they always hoped Kristen and I would get together and our families would literally become one family.

"Oh, who is it?" Mum asks, that eyebrow quirked again.

"Um, well, you've um, met him, once."

The eyebrow flicks a fraction higher. "I have?"

I nod, my chest constricting. "Jonathan's friend," I say eventually, my voice hoarse. "Dan."

Mum and Dad share the briefest glance. I'd have missed it if I wasn't monitoring them both like a hawk for any trace of how this was going to play out.

"We're not … there's not anything going on, but it would be like a date." A deep breath. "Because I'm gay and I don't know what he is but he likes me."

My hand is pulling at my hair. My scalp is starting to throb, but I can't untangle my fingers. Kristen presses her leg against mine under the table. The steady, warm weight is soothing.

"And I really like him," I say into the silence.

"Was he that lovely one with the curly hair that came here the day Jonathan went home again?" Mum asks.

I nod again. That's it. Not a single reaction to my being gay. It's so unexpected I blink at her, stunned.

Mum looks to Dad again. "He was a charmer, that one," she says. He nods and shoots a smile at me.

"Did you miss the part where I said I was gay?" I ask, breath still catching in my throat with every inhale.

"No, we didn't," Dad says, holding my gaze. "But it doesn't matter to us either way if you want to date girls or boys. We want you to be happy. You deserve to be happy."

I gape at his words. It's the most he's said to me about anything but bike mechanics and the different types of vehicle paint in years. Mum nods along with him. She reaches across the table and grasps my fingers in a tight squeeze.

I look up at Kristen and she smiles at me as if to say, *What were you worried about?*

My mouth tugs up, a smile slipping out. "He makes me really, really happy," I say, and I swear Mum wipes away a tear.

CHAPTER 29

Dan

ANOTHER DAY of school is over and again, I don't want to go home.

Because, of course, Jake Daly is still living in our spare room. He's always around, watching TV, sitting at the counter eating cereal, using the bathroom and draining the hot water.

My sister was a pain in the butt to live with, but at least I sometimes like her. No such luck with Jake. He's less bearable the more time I spend with him. That one moment of vulnerable apology has been the only hint he has a different side – the side I remember from childhood.

I'm waiting beside Hollie's car, because I've deemed that today is the day. I emailed Luke this morning to tell him. Today I'm going to tell Jonathan about our … whatever it is.

I chew my lip and fidget.

"Hey, Dan," Jonathan says behind me, and I jerk in fright. "Oh, sorry," he says, a grin tugging at his mouth.

I wave the apology away. "Hey," I say back, "are you and Hollie going to your place?"

He nods. "Hollie's working today." A pause. "Like every day. That girl needs a life."

I laugh, because it's kind of true. She's lucky though, because her work is something she truly loves, and now that she's allowed to ride again she loves it even more.

Jonathan watches me for a moment. "You want to come?"

I nod, relieved. He's aware that Jake is living with me now, and he must know that it's not an easy adjustment for me to make. Neither he nor Hollie knows what happened with me and Jake. Most of the time I'm not sure I know myself. They never ask, never push, and I'm grateful I don't have to ask for the reprieve from spending time at home.

Hollie bounds up beside me. "Hey," she beams at me. She grins at Jonathan but leans into me as I drape my arm around her. This is why I love them together so much, because nothing has changed between me and Hollie. I can still touch her, be affectionate and caring, and Jonathan doesn't go off in a jealous rage. He's almost the opposite. He appreciates the friendship I have with her, and I'll always admire him for that.

"Dan's coming with," Jonathan says, tossing his bag into the back seat as Hollie unlocks the car.

"Great." She grins at me again then slides into the driver's seat.

The wind sweeps down the hill, tugging at my hair shoved under the riding helmet. This isn't exactly what I had in mind when I agreed to come riding with Hollie this afternoon.

But here I am astride Alaska, the giant grey mare Jonathan's Aunt Beth owns. Hollie is on the big bay show jumper, Milo, and Jonathan is riding Harley. Hollie and I both laughed when Jonathan claimed him, but he's adamant he likes the little pony, and it isn't only because he's the closest to the ground. Jonathan has a point, though. Harley is a cool little horse. Alaska and Milo are both sweethearts, but Harley has the cheeky nature of a horse who thinks he's much bigger than he is. All sass, that thing.

We come to a halt at the top of the hill overlooking Beth's farm.

"I need to talk to you guys about something," I say, before I've really considered if this is the appropriate time or place.

Hollie turns to me, her face worried. Jonathan says, "What's up?"

"Luke and I have been emailing," I blurt. "Like, every day for weeks." Alaska fidgets and I place a hand on her neck to calm her and myself.

Jonathan smirks. Hollie's expression goes from worried to joyful in the blink of an eye. Neither says a word.

"We're not, um, dating or anything, but…" I can feel my blush, the heat tracking up the back of my neck, leaking across my cheeks. "He asked if I'd go to his ball next week."

Jonathan's smirk has grown to a full-out grin. "I knew it," he says.

Hollie's practically bouncing in Milo's saddle. "Oh thank god, we can finally talk about it," she exclaims. Jonathan chuckles.

"What?"

"This has been going on since we went up there, right?" Hollie knows. How on earth does she know? I croak out the question.

"Well, you were wearing his shirt when we came to his

room that day, and you had that totally flimsy story about spilling food on your own."

"Wait, what?" Jonathan interrupts.

Hollie shrugs. "I didn't really forget my phone in the car. They just looked totally sus, like we'd interrupted them. How did *you* know, if it wasn't that?"

"Luke doesn't let anyone near that drum kit, but he let Dan play. I used to have to fight him to let me near it."

I had no idea. No idea that it was a big deal to be allowed to play them. I sit there, dumbstruck. They both knew, and Luke and I have been terrified of how Jonathan might respond.

I exhale, the tension leaving my body as the relief washes through.

"You knew all along that something was going on?"

They both nod, wide grins splitting their faces.

"We didn't know you were in touch, but we've known there was something since that time Luke came here," Jonathan says.

I didn't even know then.

"If this is like you asking for my blessing or whatever, don't worry about it. I think it's cool." He smirks at me, and although I'm mortified at their knowing all along, another wave of relief washes over me.

Jonathan pulls his phone out of his jacket pocket, swipes the screen a few times and holds it to his ear.

"Did you honestly think I'd have a problem with Dan?" he says after a moment. A pause. "I suppose that's fair, but just so everyone is on the same page, I'm glad, and as I said to Dan, I think it's cool." Another pause as Luke replies. "I already knew, you idiot. You let him near the drums." Jonathan laughs, a sound of pure happiness.

Hollie's watching him, her face warmed with the same joy. He's come a long way since he moved here, the weight of the world on his shoulders.

Jonathan's watching me now. He nudges Harley over and hands the phone to me. I stare at it, a picture of Luke and Jonathan on the screen, the call still active.

"Hey," I breathe into the line.

"Hey," comes the reply. "You did it."

I'm talking to Luke on the phone and his voice is better than any memory, any imagined conversation. "Yeah," I say. "He took it all right, considering his tendencies." Luke laughs and the sound fizzes through my veins. Jonathan scowls at me, but Hollie breaks out into fits of giggles that break his sour expression. She nudges Milo closer to Harley and reaches out to lace her fingers with Jonathan's for a moment before the horses shift away from each other again.

"You know, we should do this more often," Luke says down the phone. His voice is rich and smooth.

"We definitely should, maybe even before Friday."

He laughs again. "I can't wait to see you." The fizzing in my veins intensifies.

"Same, but I'm currently on a horse on top of a hill and should probably go."

He laughs, then his voice turns wistful. "What I'd give to be there. Maybe one day. I'll talk to you later?"

"Yeah, one day. For sure. Send me your number and I'll call you later."

"Sounds good. Bye, Dan," he says, and before I have a chance to respond he ends the call. Probably for the best, because saying goodbye to Luke is something I never want to do.

I hand the phone back to Jonathan in silence. He pockets it then turns to Hollie. "Right, do these guys need more or shall we head back?"

"Heading back sounds good," Hollie says. "Wouldn't want to keep Dan from his evening plans." She smirks at me and I poke my tongue out at her. So rude, but it makes me happy anyway, because a sassy Hollie is a happy Hollie.

CHAPTER 30

Dan

JAKE IS EVERYWHERE. There are little traces of him all through the house and I'm barely holding it together.

He ignores me at school, so at least I have that to be grateful for. But in every nearly every room of my home there's now something that reminds me of him. The mug in the kitchen cupboard that he always uses, the extra towel hanging in the bathroom. At least it's not the lime-green one with the pink border that Nicole always liked.

One more night. I only need to hold it together for twelve more hours and I can escape him for the weekend.

Because I'm going to see Luke.

In the morning I'll be leaving.

The hired suit hangs on my bedroom door already. Luckily Mum has plenty of contacts through her business and could find me something last minute.

I stare at the suit as I think back over the conversation I had with Luke last night. Talking on the phone with him is a million times better than emails. We still email, but our conversations ignore the emails completely. We talk and talk but there's no reference to the emails, so when we end the call, whoever was next to reply carries on as if we haven't had a whole conversation in between. It's perfect. I'm learning a whole new side of him.

He told me a bit about his friends last night, what the plans for Friday night are, who I'll get to meet. He's nervous because he hasn't come out to them yet.

Telling his parents and Kristen was bad enough, he said, even though they reacted perfectly, like my own parents.

He keeps trying to tell Tyler, but every time he does he can't bring himself to actually say it.

My phone rings and I jolt, bringing my thoughts back to the present moment. It's not the song I have linked to Luke's name, though. It's Nicole's song.

I answer. "Hey Nic, what's up?" I try to keep my voice steady, my face calm as the camera starts up. She doesn't usually ring out of the blue.

She came to stay for that weekend, and despite the presence of the depression hoodie she seemed to be doing okay. We had a good time while she was home, then she went back to uni and her job as per usual.

"Just seeing how you're going. You've been ringing me a lot. Sorry I haven't called back before now," she says. I take in her appearance. Her hair, usually in perfectly maintained, bouncy curls, is scraped back into a ponytail. Her face is bare, not a smudge of makeup on it, and she's wearing an oversized blue hoodie that's seen better days. It's not the depression hoodie, but it's not far off it. I glance at the clock. She should definitely be getting ready for her usual Thursday night shift at the restaurant where she works.

"I'm all good, sis." I give her a grin, but it's shaky. "Aren't you going to be late for work?"

She must look to her clock too, then she turns back to the camera. "Shit, sorry little brother, you're right. But what's this about you going to a ball? Who's the lucky girl? Is this what you've been ringing me about?"

I sigh. I've been trying to ring her since the moment I told Luke I'd go with him, but she hasn't answered my calls until now. I've been trying to not let it worry me, but now I regret ignoring those feelings. She looks exhausted.

I want to tell Nicole everything about Luke, but her jumping to the conclusion that I'm dating a girl puts me on edge.

"It's that horse girl, isn't it? Hollie." She's trying to be upbeat, cheery. It's not convincing.

When Nicole is well, when she's healthy, she's funny and carefree and generous with her time, her heart. But the depression and dark moods plague her.

Hollie's depression sent her to bed for three days until I helped drag her out of it.

Nicole's worst bout sent her to hospital.

I think about all the times I've found her sitting on the couch, wearing that cursed hoodie, her face tearstained and blotchy, unable to define what is making her so sad.

"No, it isn't Hollie," I say, a little indulgently. I need to cheer her up, build that joy in her, give her something to be happy about. "She's got herself a nice boyfriend though, and she's very happy."

"So, some other lovely girl? Come on Danny, tell me. Who's the date?" She's flagging. She must have called when she had a moment of energy, but the conversation, her attempts to pretend she's okay – they're wearing her out.

I smile, sinking everything I have into that smile. "No lovely girl, Nic. His name is Luke … and he is very lovely."

Her eyes widen. "Danny! I had no idea!"

I shrug. "Neither did I until I met him."

"I'm so happy for you, Danny," she says, her voice wobbling.

"Nic," I say, my voice softening, the faked enthusiasm fading away. "Are you doing okay?"

She bares her teeth in the semblance of a smile. "Of course," she says. "I'm all good. But as you pointed out, I am indeed going to be late. Have a great time with your guy, Danny. You really deserve all the best things."

Then she's gone. Before I even have a chance to say goodbye.

The weight of that conversation settles over me. The truth of what I saw, of what I know, of what I have to do.

I climb off my bed and head for the kitchen, looking for my parents.

They're exactly where I thought they'd be at this time of the evening, in the kitchen cooking dinner and catching up on their days. Thankfully Jake isn't around right now.

I take in this everyday, normal scene. I have to destroy it. I have to tell them about Nicole, but I know what will happen. The pain will flash in Mum's eyes. Dad will pretend he's fine, but I know he's not. Mum will try to deny it until I tell her about the hoodie, about how there's no way she's getting off her couch and going to work today.

It's not supposed to be like this. But I take a deep breath and I tell them about the phone call.

Mum's eyes flash. Dad acts tough, like he doesn't feel the same feelings the rest of us do. Mum says she's sure Nicole is fine and is probably just sick.

"She hasn't got a cold, Mum," I say, my voice low. "But," I brighten, face fighting me as I stretch my mouth into a smile, "I'm already off school tomorrow, so I can go and see her and make sure she's okay."

Dad shakes his head. "You've got your thing. It's okay, Danny, I'll go and see her."

"But," I argue, "I want to go and see her; it's been ages." I can keep them from the pain. I can shield them from it.

When Nicole got sick the first time, the worst time, I was only thirteen. Mum and Dad would come home from the hospital tired, their faces drawn. Mum would cry in her room at night.

I did everything I could to help. I made dinner and snacks for Mum to take with her to the hospital. I made sure the rubbish bin was emptied and the bins went out to the curb on the right day. I'd go into Mum's work, sorting and organising equipment for hires, helping the staff covering her absence while she spent time with Nicole.

The more I realised my small actions were helping, the more I did. I never wanted my family, or anyone else, to go through that again, so I helped and helped and helped some more.

I did whatever I could to cheer them up, especially when we knew Nicole would be okay and things started to slowly creep back to normal; when it didn't feel wrong to be trying to be happy.

I spent hours after school, and often during school time, at the hospital with Nicole. We read books together and watched movies.

I took dozens and dozens of photos on our old digital camera and Nicole would study them all, choosing her favourites.

I printed them all and made her a huge poster. It's on the wall of her new flat.

Gradually she came out of the depression and life went back to normal – mostly. Every so often she'll have a blip, like the one she's having now, but she's never been so far from home while having one.

I don't want her to go through it alone. And I know I can help Mum and Dad by going. I always handle Nic's dark moods the best, somehow knowing what to say and what to do to help.

My family needs me. My sister needs me. I'm not going to frolic off with some guy.

A pang slices through me at the thought.

He's not some guy. Luke is not just some random guy. He is *the* guy. Surely he'll understand.

Dad places his hand on my shoulder, locking in eye contact. "Dan, I know you want to see her, but you should go with your plans. She wouldn't want you to miss that. I'll take care of Nic, I promise." He squeezes my shoulder then turns and leaves the room, pulling his phone out of his pocket, already making plans.

CHAPTER 31

Luke

I CAN'T BELIEVE Dan will be here tomorrow.

In twenty-four hours he'll be right around the corner from my house, getting ready at Jonathan and Kristen's. For some reason our parents deemed this the most suitable plan, and even though we'll spend tomorrow night together at Tyler's house, on Saturday night Dan is back in Jonathan's old room.

I'm currently walking with Tyler to the park down the road from home again, and for the first time it's not him wheeling my bike: it's me. I still haven't quite got steady enough to want to ride directly there, but I need the solid feel of the bike beside me right now, like an anchor preventing my emotions – my excitement and anxiety – from sweeping me away.

Tyler and I are walking in silence, but it's not uncomfortable. The only uncomfortable part is what's going on in my own brain.

I need to tell him about Dan but it feels like the weirdest thing to bring up in conversation, like it's really self-centred to have to say it. I've tried to tell him so many times, but each time I can't go through with it.

"So, about tomorrow," I say eventually, and immediately I feel like I've got a raging fever. My hands aren't shaking, but only because I've got my bike handlebars in a death grip.

Tyler pulls his gaze to mine. "Yeah? You're coming to my place before, right? And after?"

I nod. "It's okay if I bring my date with me?"

A strange expression crosses his face. I can't quite figure out what it is, or even if it's positive or negative. "Yeah, of course. We've been over this. There's plenty of room."

I fiddle with the brake lever under my fingers.

"Are you nervous?" Tyler grins at me.

A blush heats my cheeks. "Yeah, I really am." I hold out a hand, showing him how badly it's shaking.

He laughs at me. It's okay though, because I'm mostly laughing at myself too.

"Who is this mysterious date of yours, anyway?"

The moment's arrived, I suppose. The moment when I tell him about Dan, and in doing so, about myself. "It's someone I met through Jonathan," I start.

Tyler beams at me, though it seems a little forced around the edges. "And you're nervous about this why? It's clear she already really cares about you."

Wait, what?

Who already cares about me? And she? Who does he think I'm going with?

He carries on before I have a chance to process my thoughts.

"This is like the first proper date, right? Where it's either going to go from friends to something more, or it's going to crash and burn?" He pauses, blinks a few times. "I'm really sorry. I'm sure there won't be any crashing and burning."

"Wait, wait, wait." I hold a hand up, stopping and turning to face him. "Who exactly do you think my date is?"

"Kristen … Right?" He shuffles his feet, rubbing the back of his neck with one hand.

I laugh. Right in his face, loud and completely out of the blue. It happens more often now than it did, but I'm still surprised every time. I clap a hand over my mouth to shut myself up. His eyes widen at me, his face slack.

"Um, no, most definitely not Kristen," I say, when I finally get the laughter to subside. It threatens again and I start to snort but manage to suppress it. "I truly love her, but not like *that.*"

"Oh," Tyler breathes, and abruptly turns to start walking again. "You said you met them through Jonathan and I assumed, well, his sister."

The smile is still tugging at my lips. "No, it's Hollie's friend, from down there."

"Ah." A nod. He fiddles with the straps of his backpack. We've reached the park and I drop my own bag, then wheel the bike to the flat patch of ground I usually start my rides from.

Tyler is standing waiting for me, looking decidedly awkward and uncomfortable.

"Are you going with anyone?" I ask, suddenly unable to recall if he's mentioned having a date. I've been so caught up in my panic over Dan that it's quite possible he did say something and I totally missed it. "Sorry, my head's all over the place. I can't remember if you said you are."

He shakes his head. "I was kind of hoping to ask someone." He shrugs, and his eyes don't quite meet mine. "But it didn't quite work out." He pats the seat, indicating I should get a move on. He gives a tight smile as I swing my leg over. It's a movement that's getting gradually easier but is still awkward as hell. Tyler continues speaking. "It's okay though. I'm looking forward to going regardless."

"Yeah," I say. "It should be good."

I push down on the pedal and the bike moves forward. A few wobbles, another rotation of the pedals and it smooths out. This feeling, of riding again, it hasn't got old yet. I'm not sure it ever will. I ride in a loop around the park, straying further and further from the safety net that is Tyler each time. He jogs around the park, staying close-ish, but I haven't had a near fall since the very beginning.

I stand on the pedals as the bike rolls down a gentle slope. The balance isn't quite what it used to be, but it feels good all the same. I let out a small whoop of celebration at the feeling, then skid to a stop as a thought hits me. The stop is abrupt and messy as hell. I stumble a bit and Tyler is beside me in a moment, helping me steady the bike. He's breathing hard, clearly having sprinted to catch up with me.

"Who is it?" I ask, adrenaline coursing through me. "The person you wanted to go with."

He glances up at me, taking in the fact that I'm physically fine, that my erratic manoeuvre hasn't harmed me in anyway. He breaks eye contact to reply, though. "Oh, it doesn't matter," he says, his face flushing hard, and not from exertion.

"Who was it?" I repeat. "Come on man, I swear I won't judge."

He sighs and rubs at his neck again. "Kristen," he mumbles after a long pause. It's quiet but I catch it clear enough. His cheeks flush bright red.

"I freaking knew it," I exclaim. "Is this why you're friends with me?" It's a joke, I think. I try not to consider what it actually means.

"What?"

"I knew you liked Kristen. Sorry, I didn't think about it properly before. You should ask her to go with you tomorrow."

"Oh, oh no, I don't think so," he says.

I climb off my bike and together we walk back to the picnic table. I try to think of ways to convince him to ask her. We reach the table and I slide onto the seat, leaning my bike beside me.

I tap my knuckles against the wood of the table, thinking back over Kristen's interactions with Tyler. Did he simply not ask her because he thought she was already my date?

I'm about to lay out for him all the reasons he should ask her, to argue that he should ask her, to tell him that Kristen doesn't have a date as far as I'm aware, but I'm interrupted before I can even start.

"How was your ride?" Kristen skips up and slides onto the seat beside me.

"Yeah, good," I say. "I haven't done much yet."

Tyler immediately stands. "I'd better head off," he says. "I'll see you at my place tomorrow night?"

I nod, stunned. It's not like Tyler to leave me here to ride without him to supervise me. "Sure," I say.

He grins down at me, but it's a little tight around the edges. "Good. See you then. Can't wait to meet this girl of yours."

I flinch at his words but think I manage to hide it enough. He doesn't react, so I must have.

He looks to Kristen and gives her a little smile, ducking his head to hide his blush before striding away. He ran here all the way from his house, and is now intending to run home again, just to avoid Kristen.

A hand connects with the side of my head. "You haven't told him?" I turn to face Kristen and wince.

"Er, no. No, I have not."

I should have. I should have told someone other than Kristen and my parents that my date to the ball is a guy.

But it was bad enough telling Mum and Dad, and I really can't be bothered with the build-up of it all.

That's a huge lie. I have tried. So many times. But the words never come and the ball is virtually here already and this was my last chance, my last attempt. It's really too late to do anything about it now. I'm not telling the whole school beforehand; I figured walking in with Dan would be announcement enough.

"You're either being a total boss about this or you're really bloody stupid," Kristen says.

"Oh, I'm being a huge chicken, there's no doubt about that."

Kristen shakes her head, lips pursed in disapproval. "Luke, there is absolutely nothing chicken about what you're doing. It's not like you're out everywhere."

The knots in my gut tighten at her words. They've been there for days now, snarling ever tighter with every passing minute. "Don't," I say. "Let's not talk about it, okay?"

She watches me closely, then nods. "Okay, if you're sure."

"Yup," I say, standing up from the table. "And hey, before we head back, go talk to Tyler for a second." He's thankfully still nearby, standing under one of the trees edging the park, tapping away at his phone. I'm super grateful to whoever messaged him and needed an instant reply.

She looks at me, head tilted in question.

I shake my head. I'm not telling her, but I'll give both my friends the opportunity to do it for themselves. "I think he wanted to talk to you, that's all. And go now, because he's about to leave."

She's still looking at me sideways as she turns away, hurrying after Tyler. She calls out to him and he stops. He flashes a look in my direction, and I give a mocking salute.

They talk for a few minutes as I carefully walk my bike across the park.

"Catch you later, Luke," Tyler calls, shooting me a look that says he knows exactly what I'm playing at and he doesn't approve, then turns and heads for his place. Kristen waits where she is, her cheeks pink.

"You ass," she says, whacking me on the arm as I approach and taking the bike from me.

"Did it work though?"

"Yes," she breathes. "Yes, it worked."

I grin. "Excellent."

CHAPTER 32

Dan

AS DAD WALKS out of the room I'm reassured, because I know he's right. He will look after Nicole.

But I'm also left at a total loss because I don't know what to do to fix this; to shield my parents from it, to help Nicole.

It's in this moment of despair that I notice Jake is standing in the kitchen. Mum is speaking softly to him. His eyes flick to me, to Dad's retreating form then back to Mum. He nods and she follows Dad down the hall.

Jake goes straight for the fridge and starts pulling things out to make a salad, as if nothing is going on except that he's suddenly decided to be helpful.

"I'm coming with you," I shout down the hall. I don't care. I don't care that Jake can hear me, I don't care that for once I'm causing my parents stress instead of joy.

"Dude," Jake says, settling onto a barstool with a chopping board and knife. "I know it isn't my business, but they're right, you should go do what you were planning to do."

"You're right, it isn't your business," I snap at him, fury raging through me. "Who the hell do you think you are swanning around here like you own the place? Telling me what to do?"

His head snaps up as my anger builds. "Danny," he says, his voice low. "I – I didn't mean to. I know you hate me being here and I'm sorry that you're stuck with me. But your dad can handle what's going on with your sister."

"You don't know anything about it, so you don't get to decide that."

"Maybe I don't," he says, his voice weirdly calm and serious, considering who I'm talking to. "But your parents do know. It's not your job to fix this."

"But—"

He cuts me off. "You're going to give up going to this ball or whatever it is you're going to? To do something that someone else can take care of? Someone who's better suited to handling it? What's your date going to say? How're they going to feel?"

"It's fine," I snarl. "Luke will understand. He'll understand I need to be with Nic."

Jake doesn't bat an eyelid when I mention Luke. I don't care anymore.

"He'll understand. He's not like you." I spit the words across the kitchen and we both freeze as they register.

"What do you mean by that?" Jake cocks his head, tipping his chin up in that arrogant way that makes me want to throw things at him.

"I mean," I say, my voice harsh, "that Luke will understand and he won't ditch me, the same way you did when I had to be there for Nicole."

His eyes widen and his head loses the cocky tilt. "What do

you mean? About me ditching you?" He looks stricken as the silence extends between us. "Tell me."

"It doesn't matter."

"It does matter. It matters to me." His voice is pleading, almost desperate. "Danny, tell me. Please."

I stare at my past best friend, realisation settling over me. He doesn't know. I always assumed he knew what happened when our friendship fell apart. But maybe he doesn't know.

"When Nicole first got sick," I say, my voice wobbling, "it was like you disappeared out of my life. You never had time for me anymore. Whenever I came to school you were with your new friends. I didn't fit there and you wouldn't talk to me. You barely acknowledged me."

Jake's face has gone slack. He bites the side of his thumb.

"Shit, Danny," he breathes, his voice shaking too. "That's why you were always busy back then? Why you missed so much school the first term at high school?"

I nod and take a deep, shuddering breath. "I really needed you and you weren't there." My voice cracks so I slam my mouth shut.

"You were never around. I'd come over after school and you wouldn't be here. When you *were* at school you hardly talked, but you were hardly there and I couldn't figure out why. I thought you were done with me. I thought you'd started hanging out with new people."

"I only did that because you did." I slump into a chair, resting my head in my hands. "Then you turned into such an arrogant jerk that I didn't want to be friends with you anyway," I mutter.

He bites his thumb again. "I was jealous of you," he says, shocking us both speechless. The silence expands between us before he eventually starts talking again. "I saw you with your mum or dad and they were always so focussed on you, while my parents were splitting up and Mum was talking about leaving the country." He stops and taps his fingers against the bench top, tilting his head to take in the ceiling for a moment. "I could have gone with her. She asked me to go but I didn't want to leave everything behind, like you.

"So I stayed, then I got to school and you'd sit there like you were bored out of your head and wanted nothing to do with me. You'd disappear for days and I had to find someone else to sit with. By the time you came back … I guess it looked like I didn't need you anymore. But I did.

"You became this whole other person. You made all these friends and everyone loved you. I was jealous." He takes a shaky breath and shrugs a little. "But," he says like he's trying brush off the huge revelation he's dropped on me, "all of that aside, your dad can take care of Nicole, and I bet this Luke guy really wants to see you. It's not up to you to save everyone. It's not your job to make everyone else more important than you."

"What do you mean?" My head is still in my hands. I'm too shocked by what he just told me to even look at him. I have no idea what he's talking about now.

"You do everything for everyone else, whether it helps you or not."

"That's what being a nice person is, Jake," I say.

He shakes his head. "No, I mean you take it too far. You do things for other people even if it's going to harm you. You're always putting other people's feelings first. Don't think I don't see the way you fuss over Hollie, always making sure she's okay. And you didn't say a thing when I moved in here. Your mum doesn't even know we aren't friends anymore."

"Yes she does," I mutter.

"Okay, but she doesn't know how little you tolerate me. You just sucked it up and pretended like everything was fine so it wouldn't upset her. Going to see Nicole now, it's going to ruin something that should be great for you. You're willing to throw it all away for this weird thing where you have to save everyone else."

"Because she's my sister!"

How he keeps his voice calm I don't know, but he carries on as if I haven't just shouted in his face. "And when she's doing better, is she going to hate herself at least a little bit if you give this up for her?"

I glare at him, grasping for words.

"That was a low blow, I'll admit," he says, proving the arrogant jerk hasn't completely disappeared. It's a strangely comforting thought. "But it's time you did something for yourself. Nicole will be taken care of. You go do this for you, and for Luke. I have no idea who he is, but if you don't go you're letting him down." He pauses. "Yeah, that was a low blow too." He stands up from the counter. Somehow he's made an entire salad during this conversation. He rinses the chopping board and knife, putting them in the dishwasher like it's the most normal thing in the world to throw all these truth bombs at me over meal prep. "Think on it, but you know I'm right."

He strides from the kitchen and I glare after him. Because I don't need to think on it.

I know he's right, the bastard.

CHAPTER 33

Luke

MUM ADJUSTS the collar of my suit jacket – again – and gives me a watery little smile. I pull a ridiculous face and she laughs. It's much better than the teary state she's been in about me going to my Year Thirteen ball.

The front door bangs open and Kristen shouts down the hallway. "We're here!"

"Kris, have some manners," Carol's voice scolds her.

My heart skips, leaps, trips over its own feet and falls off a cliff. If Kristen and Carol are here, it means Dan's here too.

He drove up this morning and went to their place to get ready. Jonathan and Kristen arranged it like they were secret agents. I told them Dan could come straight to my place but Kristen insisted he go to her place first. Something to do with building intrigue and romantic tension that I didn't quite follow.

Kristen appears in the doorway to the lounge, her dark purple dress sparkling with every movement. "We left him at the door," she says to me, tilting her head in that direction. "Figured we should give you a moment without an audience."

She winks. Or tries to. It's never been something she's been able to do.

My heart falls off another cliff. He's at my door. He came all this way. Mum gives me a little shove from behind, propelling me forward. It's only a light touch, but it's a nice realisation that people aren't scared to touch me anymore.

I take a deep breath, steeling myself as I turn the corner into the hallway.

There he is, standing in the entryway, waiting for me.

Dan.

He smiles as I move closer, his eyes roaming over me.

"Hey," I say, stopping in front of him.

"Hey," he says back.

Oh, I'd totally forgotten how gorgeous he is. Like, I knew, but in real life it hits different.

I looked him up online a couple of times since I saw him, and Jonathan sent me a picture of him, Hollie and Dan the day we fessed up about our emails. But as he's standing in front of me right now, with his golden curls tumbling into his eyes and the dark blue suit that may or not actually be shimmery, I'm struggling to catch my breath.

His lips tilt up as he takes me in. "Only one crutch?"

I grin. "Only one," I say. "Sometimes not even that, but not tonight. Sorry."

"No, don't apologise. That's awesome. Well done."

I want to touch him. I want to slide my arms around his waist and pull his head into my chest and at the same time I want to kiss him so badly I might pass out with the need.

"You ready for this?" His voice is soft. "Kristen said you haven't told any of your other friends."

I shrug. "I'm ready, and they'll find out soon enough." We're inching closer with each murmured word.

"Honey," my mum calls. I huff out a sigh. "You need to go soon, and I need photos first."

I close my eyes. Take a breath to calm down. Mum and her photos. Totally mortifying. Is it always like this when bringing someone home to meet the parents?

"I'm sorry," I whisper to Dan. "She's … relentless."

Dan laughs again. "Don't worry about it. Mine's the same."

I turn and make my way back down the hallway. Dan falls into step beside me and slides his hand into mine. My heart's getting a real acrobatic workout today. I glance down at our entwined fingers and my grin matches Dan's as we re-enter the lounge, ready to face my mother and her camera flash.

We escape, barely and late, but we make it out after several hundred photos. I'm still seeing little white flashes in my eyeballs.

Dan was perfect with my family. Not that I was expecting him not to be. We walked back into the room and I know that my parents and Kristen's were trying to be cool about it all. Kristen, on the other hand, let out a loud "Awwww", then presented us both with a flower that she pinned to our jackets. They were tied with charcoal grey and blue ribbons. The scheming little wretch.

I introduced Dan to Mum and Dad and they chatted easily. I'm pretty sure Dan could charm a rampaging hippopotamus with a few words, so my parents were nothing.

The several hundred photos were taken. Kristen managed to distract the parents long enough for us to make our escape.

We barely had time to talk inside; only a few passing comments, not the in-depth catch-up I've been craving. As we step out onto the porch Kristen rushes past and jumps into the backseat of Dan's car. Dan heads straight for it too, but I catch his hand, pulling him back to me.

He startles, maybe at the fact I can actually pull with a little bit of force these days. Not a lot, but enough to get him to stop. Haley's workouts have been paying off.

"Hey," I breathe, stepping in close to him.

"Oh, hey," he says. "We really should go, you know."

"I know, but I wanted one second with you before we do."

He smiles, but it doesn't quite reach the same intensity I remember. It's like the dial isn't all the way up.

"You all good?" I ask him, the nervous knot twisting in my gut.

"Yeah, yeah, of course," he says. "I'm all good." Then he leans in and presses a kiss to my lips. It's like the very first time. A moment of soft, warm pressure, then he's gone.

I follow him to the car, climb in and sit in silence as we head for Tyler's.

Something's not right about this. Dan is here, sitting right here beside me, but it's not like it was before. It's not like it's been the whole time we've been emailing. He's stiff and tense and has barely said anything to me. Even Kristen can't get him to talk.

As we pull into Tyler's, Kristen reaches over my seat and

gives my shoulder a squeeze. "Give me a few minutes first, all right?"

I spin to face her. "What—"

But she cuts me off. "I want a minute with Tyler first before you swoop in and go all big-brotherly on me."

Pink stains her cheeks and I realise that Kristen likes Tyler way, way more than she's let on this whole time. "I won't say anything about you." She pats my shoulder and hops out of the car, striding for the house in her towering heels and the confidence of a fantasy novel queen.

I watch her go, delaying the moment I need to turn my attention back to Dan. I don't know why I'm putting it off. I've wanted to see him for so long, and now he's here I don't know how to talk to him. When I finally turn to look at him he's studying his phone.

"Everything okay?" I ask, hating that this is the second time in barely fifteen minutes that I've asked him.

He shoves the phone into his pocket and rubs a hand over his face. "Yeah. Sorry, it's been a weird day. You ready to do this?"

I glance back at the house. I'm about to do this. If I walk in there with Dan there's no going back. There're at least twelve of my friends in there, some probably with partners I don't know.

I tug at my hair and the pressure in my stomach builds.

My car door opens. I didn't even notice Dan getting out but there he is, beside my door, holding his hand out for me.

I climb out and settle my crutch on my arm. Dan closes the door quietly and turns to face me. He takes my free hand in both of his, running his fingertips over my knuckles, across my palm. It sends shivers through me, and my blood starts singing as it races through my body.

"You can do this." His voice is steady, his attention fully focussed on me, the most it has been since he arrived. "You are strong and brave and amazing and so frickin' gorgeous. You can do this. I know you want to do this, otherwise you wouldn't have asked me to come." His smile wavers, but he forces it still. I can tell it's forced because it doesn't quite sparkle in his eyes like one of his usual smiles. "But if you want, we can just be friends tonight. I don't have to be your date."

I shake my head. "I want to do this with you as my date. It'll be worth it," I whisper, and the smile he gives me really is worth it. It's still not the megawatt grin I saw so often the last time he was here, but it's a beautiful smile nonetheless.

"Shall we, then?" He offers me his arm and I take it.

The house is creeping closer with every step. My blood stops singing and starts roaring. My breath is coming so fast and hard I barely feel it, but I can't catch it. We reach the front door. I'm seeing camera flashes again.

Dan opens the door.

CHAPTER 34

Dan

I'M STILL NOT sure I should be here, standing on the front porch of Luke's friend's house. Not with everything happening with Nicole. It feels so wrong.

But Mum and Dad refused to let me go to her. Mum said if I didn't go and see Luke as planned then I could go to school and help her at work this weekend.

I reluctantly gave in, the conversation with Jake echoing in my head.

I've wanted to see Luke for so long, and now I'm here but my mind isn't. It's making me feel like shit because I should be giving Luke my full attention. I should have my entire focus on this boy in a suit standing beside me, looking like a goddamn dream.

The anxiety over my sister though: it's gnawing away at me and my distraction is making Luke nervous.

He could be nervous in general, I suppose, because tonight is a big deal for him, but I'm pretty sure it's because I'm a mess and making him feel super uncomfortable for inviting me.

I'm trying not to think about it. I'm trying not to think

about Nicole or Luke regretting asking me, but it's hard, especially with the way his hand was shaking as I helped him out of the car.

Tyler's house is massive. I can see why everyone is meeting here first for photos. It's a two-storey sprawling home that in my book qualifies as a mansion. Sweeping driveway framed by stunning trees, manicured lawns, probably a pool and tennis court out the back.

Luke and I are standing on the porch, the tension radiating off him. He's wound so tight his fingers are digging into my forearm.

He hasn't told anyone about me aside from Kristen and his parents. I'm not sure what to think about that. I really hope he didn't tell his friends with the hope that I'd bail and it wouldn't matter anyway.

I shrug those thoughts off. I need to focus. I need to think about Luke here beside me and how I'm going to make sure he has the greatest night ever.

I take a deep breath and push the door open, and the weight of Luke's hand on my arm disappears as all eyes fall on me. The group is gathered right in the entryway, a few parents taking photos of a group of girls posing on a sweeping staircase. This house is so fancy. There must be fifteen or sixteen teenagers standing here staring at me like I have seven heads.

I immediately spin away from them, looking for Luke, because he's not by my side anymore. He's standing on the edge of the porch, heaving great shaking breaths. My stomach drops out and I step towards him. I reach him in two strides, urging him to sit.

He tucks into himself, still struggling for breath.

"Luke," I say. "Luke, look at me." My hands are on his

face, turning it to me. God, the feel of his jaw under my palm. This is not the time for thoughts like that, so I push it away.

Luke slowly lifts his grey eyes to meet mine. "Breathe," I whisper. "Slow, steady … That's it." I smooth my hands down his neck, across his shoulders, holding him here with me and not letting him slip away.

After a moment he steadies, breath making it into his lungs. But his eyes, they tear at my heart. "I'm sorry," he whispers, voice breaking. "I don't know what I was thinking. I can't do this."

I stroke his hair. His breath is beginning to settle, the panic ebbing away, leaving him looking drained and exhausted. "You can do this," I promise him.

"I can't," he growls. "You barely know me; you don't know if I can do this."

"I know enough," I say, willing my voice to stay steady, willing it not to show how much that hurt. He's lashing out because he's upset. I know that. I try not to let it break my heart a little. I try not to think that I might have come all this way and Luke can't even enter a room with me. I try not to think that I could be with Nicole. That I *should* be with Nicole.

He lifts his gaze to meet mine, his eyes glassy with tears. "I thought this was what I wanted … but if it was, why can't I do it? Why does it feel like too much? Everything feels like too much. I can't do it." He wraps his fingers around my wrists and it anchors me. "I'm so sorry, Dan," he whispers.

I've been totally blindsided. I don't know what to say, what to do. If his fingers weren't pressed against my pulse holding me here, I don't know what I'd be doing. I'm frozen, staring into his eyes.

"Luke." Kirsten's soft voice breaks into our silence as she

lowers herself to the ground in front of Luke, gorgeous dress, sky-high heels and all. I slide sideways, taking a seat on the step beside him. He releases one of my hands but clamps his fingers tighter around the other as if he thinks I'm going to run.

"Luke," Kristen says again. "You're okay. Everything is going to be okay. We're here with you." She glances behind us and a scowl creases her brow for a second before she refocuses on Luke, pressing her fingers into his knee that's bouncing with agitation.

I take a peek over my shoulder and realise there's a group of people there, staring. Watching. Listening.

A tall guy in a classic black suit lowers himself to sit on Luke's other side. He places a hand on Luke's back and our eyes meet above his head for a second before he leans down towards Luke. "Hey," he says, then pauses, obviously deciding how to say whatever it is he's about to say. Luke's grip on me tightens. "If anyone ever gives you the tiniest bit of shit, we've got your back." He turns to the small crowd gathered behind us, silhouetted by the lights inside the house. "If any single one of you has a problem with Luke, then you can get the hell out, right now." No one moves.

"We love you no matter what," a girl says, and I recognise her red hair though I can't recall her name. Murmurs of agreement from the group.

"Good, now go away," the blond guy says, and Luke snorts a tiny laugh. I feel the relief wash over me. He's going to be okay.

Luke's death grip around my wrist slackens as his body gives, the tension releasing. The guy sitting across from me waves for the others to go back inside. They slowly drift away, leaving only me, him, Kristen and Luke on the porch. The guy pats Luke's shoulder. "You all right, man?"

Luke slowly pushes away from me, sitting himself upright. He can't meet the other guy's eyes, or Kristen's. He won't even look at me. "I'm really sorry," he whispers. "I'm sorry you came all this way." The apology is directed at me.

"Don't," I say, at the same time as the other guy. He stops talking, gesturing for me to continue. "Don't apologise," I say. "You don't need to apologise for your injury, or for a panic attack. If you don't want to do this, you don't have to." I swallow, hard, but force the next words out. "You don't owe anyone anything. You don't owe anyone an explanation; you don't owe me anything either. If you don't want me to come as your date tonight, I won't. I'll go back to Kristen's and we can hang out tomorrow."

The words taste like poison in my mouth. I don't want him to take me up on that offer. But I'm not going to force this on him. It has to be his choice. He has to want this and be ready for everything it's going to mean.

He shakes his head and I try to hide my exhale of relief. "I want you to come with me, but there's been so much change. I'm only just figuring how to be happy again and everything keeps changing. It's too fast. I can't keep up and this is going to change everything all over again."

"It's not going to change everything, Luke," Kristen says. "Maybe some things, yeah, but not everything. Maybe the good will outweigh the bad. Because Lukey … you deserve to be happy. You deserve to have someone look at you the way Dan does. There is no set quota on how much happiness you're allowed. If you're worried about going over the limit, don't be. There is no limit, Luke. Not to the amount of happiness you deserve."

He's staring at the ground, letting Kristen's words wash over him. I wonder what she means about the way I look at him. She's right about the happiness he deserves, though. He deserves it all.

"I'm so sorry," he whispers to his knees, the fingers of his free hand coming to tangle with mine.

"Luke." I turn him to face me again with my fingertips against his jaw, but the grey eyes stay downcast. "You don't need to apologise to me for who you are. I always, always think you're amazing."

"Even if you came all this way and I can't even walk in the door?"

"I'm not here to go to a ball with people I don't know, Luke. I'm here for you, and if this is as far as we go, then that's fine by me. But for the record, I still know you can do this. And I know that doing the hard, scary things usually gives you the best experiences." I take a deep breath. "But only – *only* – if you want to do this."

"You spent months thinking Johnnie hated you for who you are," Kirsten says, and so many pieces click into place inside my brain. "It makes sense you'd feel like this. But you've got all of us. No one's going to give you shit surrounded by us. I will destroy them." There's such violence in her voice that I don't doubt her for a second.

"What she said," the blond guy sitting on Luke's other side says. "Dan's right, Kristen's right. If you want to do this, you absolutely can. I don't think you realise how strong you are. Plus, you've got all of us. I think you'll regret it if you go home now. I know it's just a stupid school ball, but man, you deserve a bloody good night. And Dan did drive all this way to see exactly how crappy our school is."

Luke laughs a little more this time.

"Take your time, we've got plenty, but it would be really cool if you could come," the guy, who must be Tyler, says as he stands up. He holds his hands out to Kirsten, who takes them and climbs to her feet. She rearranges her skirt then places her hands on Luke's shoulders. She leans in and whispers something in his ear, which elicits a smile, then kisses him on the forehead. "You're so loved, Luke."

Then we're alone again.

"Don't even think about apologising to me," I say as Luke opens his mouth. He snorts, then bursts into a real laugh. The relief washes over me. He's back from whatever dark, terrifying place he was in. He leans into me, the laughter shaking through his body.

"I'm really, really scared." His voice shakes. "I feel like I'm a whole different person than I was a year ago, six months ago, a month ago. It's hard to keep up with everything that's happened."

"I know," I say. "But I honestly think you can do this. I know you wanted to do this, but it's okay if you're not ready. Like I said, you don't owe anyone anything, not even me. We don't need to share it with anyone else unless you want to. I told you before, whatever we have going here, it's only ours. No one else matters."

He takes my hand in his, weaving our fingers together. "What do you want to do?"

"Well, I'll do whatever you want to do, because in the end it's your decision, your life, your school, and you have to be ready to do it. But I really, really would love to dance with you, especially if there's a disco ball."

Luke laughs again, leaning his head on my shoulder. My heart stammers and I might die with how badly I want to touch him *everywhere*.

"I suppose we have the rest of the weekend to hang out just us. And I couldn't possibly deprive you of the disco ball."

"I don't really care about the disco ball," I say into his hair. "But don't deprive me of you."

CHAPTER 35

Luke

THE FRONT of the school is festooned with lights. It's lit up like it's daytime. Despite it being my boring old average school, *and* I've seen it like this before, I have to catch my breath.

Seeing it like this throws me back in time to last year's ball, when I arrived with Jonathan, both of us strolling in without a care in the world, thinking we were invincible, together to the bitter end.

We never even considered there could be a bitter end. There were only glory days for eternity.

What a difference a year makes.

Dan pulls into a parking space as close to the entrance as he can, which isn't particularly close considering my meltdown has made us late.

I almost lost my nerve to go in that door again, but Tyler had my back and Kristen and Dan were by my side. The murmuring conversation died as I stepped into the room, my face tight and hot from the tears I'd shed on the porch.

Stacey was the first to reach me. She wrapped her arms around my waist, squeezed me tight then released me to turn to Dan. "We've met before, yes?" She eyed him like she'd like to eat him.

He grinned. "Yeah, we have, at the beach that day."

The corner of her mouth tilted up. "I now understand why you didn't stay to hang out." She winked at him.

Dan's laugh rang loud through the room, his eyes sparkling. He shrugged. "You might be onto something."

A couple of others approached me and gave me hugs or slaps on the back. Told me they were proud of me, accepted me, would support me.

Then someone's mum clapped her hands and hurried us all into formation for photo after photo after photo. Parents and their cameras.

Kristen went with Tyler to the ball, leaving Dan and me alone in his car. Country music thrummed softly through the speakers. When I questioned him on his choice he laughed and blamed Hollie. "But," he said, "I like it. It's fun, or painfully romantic, or both at the same time."

"You know that most of what Jonathan and I played was country, right? Or at least country adjacent."

He stared at me, lips parted in surprise. Then he laughed. "I thought he adapted to Hollie's music really quickly."

Now, I sit here in the car realising I have to go through the walking through the door thing again, except it'll be about five hundred times worse than when it was just a handful of my own friends. This is half the school, including teachers. By Monday everyone at school, and a whole lot of people outside of school, will know. The same feeling from before hits me. The one that took over every time I got close to telling Tyler who my date was. The inexplicable feeling of both too hot and too cold at the same time, the shakiness, the tremulous stomach and the overwhelming desire to flee.

Dan slips his hand into mine across the centre console of his car. He squeezes softly, his thumb caressing the back of my hand. "You can do this," he says, voice low. "I know you can." He gestures behind us and I notice Tyler, Kristen and a bunch of others have gathered there. My support crew.

"Thank you," I say, voice catching on the words. "I couldn't have done it without you."

He flashes a cocky grin. I want to freeze frame this moment and keep it forever. "I'm sure you could have found some other guy to walk in with. They wouldn't be as cool as me though."

I laugh, and it feels so good. I lean in and brush my lips against his. A shiver runs down my spine. I can't wait until we're alone and I can kiss him properly.

"Come on," he says, his voice soft. "They're all waiting for us."

I take deep breaths, straighten my suit and climb out of Dan's car.

He was right. They are waiting for us. As we walk towards the entrance, my friends form a tight group around us. Kristen and Tyler are on one side of me, Dan on the other. I grip Dan's hand so tightly I'm probably crushing his bones, but he doesn't comment and doesn't even wince. He just holds me firmly. Steadily.

Somehow I'm at the front of the group when we reach the foyer. My steps slow but Dan tugs gently on my hand, and just like that we're through the doors and inside the building.

There're a couple of people milling around, but Dan keeps hold of my hand. Another tug and we're making our way across the room, brushing past the murmurs and whispers, the double-takes and wide eyes. My breathing spikes, but no one approaches us. No one scowls or glares. There's surprise, but not aggression.

We push into the swinging doors to the hall and we're inside, the music already pounding through the dim space. Coloured lights flicker, balloons and a few sparse decorations cover the walls and ceiling. Everything is bright and shimmering. Glitter and sequins and sparkles. But the real highlight is the mass of students in the room. Brightly coloured dresses of all styles, glitter in hair and on exposed shoulders, ties and corsages. And above it all, a glittering disco ball.

"Good to see you keep your promises," Dan says, leaning into me as his eyes land on it.

I chuckle. I've laughed more around this boy in the few times I've seen him than I have the entire six months since my injury. And every time that sound bubbles up inside me, the feeling inside me changes too. The laughter is slowly but surely scrubbing away the pain.

We move into the room, Dan taking everything in but following my lead. I'm just going with the group though, letting us be led by them, not quite ready to break from their protective cocoon even though we've barely had a glance since we set foot in this room. I know it's coming.

As if I've thought the moment into existence, a guy stops in front of me. I don't know him but his face is vaguely familiar, so definitely someone from school.

I stop as the guy blocks my way. Dan, as always, is beside me. Tyler must have noticed the shift in the air because he stops too and turns back, crossing his arms and assessing the guy in front of me, then stations himself at my shoulder.

Everything in me seizes up. I can feel the panic building in my chest, the heat behind my eyes then crawling across my cheeks. Any second now the trembling will start and the urge to vomit will threaten. But Dan's hand is sure in mine and I can feel the heat of Tyler's presence at my shoulder. I glance sideways and can see Kristen. She reminds me so much of her brother, and something in me settles.

The stranger looks me up and down, his gaze lingering on where Dan's hand is linked with mine. His lip lifts in a sneer. "Are you a—"

I cut him off. I don't need to hear what he's going to say. "It's not any of your business."

He sneers some more. "Is that why Jonathan left in the middle of the night? Lover's tiff?" His mate standing beside him sniggers. A gorgeous girl in a slinky silver dress pulls at his hand, telling him to shut up, sending me silent apologies with her eyes.

"Ooh, did you turn gay when you spent all that time in hospital? Probably not many hot girls in there," the guy says, ignoring the girl.

"I don't even know who you are," I say, willing my voice to stay steady, strong. "I don't care what your pathetic opinion of me is. Now if you'll excuse me, I've got a date I want to dance with."

I glare at him then stroll past, as best I can still using a crutch.

"God, you're such a fucking asshole," the girl hisses at the jerk. "I'm fucking done with you." She drops his hand and turns to us as we pass. "I'm really sorry. You guys are gorgeous together. I hope you have a good night. If he gives you any more shit let me know. I know all his weaknesses." She flashes us a delightfully wicked grin and Dan laughs.

"I like her," he says as the girl shoves past her ex-date and storms away.

"Yeah?" I ask, turning to him. The asshole has already blended back in with the crowd. When my eyes meet Dan's, everyone else in the room fades into the background too. "Here I was thinking you liked me. How did I get it so wrong?"

He steps closer to me, slips an arm around my waist, his palm across my lower back, fitting us together. My heart hammers. We haven't been this close since that time we made out on my bed and he was shirtless. My head spins at the memory, at the way his thighs are currently crowding mine, the way his eyes are sparkling under that goddamn disco ball as he tilts his face up to me. "Oh, the way I like you is *completely* different to the way I like her."

My hand lands on his waist. His free hand brushes against the hair at the back of my neck. I don't even know how his hand got there without me noticing. My gaze is locked on his and all I can see is his eyes, the line of his nose and the curve of his mouth, so maybe that has something to do with it.

His thumb brushes the hinge of my jaw, right below my ear, and it sends shivers rippling through me.

I'm so glad he's here to hold me up because I'm losing control over my knees.

"I do have to agree with her though," Dan says, voice low and husky. We're so close I can feel it rumbling through his chest. "We are gorgeous together."

I say nothing. I don't have enough breath or coherent thought to produce words.

"And you're *such* a badass. The way you looked at him." Dan's mouth curves up into a wicked smile, like the random girl's but so much better because it's his mouth. "It was the way you'd look at something gross you accidentally stepped in."

A breathy laugh escapes my lungs. I should be upset. I should be shaking, crying in the corner. But somehow, I don't feel like I need to be. I certainly don't want to be. I want to be right here on the dance floor with Dan's hand running up and down my spine.

I can't believe he's here – finally. He's here, not some flimsy daydream, but solid as a rock.

Solid and really, really hot, with his body pressing up against mine.

I curse at the stupid brace under my clothes and wonder what it will feel like to not be wearing it and have him against me like this. I wonder if he'll be around long enough to know me when I've thrown it in the bin or burned it; when I never have to wear it again and can truly feel the press of his palm against my skin.

I hope that day comes. I push away thoughts of it not happening.

I drop my head lower, our noses grazing. His face is so close to mine it blurs, and our breath mingles.

A breath before our lips touch he speaks again. "Are you really going to dance with me?"

My head is spinning so hard and I'm fighting with every-thing in me to keep standing. I'll do whatever he wants if he'll kiss me. "If you want to," I breathe.

His mouth curves and I'm too close to actually see it, but I can feel the way his face moves into the delicious smile. "Good, because I really want to do that." Another breath. I'm shaking. "There's something else I really want to do."

I close my eyes, trying to concentrate. "What's that?" I grit out.

"This," he breathes as he finally – *finally* – presses our lips together.

I melt into him. I forget the crutch looped over my arm as I wrap both of my arms around him. It bangs against his leg but he ignores it totally. He slides his tongue along my bottom lip and my knees buckle.

Any residual idea that Dan and I are only friends flees my mind. There is no way, absolutely no way I could ever be "just friends" with this boy. How would I ever look at that mouth and not want to kiss it? Look into those eyes, bottomless depths of the softest, kindest brown and not want to know every little thing that goes on in the brain behind them? See those hands and not want them in mine, or on my skin?

This stupid wall I've tried to keep in place despite all that email flirting and all the previous kissing teeters and tumbles. There's nothing left; not a single brick remains, only clouds of dust being blown away by golden curls and a wicked grin. And those hands.

We break apart, both sucking in shaky breaths.

"Take me dancing, sweetheart," Dan says after a moment, that heart-stopping grin curving his lip again.

I barely have the wits to gather my crutch back before I tangle our fingers together and lead him to the dance floor.

CHAPTER 36

Dan

SEEING Luke with his friends is different than I expected.

Luke at this ball is different.

Luke being out, confronting that jerk, dancing with me. None of it is how I expected this to go.

He wasn't like this when I was here with Hollie and Jonathan. It wasn't noticeable, but seeing him now I know how much he was holding back; how much he was tiptoeing around me and Jonathan.

Since that heart-crushing moment when that asshole confronted Luke and he absolutely destroyed him with his voice and the most epic look of disdain I've ever seen, Luke has let loose.

I couldn't help but hold him close and kiss him right there and then because I was so stupidly proud of him. I don't think I've ever been prouder of anyone in my life, and I've seen some people do amazing things.

And here he is now in the middle of a dance floor, surrounded by friends, a smile spread over his face. The weight of the accident, the pressure of coming out, the stress and worry over everything that has happened to him over the past six months has lifted. Even my being distracted isn't affecting him anymore. In fact, he's been distracting me from it, for which I'm grateful. The relentless worry has been exhausting.

Tyler grins every time his gaze lands on Luke. I swear I caught Kristen wiping away tears as she watched him dance, carefully but barely using his crutch.

We danced together until sweat ran down my temples and my breath came in short puffs. We started slowly, both of us reluctant to break the touch between us. But slowly we fell into the rhythm of the music, which called for more than holding each other and swaying.

I pulled away eventually, needing a moment to catch my breath and find a drink. I brushed Luke's wrist, indicating my intention with the tilt of my head. He tried to come with me but I made him stay. I reached up and brushed a kiss against his damp cheek. "I'll be right back," I said into his ear.

My skin still tingles where he brushed his fingertips as he pushed my hair back from my face. He smiled and watched me go.

This whole day has been hard. On the drive up I was caught between the excitement of seeing Luke and the guilt of letting Nicole down, even though Jake's words kept strumming through my mind.

Whatever choice I made, I was going to let someone down. Jake was right about Nicole, too. She'd be furious if she ever found out I stood up Luke to go to her instead.

If she gets better.

I've been trying not to think about that all day. Instead I thought about Dad being with her, finding her doctor, taking her to hospital if he needed to. Making her get up, shower and go outside, eat something that didn't come directly from a crinkly packet.

Dad is with her and he'll keep her safe.

Seeing Luke's face helps. He keeps me here in the present with him. Every time he touches me it grounds me here, helps me remember that I want to be here. I really, really want to be here with him.

I know I'm drifting in and out though. No matter how hard I try, I can't keep my full focus on the moments right in front of me. On the drive between Luke's and Tyler's houses I was with Nicole. But the moment Luke needed me, those minutes on the porch, he was all I could think about.

I'm used to being needed. I thrive on being needed. Hollie needs me, and being there for her when her dark moods strike, helping pull her back out of them: it's easy for me.

My thoughts stray to her. She messaged earlier telling me to have the best night ever and that she couldn't wait to hear all about it.

I wonder about Mum, who's home alone this weekend except for Jake.

Then my thoughts spiral to Dad and Nicole and I worry some more about how they're doing.

I'm being pulled in too many directions. Too many people need me. I've never had this before. I've always been able to help everyone when they need me, give everyone what they need. But right now, I can't.

Jake's words echo again. Him telling me I need to do something for myself, to stop giving everything I have to everyone else. I wonder if he has a point.

I finish the drink in my hand. It's already warming up but it's better than nothing. I head back to the dance floor, ready to fling myself back into the fray and try to lose all these thoughts tumbling around in my head.

My eyes lock on Luke, his head tilted back, the little squares of light from the disco ball scattered across his cheeks. He turns, chin lowering, and his eyes meet mine.

My pulse booms. Any refreshment the drink brought evaporates from my tongue. His tie is loose, the top button of his once crisp white shirt unbuttoned. Kristen twirls by him, giggling as she bumps into him. He gently steadies her, but his eyes never leave mine.

My feet move towards him. Every step brings another detail into focus. Another perfect, gorgeous detail.

My phone vibrates in my pocket. My steps falter. No one should be calling me now. The only people who ever call me know exactly where I am and that I'm not exactly up for taking calls right now. It's also super late, so no one in their right mind would be calling.

I pull my phone out. A cold shiver goes through me as I register the name on the screen.

Nicole.

Nicole is calling me.

I turn away from Luke and crash through the doors into the foyer, lifting the phone to my ear as I go.

"Nic," I say down the line, my voice hoarse and scratchy. I don't know if it's the emotion of hearing from her, or from having to shout everything I've said for the past two hours.

"Danny," she sobs. My heart splinters. "Oh, Danny. I'm so sorry."

"No," I say, my voice shaking. It's not only my voice, I realise. My whole body is shaking.

Nicole's never called in the middle of the night before. She doesn't usually call at all if she's feeling bad. Dread looms over me.

"You don't apologise, Nic, don't you ever do that, okay?" My voice is breaking, shattering, but I patch it together, force steel into it so I can hold it together for my sister. I pull my phone away from my ear and fire off a text message to both my parents, hoping that one of them is awake; that if Dad is asleep Mum can call him and get him to Nicole. I hit send and replace the phone at my ear.

"I got your picture," Nicole says. The picture I texted her of me and Luke earlier, when I first arrived. He was looking at me all starry-eyed, like he couldn't quite believe I was standing in front of him, real and solid. "You're so gorgeous, Danny," Nicole says. "And that boy, the way he's looking at you." She draws a heavy breath. It leaves her in a sob. "He'll look after you, Danny."

Everything inside me vanishes. I'm hollow, only a gaping black hole inside my soul. "Nic, don't say that."

"But he will. I'm so happy you found him and I'm so sorry for ruining your night. I just needed to hear your voice. I wanted to tell you how much I love you. I wanted to tell you he loves you. Luke, I mean. I can tell by how he's looking at you."

"Nic, it isn't like that with him. It doesn't matter," I say, desperation stretching my voice thin. "I need you, Nic. I need you to look after me. Not Luke. You, Nic. Always you."

"I love you so much, Danny." She's not hearing me. She's not hearing what I'm saying.

"I love you, Nic, please Nic. Don't – don't do anything you can't take back. You can't leave me, Nic. I need you."

"I'm so tired, Danny. So tired. It never goes away." Her voice is soft now, like she's sleepy.

Where is Dad? Why is he not with her yet?

"Nic, please." I'm begging. Any pretence of being strong is gone. "Don't do this to me, Nic. I love you. Please don't let me go."

A noise. A deep voice down the line. "Nicole." Dad's voice. I sag in relief.

"I've got her, Dan," he says down the phone. "I'll take care of her. Danny, I'll call you as soon as I can. I promise. We love you."

"Okay," I whisper as the line goes dead in my hand.

CHAPTER 37
Luke

NICK.

I love you, Nick.

Don't do this to me.

I need you.

It's not like that with him.

It doesn't matter.

You can't leave me, Nick.

Dan ran from the auditorium so fast, with an indescribable look of panic twisting his face, I followed him without hesitation.

I wish I hadn't.

It took me a bit of time to get to him, out in the foyer. But I was there in time to see him crumple onto the floor, missing the seating by less than a metre.

He sat on the floor of my school, sobbing down the phone to this Nick person, begging them not to leave him.

He's spent the night with me, touching me, igniting flames in my bloodstream with even the briefest brush of body against body.

He danced with me, kissed me. He drove for hours to do this with me. And now he's crying – actually crying – over someone else. He's still on the floor, his phone clutched to his chest as he shakes and sobs.

I don't understand. I don't understand why he's here if he wants to be with someone else. I don't understand how Jonathan could have let this happen, either. Surely if Dan had a boyfriend, Jonathan would never have let me get involved.

Maybe I'm the one fooling myself. Maybe Jonathan didn't realise how seriously I'd got into this thing with Dan. If Dan himself is calling it just a friendship, then I've clearly got myself confused.

I thought the wall I'd built up over the past few months was rubble, but already it's piecing itself back together, preparing the defences.

I really, really hope there's some logical, non-heartbreaking explanation for what I've just witnessed.

Dan sniffs, exhales loudly, shifts on the floor. He obviously catches sight of my shoes because his gaze slowly lifts, trailing up my body.

He's given me a look like this before, his eyes lingering on me. Then, it made my skin flame, my blood sizzle. This time, though, shards of ice splinter through me, stabbing me all over.

There's nothing heated in his gaze, nothing appreciative. There's nothing there at all.

His eyes are red, tears streak his cheeks and there isn't a single emotion I can identify in his face, even when those eyes lock on mine.

"I need to go," is all he says.

Any last remaining shred of hope disintegrates. Despair

shoots through my heart, punches me in the gut. My head spins with betrayal.

"What the hell was that?" My voice is harsh. It's rough and clipped, filled with raw, broken emotion.

"I – I need to go. I can't explain now, I need to go." He's already fishing his keys out of his pocket.

"What?" I'm dumbstruck. "That's it? That's all I get? Where are you going?"

"Home. I need to go home." He finally seems to actually see me. "I'm sorry," he says, and turns for the door.

"That's not good enough," I growl, reaching for him, grabbing his wrist and pulling him back. Again, this same movement only a few hours ago would have set my heart racing, now I'm just angry, devastated. "I don't get it."

"I – I can't explain now." He's turning away.

"What do you even want from me?" I cry. "I didn't want any of this, but you tore through my life and I got swept up in all your promises, all those bloody promises. When I finally, *finally* accept that I've fallen so bloody hard for you and everything I tried to do to keep you at a distance was a waste of time, you turn tables on me and you're going to walk out on me? I did all this for you and you're going to leave me here?"

His face goes even paler than it was a moment ago, which I wasn't sure was possible. His expression twists, something like despair tangled in the emotions there. He takes a step towards me and lifts his hand to brush his fingers along my cheek.

"I'm so sorry, Luke." His voice breaks over my name and something in my chest does the same. "I can't be who you need me to be."

I don't know what he means, but before I have the chance

to ask, his phone rings. He glances to the screen then back to me.

I will him not to answer the call. I will him to explain what's going on.

"I'm sorry," he whispers, voice wrecked. "I can't do this now. I'm so, so sorry." He blows through the outer door, out into the night.

I'm so shocked he chose to walk away that I stand there shaking, too scared to try walking in case my body gives out on me.

All the physiotherapy, all the workouts, strength training, exercises; it's like they never happened.

I feel as weak and broken as I did six months ago.

CHAPTER 38

Dan

I RUN FROM LUKE.

From the shock and pain and desperation on his face. The feel of his cheek still tingles in my fingers. I hate that I caused that look on his face, but I can't worry about that right now.

I burst through the door, already lifting my phone to my ear.

"Mum." My voice is raspy, like I've swallowed gravel.

"Danny, honey," she says. Her voice is shaking. Like mine is shaking. Like all of me is shaking. I can't get it to stop.

I'm in the middle of the carpark outside the school when my steps finally slow. It's raining. Not a lot, only a light drizzle, but enough to make the fairy lights around the entrance fuzzy and the asphalt carpark reflect the glow.

If my world wasn't falling apart it'd be fucking romantic.

"Is she okay?" My voice breaks again. I let it. I can't fight it anymore.

"Dad's taking her to the hospital," Mum says, worn and weary. "He thinks she might have taken something. We're not sure. But she's in the best place she can be, and she's safe."

Someone may as well have kicked me in the guts. I can't draw a breath. I gasp and wheeze, bracing my free hand against my knee.

Nicole, my beautiful Nicole. I should have been with her.

"I'm coming home," I say, finally able to catch my breath. I'm pulling my keys out of my pocket already.

"Oh, honey, no."

"But I need to. I have to come home." Why doesn't she want me to come home? Why doesn't she want me there?

"Not tonight, honey. It's too late. You're upset. It's not safe for you to drive. I wish you were here, I really do, but do not drive."

"I can't stay here," I whisper. The image of Luke's face flashes through my mind. The devastation. "I don't know where to go." I don't know if I'm talking to Mum or myself.

"You were staying at Luke's friend's place tonight, yeah? Not at Luke's?"

"We were supposed to stay at Tyler's. I can't go there now."

"I understand. Go back to Luke's. Stay there tonight and see how you're feeling in the morning; if you'll be okay to drive. If you aren't, I'll come and get you."

"But you need to go to Nic." She can't come and get me. She needs to get to the hospital. She needs to see Nicole, make sure she's okay.

"Not until you're back safe, okay?" Her voice is thin and tired. "Can you get back to Luke's? Stay there for the night?"

"Yeah, yeah I'll do that," I say. I can't tell her about Luke. About what I did to him, leaving him standing there looking completely broken. She doesn't need that burden too. "Call me as soon as you hear about Nic," I say. "I don't care what time it is. I won't be asleep."

"I know, honey. I'll call as soon as I hear anything." She pauses. I hear her draw a heavy breath. "Danny, I'm so proud of you. She's safe because of you. I love you."

"I love you too, Mum." The sobs fight to break free but I manage to suppress them until she tells me we'll talk soon and ends the call. Once I know she's gone I let them loose and they tear through me. I lean my head against my car, the drizzling rain nestling in my hair. The glass of the car window is cold, blissful against my tear-ravaged face.

I stand with my face pressed into the cool glass until I'm soaked through, but the devastating sobs have subsided. Once I can breathe somewhat normally again, I heave myself upright, climb into the driver's seat and start the ignition.

I pull out of the carpark and drive. I don't know where I'm going. All I know is I cannot go back to Luke's.

CHAPTER 39

Luke

DAN IS GONE.

I don't know where. But he isn't here.

I stood in the foyer trying to regain some control – of my breathing, of my feelings, of my face – until I saw Dan's car pull out of the parking lot and disappear into the night.

I walk back into the ball. Everything is hazy, like a snow globe that's been shaken way too hard. The room full of colour, glitter, music and laughter is completely at odds with what has happened. I glance up at the disco ball and want to smash it into tiny pieces. It already feels like shards of glass are tearing into my soul, so maybe actually smashing something to smithereens would help.

I edge around the room, finding a shadowy corner to sit and figure out what the hell to do next.

I'm supposed to be staying at Tyler's tonight, with Dan. My backpack, filled with spare clothes and my sleeping bag and pillow are all in Dan's car. Unless, of course, he turfed them out in the carpark.

Even my own house keys are in his car, carelessly dropped

into the centre console. I can't go home, even if I have a ride. I suppose Mum will let me in, if she's still awake.

Going to Tyler's though, with the whole group of people – it's too much. I'll have to explain what happened, which is going to be downright impossible because I don't even know.

I know I'm missing something; the thing that might explain the personality transplant Dan just had, but I can't find that missing piece.

I find a shadowy corner and settle down to wait out the rest of the evening. My body is too exhausted to even pretend everything is okay. I sit and watch my classmates sing and dance and laugh and kiss under those stupid twinkling lights.

Despair fills me. So similar to the feelings after the accident, when I thought I'd never use my legs again. So similar to the feelings I had when I realised Jonathan had walked out of my life, seemingly without a backward glance.

I think of that time when I lost my best friend, and realise I feel the exact same thing now. Because over these weeks of emails, that's what Dan has become. Jonathan will always, always have a special place in my heart and in my life. But things are different now, even if neither of us wants to admit it. It isn't the same after the rejection and heartbreak, even if it was pure misunderstanding and confusion on both sides, even if neither of us meant it. The distance is there now. I tread so much more carefully around his feelings than I did before, terrified that if I lay too much on him I'll hurt him again without meaning to.

My accident broke me physically but it broke him mentally, and he's only now beginning to rebuild himself. I can't talk to him about the horrid little details of life now, of my fears, of the loss I've felt, because I know he'll pile it on himself, blaming himself, even though none of it was ever his fault.

But with Dan, I could tell him anything. I never shied away from it. I never even had to think about it. I simply wrote whatever came to mind and he accepted it; all of the good and all of the bad. It felt like he wanted to know all of me, the best parts and the worst.

And now he's gone.

I'm alone again. Even in this huge room filled with people, I'm alone.

Tyler and Kristen are amazing, but it's not the same.

I need Dan. If this happened with anyone else, I'd go to Dan and he would talk me down, talk me through it and leave me feeling calm and like I could handle anything. But what do I do if I don't have him anymore?

Kristen slides into a seat beside me, surprising me from my musings.

"Hey," she says. "Where's Dan? We're pretty close to leaving."

I shrug, unable to make eye contact with her. "I don't know."

She glances around as if he'll materialise, as if I simply haven't seen him nearby. "What do you mean? I assumed you guys were making out somewhere … but…" She's staring at me hard now, but I keep my eyes lowered. "Luke, what happened?"

My head starts shaking. My eyes are burning and my breath is already hitching. *I* don't even know what happened. How am I supposed to explain it to her? She places a hand over mine. "Luke, what happened? Where is he?"

"He's gone," I say eventually. I force my breath to steady.

"He took some phone call, then he just … he left. He didn't tell me why."

Kristen opens her mouth to speak, then closes it. Reshuffles on her chair. She's speechless. Her mouth opens again but she still doesn't say anything, because what is there to say?

She pats my hand, holds up one finger – an indication for me to wait – and disappears back into the crowd. Moments later she returns with Tyler in tow. Their fingers are linked loosely together as he trails behind her and he's gazing down at her with total devotion. A pang hits me as I realise I was looking at Dan like that barely an hour ago.

"Let's go," she says to me, hauling me out of my seat.

"What? No. Finish your night," I say, stumbling as she pulls me to my feet. I manage to get upright, my crutch in place, but my body is tired. My legs aches, my back is stiff and tight. I'm going to hurt so much tomorrow, and for what?

"We're all good, there's only five minutes left anyway," Tyler says. "Come on, man, let's get out of here."

We wind our way through the crowd. It's starting to thin already. We make it to the foyer and my eyes land on the spot Dan collapsed on the floor in a moment of total devastation. Nick must have been really something. The thought crosses my mind, but even as it does that little niggle that tells me I'm missing a vital piece of the puzzle tugs at me.

Still, the empty space where Dan's car was parked taunts me as we pass. I avert my eyes and Kristen holds my hand, but none of it dissolves the dull ache in my heart. She helps me into the front seat of Tyler's sedan, noting my fatigue.

The moment Tyler starts the engine, my phone rings.

My heart skips several beats as I fumble to get it out of my pocket. All my movements are slow and clumsy at this point though, and it takes far too long to retrieve it.

Mum.

Not Dan.

Why is Mum calling me in the middle of the night?

"Hey, Mum," I say, answering the call with nervous trepidation. "What's up?"

"Hey, Luke." A pause. "Is Dan with you?"

"Wha…what?" My voice croaks, but I manage to get the word out eventually.

"Is he with you?" Her voice is tight with concern. How does she know something's happened?

I sigh, my voice trembling as I tell her no, he isn't with me.

"Oh," she says.

"He told me he was going home. He ran out, telling me he was going home, and I haven't seen or heard from him since. That was an hour or so ago." Something unsettling is twisting in my gut. That thing telling me that I don't have the whole story. It's telling me that something is very, very wrong. "What's going on?"

There's nothing but Mum's breathing down the line for a moment, two, before she finally speaks. "Dan got a phone call tonight," she says, eerily calm. "From his sister." Another breath, this one shaking. "She – she's very unwell. She tried to say goodbye to him." Mum's voice is beginning to splinter. My breath is catching, tightness in my chest making it hard to breathe in or out. "While he was on the phone with her Dan texted their dad, who was at her place, and he got her to the hospital." Mum takes another shaky breath. "Nicole is being looked after now, but Dan never came back here."

Oh my god. My chest is caving in. The uneasy feeling in my stomach is gone, replaced with a deep, hollow horror.

Nicole.

Nick.

He's never mentioned his sister by name. He always just calls her "my sister".

Not a break-up. A different kind of goodbye.

"Where's Dan?" I whisper, suppressing the roiling in my stomach. Tyler is still driving. He's glancing sideways at me repeatedly, clearly listening to the conversation while trying to focus on the road. Kristen's hand snakes over from the back seat and grasps my shoulder.

"I don't know," Mum says. "His mum phoned me right after she spoke to him and said he'd be staying here tonight, instead of at Tyler's. I think she assumed you'd be here too. But he never showed up."

"I didn't know. He didn't tell me. I thought – I thought…" I trail off and suck in a searing breath. His sister tried to say goodbye to him. Does that mean … Did she hurt herself? I wave my hand at Tyler as my stomach lurches and he pulls over. I stumble from the car. Somehow my body is moving in this strange burst of energy. Adrenaline, probably. I trip on the curb and my knee hits the concrete footpath. I don't care. I stumble further, crawling onto the verge.

I take deep gulping breaths, but even then I can't get enough oxygen into my lungs.

Kristen races out of the car behind me. Her hands fall on my shoulders and run through my hair as she tries to soothe me. I've lost track of my phone; I must have dropped it. I scramble around in the dark looking for it. It's too dark and my eyes are blurred with tears.

"Tyler's got it," Kristen says, grasping my face between her hands and forcing me to look at her. "Tyler's got your phone. He's talking to your mum. We'll figure it out. We'll find him."

I give a short nod and slump forward, lying down on the wet grass verge beside the road. The car rumbles quietly at the curb as Kristen slides towards me, placing my head in her lap, trailing her fingers through my hair. Tyler's still talking to Mum.

"He wanted to go home," I whisper. "What if he did? What if – what if…" The urge to vomit overwhelms me again. Kristen's cool, soft hands swipe across my cheek, my forehead. The urge subsides.

Tyler ends the call and lowers himself to the grass beside Kristen.

"Could he be at my place?" Kristen asks before Tyler has a chance to speak.

Tyler shakes his head. "Your mums have spoken. He's not at either of your houses. His mum told him not to drive home and he said he wouldn't. We have to assume he hasn't."

"We have to hope he hasn't," I say, tears still leaking from my eyes and running silently down my face. Kristen catches them all.

"Do you have any idea where he might be?"

I stare up at the sky, catching sight of my friends leaning into each other, Tyler tucking Kristen under his arm and into his side as I throw my mind around, trying to think about places he might go.

"I barely know him," I whisper. "How am I supposed to know where he'd go?"

Tyler sighs. "I know. It's not like it's his hometown either, where he's got special places he could go."

At his words I try to sit up, realisation hitting me. Unfortunately my body is still exhausted, even more so since I tumbled out of the car.

Kristen pushes me upright.

"I might know where he is. It's a long shot, but it's the only place I can think of. If you take me home I can get Mum to drive me there." There's a tiny golden glimmer of hope sitting in my heart. The one place here that might hold special meaning for Dan.

"No way. We'll drive you," Tyler says, climbing to his feet and holding out his hands for me. He helps me back to the car and I let him, because as stubborn as I am about having people help me, I can't do this alone. Not right now. I need someone else. He helps lower me into the car then heads around to the driver's side. Kristen slides into the back.

I tell Tyler where to go. He raises an eyebrow at me, like he's not sure this is the greatest idea I've ever had, but he puts the car in drive and a few minutes later we're heading out of the city.

I flick Mum a text to tell her we might have an idea where he is and I'll let her know as soon as I can.

She sends me back a *Please do,* then after a moment, *I'm so proud of you.*

I clutch my phone to my chest, right above my heart, and cross my fingers that I've got this right.

CHAPTER 40

Dan

MY PHONE RINGS AGAIN.

I glance at the screen and cancel the call.

The list of declined calls and ignored messages are piling up.

Hollie.

Jonathan.

Luke.

I ignore them all, even the ones from Luke, despite how much my heart aches every time I see his name flash on my screen.

I'm waiting for one call and one call only. I won't risk missing it by being on the phone with anyone else. My phone battery percentage is dropping dangerously low, so I'm too scared to even read and reply to the text messages.

I readjust my position, the movement causing a trickle of rain to slip inside the collar of my shirt. It causes a shiver, but then it passes as it melds with the rest of the water plastering the dress shirt to my body.

I push the hair back off my face, flicking more water from the ends as I do.

And I sit here, waiting for my mother to call me to tell me if my sister is alive or not.

238

CHAPTER 41

Luke

TYLER PULLS into the gravel parking area and his headlights illuminate the car parked there.

Dan's car.

I found him. I sag with relief.

As we got closer and closer my apprehension grew. I was terrified we'd driven for what felt like eternity for nothing; that he wouldn't be here.

"Tell Mum," I say, pushing the door open before the car has even come to a complete stop. Kristen nods, not looking up from her phone. She's been frantically tapping away the whole drive out here. Every so often she muttered something about Jonathan, or Hollie, or answering calls or voicemail, so I assume she has them trying to reach him too. It doesn't sound like he's answered any of us.

I stumble and trip my way across the parking lot, barely able to lift my feet at this point, my single crutch not nearly enough support.

There's no light out here except for the glow of Tyler's

headlights. There's no sound, not even when I call out for Dan. For a moment I wonder what I'm going to find.

He's not in his car, but as I round the front I see him perched on the railing, looking out over the beach we held hands on.

I shuffle towards him. He doesn't turn at the sound of my approach. He doesn't even turn when I lean against the railing, letting out a low moan of pain as I do. Too much. This night has been too much for my body.

But I lean on the railing, right where he kissed me for the first time, and look up at him. His hair is plastered to his head, his shirt to his body. There mustn't be a dry spot on him, despite the drizzle only being light. He's been out here a while.

I reach over and take his hand. It's freezing. He doesn't move, doesn't flinch or react in the slightest.

"Dan," I say. I squeeze his hand. Nothing. "Will you tell me about your sister?"

He jerks at that. His entire body, like he's been electrocuted.

"What's her name?"

"Nicole." His voice is rough with emotion and disuse. Nicole. Nic. My heart twists.

"How old is she?"

"Twenty-three."

"What's your favourite thing about her?" I keep my voice soft and non-threatening and the questions simple, like my therapist has done with me over and over. My mental therapist, as opposed to my physical therapist.

"She's funny. Like, really funny. She has a stupid joke or bad pun for every occasion. She's kind too, always so kind. She used to read to me when I was a kid and couldn't read whole books on my own. She'd help me. And she's so smart. She never believes it because she can't do math, at all, but she's so, so smart, just differently smart."

"She sounds amazing," I say, trailing my thumb across the back of Dan's hand.

"She is," he says, voice barely audible. "I don't know what I'd do without her."

"Have you heard from your mum yet?"

He shakes his head, water dripping from the ends of his hair and running down the length of his nose.

I reach up and swipe the moisture from his face, likely a mix of rain and tears. He shivers.

I want to scream at him. Shout at him that he should have told me what was going on, ask him why he didn't tell me. I want to rage at him for causing everyone so much distress. But I gaze up at him and all I can see is the boy I've given my heart to, looking completely lost and broken. I know that feeling, so instead of shouting and yelling and demanding answers, I swallow my own feelings and squeeze his hand tightly in mine.

"Come home with me," I say, willing him to agree.

"But don't you—"

I shake my head, smooth the hair back from his face, wipe away more moisture from his cheeks. "Come home with me," I say again. "Please."

"I don't know how to help her."

"You did everything you can," I say. *He probably saved her life,* I think, but I don't say that because we don't know enough yet. "But you need to come home with me so your mum doesn't worry about you, too."

He looks at me then, properly, for the first time since I

arrived. "How did you find me? How did you know to look for me?"

"Your mum rang mine, and when you never went home like you said you would, she got worried. If you weren't at my house, or Kristen's, this was the only other place I could imagine you going."

"Is my mum freaking out?" His eyes flash with pain and worry.

"Your mum doesn't know you aren't tucked up in bed at my house. We didn't want to worry her any further."

He sags in relief. "Oh god. Thank you." He breaks then, his body crumpling as sobs overwhelm him.

Tyler approaches us slowly, Kristen by his side.

"Come home with me, Danny," I say, pleading this time.

He looks down at me, glances for a moment to Tyler and Kristen, then back to me. "It wasn't supposed to be like this," he whispers. "You were supposed to have an amazing night. You would have, if it wasn't for me. I shouldn't have come."

"I did have an amazing night, with you. But none of that matters now. All I want now is for you to come home with me."

I don't know how to make him agree; to get out of this rain and come home so we can look after him. "Please," I say again. "We want to look after you."

He stares at me. The misty rain lit golden by Tyler's head-lights is falling around him, and aside from his pain-ravaged expression he looks breathtakingly beautiful.

He looks like he's going to argue some more, but then he tilts his head. The tiniest nod.

He slowly turns himself on the railing, stiff from sitting in the cold so long. His feet touch the ground and he staggers. He falls into me and my body spasms as it catches his weight. The moment is a role reversal of the first time we met, and the things it does to my heart, my body, are the same, but about a thousand times more intense.

Tyler slips Dan's arm over his shoulder and leads him towards the vehicles. Kristen falls into step beside me, then pulls open the door to Tyler's car and we watch in silence as Dan climbs slowly into the back seat. Tyler ushers me in after Dan, helping me up into the SUV.

Dan turns to me, a dazed look glazing his eyes, but for a moment they focus solely on me. "You're hurting," he whispers. I adjust myself in the seat then slide him closer to me, tucking him into my side as his head falls onto my chest. "I'm so sorry."

"Don't say sorry, don't ever say sorry, not for this," I say as I pull him closer, tangling my fingers in his hair as I hold him tight against me, refusing to let go.

CHAPTER 42

Dan

I'M SO COLD.

I must have been sitting at the lookout for hours before Luke and his friends found me. It wasn't until I looked at them standing there in the rain, bedraggled and soaked, that I considered I must look the same.

I hadn't noticed the cold, or the rain, or the time, as I sat there ignoring all those calls.

"Hollie," I say, into the warm expanse of Luke's chest. "Hollie was calling me." I'm wracked by a bout of shivering so severe I think my teeth might fall out. Luke slips his hands into my hair, grasping the strands, pressing his fingertips against my scalp. He's holding me here, keeping me here with him.

"We thought you might answer a call from her, but she knows we found you. They know you're safe."

I release a breath and sink into Luke. He's holding me so tightly.

The ache in my chest is immense as I worry about Nicole. The worry I always feel for her has expanded, reaching further than I ever thought it could. I've thought about how I'd feel in this situation, what it would be like if I lost her, but the reality of the feeling is worse than my imagination could ever have conjured, and I still don't know the severity of the situation. I don't know if Nicole is okay.

I try to focus on Luke's touch on me, the steady beat of his heart and rise and fall of his breath. I hope it will steady me, but then I think about the way he walked back to the car after he'd finally burst me out of my stupor. He's in so much pain. His body must be exhausted. But he didn't give up on me.

I slide my hand up and rest it against his chest, where he covers it with his own. He slips my phone from my grasp, tucking it under his leg, and when I try to grab for it he entwines his fingers with mine, resting them against his heart once more.

"You—" I start to say, but he cuts me off.

"Dan, we'll talk later. Rest now." His voice is soft but resolute.

I can't rest, though. How could I even contemplate resting when Nicole might be … she might be dead. A shudder ripples through me at the thought, but Luke continues to hold me, his fingers running through my hair as he murmurs comforting things in my ear. Things like "I'm here," or "You're safe," or "I've got you."

Without my permission my body relaxes and my eyelids droop, and despite me fighting it, I begin to drift away.

My phone is ringing. I jerk, reaching for the sound. I can't find it. Panic swells over me. I need to get to my phone but I can't. I'm wet all over and my clothes are sticking to me.

What's going on?

A hand settles on my head, gently pulling it back to rest against a warm body. A deep voice is talking. Someone answered my phone. Everything is still foggy.

The person talking is the same one holding me against him. I can feel the vibrations of his voice through his chest. Fingertips slide against my scalp, and it all hits me at once.

Nicole.

Luke.

I'm with Luke.

Luke came to get me and he must now be talking to my mum on the phone, hearing about Nicole.

"He's okay," I hear him say. "He's upset, but he's sleeping."

I try to sit up and reach for my phone.

He gently presses his fingers into my scalp, and it feels so damn good I relax again. He's ending the call. Saying they'll talk soon, hanging up and tucking the phone back under his leg, out of my reach.

Before I have the chance to speak, Luke is already answering my questions. "She's okay, Danny. She's in the hospital, but she's okay. She's going to be okay."

Okay.

She'll be okay.

The tears hit like a bolt of lightning. Completely out of nowhere but unavoidable. Great shuddering sobs overwhelm me. I cling to Luke, pressing my forehead into the side of his neck, and he wraps both arms tight around me.

"She's safe, Danny. She's safe and going to be okay. Because of you."

I let the words roll over me, repeating them over and over as I let myself be held.

I'm dripping all over Luke's kitchen. The backseat of Tyler's car must be soaked. The thought registers, but I can't seem to care about it. I should feel bad that I probably ruined it, but I can't concentrate on what's happening right in front of me, let alone on that vague concern.

Kristen drove us home in Tyler's car. I assume he drove mine back, but it's another thing I don't have energy to deal with

Luke is arguing with his mum as I stand here soaked through. I'm so cold. I want to lie down and forget this night ever happened.

"Mum," he says. He sounds annoyed, probably with me. It seems ridiculous that I spend months pining after him and when I finally – finally – have my chance, I blow it so spectacularly. I can't even bring myself to care all that much. I will some other day, but not right now. I try to focus on what he's saying. "Wherever he's sleeping I'm sleeping there, too. You may as well let him stay in my room. I'm not leaving him alone."

His mum sighs. I can't recall her name. Why can't I remember it? She met us at the door when Kirsten dropped us off a few minutes ago. Luke's mum hugged us both and dragged us into the kitchen, where she wrapped us up in towels and tried to feed us. I have zero appetite. I don't think I'll ever want to eat again.

Luke begrudgingly took a plate of food. He's clutching it so tightly it might shatter. I reach out and pry the food from his hand, setting it on the table.

"Fine," Luke's mum says, holding out a box of pills. "Eat

that, take one of these and sleep. But the door stays open." She looks all cross and stern, but then her expression softens. "I'm very proud of you," she says as she steps into Luke, giving him a gentle hug. "I love you. Now, go to bed."

She turns to me and gives me a soft smile, but doesn't say anything as she leaves the room.

"Come on," Luke says. I pick up his food and follow him as he slowly makes his way to his room, each step slow and painful.

We should be at Tyler's now, curled up in sleeping bags side-by-side in a corner somewhere, my arm around him. We should have been asleep hours ago and Luke wouldn't be pushing himself so far past his body's limit. I was supposed to make tonight better for him and I've done exactly the opposite.

Luke takes the plate from my hand and puts it on the bedside table, then faces me.

His fingers reach up and brush against my cheek. My breath stutters.

"Come on, let's get you dry," he says, then slides his hands across my chest and shoulders and slides my suit jacket off. He throws it haphazardly over a chair before focusing on me again.

I haven't moved. I should be taking these wet clothes off. But I can't seem to do anything at all.

Luke's hands shake as he reaches for the buttons on my shirt. He gets two undone before his knuckle brushes against the skin of my chest and the heat sears through me.

I grab his hand, stopping him before he can undo the next button. This isn't how I want this to happen. I don't want him taking my clothes off with pity in his expression. If Luke's going to be undressing me I want it like the last time he took off my shirt, when my skin was scalding and every touch was like fire. When I was dizzy with the desire to touch him. I don't want it in this vague foggy state when he's only helping me because he feels obliged to.

"It's fine," I say, and I'm startled to hear how rough my voice sounds. "I can do it."

"Let me help," he says, voice low and soft, as smooth as silk.

"I don't need help."

He shrugs, and it causes some kind of emotion to flicker in me. I can't identify it, but being able to feel something other than the hollowness of the past few hours is something and I embrace it. I cut Luke off before he manages to speak.

"You don't need to look after me, okay? I'm fine. I'll be fine."

"Danny, I want to look after you." His hand is cupping my cheek, his thumb brushing the skin right below my eye. I want to lean into his touch. I want to let him wrap me up and tuck me into bed. But through the haze and pain and chaos of tonight, one thing has stuck with me: his words right before I walked out of the ball. Him telling me he doesn't want any of this. He doesn't want me.

"No you don't," I snap. "It's okay. I get it. Don't pretend. I'm sorry I ruined your night. You didn't deserve that. I'll stay tonight because I have to, but I'll go home tomorrow and leave you alone. For good."

The words flow out of me, and before I can meet Luke's eyes I turn away and tear the shirt from my body.

CHAPTER 43

Luke

DAN FUMBLES with the rest of the buttons on his shirt then grapples with the wet fabric, trying to unstick it from his shoulders.

He's going to leave me for good? He can't mean that.

I push through the stiffness and pain in my own body and step towards him, grabbing onto the saturated shirt and helping him pull it from his shoulders. He's facing away from me and I can see the tension lining the muscles of his back.

"Please don't," I whisper, and I don't know if he hears me as he fists the shirt in his hands.

"Don't what?" he asks after what feels like an eternity of me fighting the urge to reach out and touch him. There's a huge chasm between us, one that I don't know how to cross. All I know is that I want to. I thought we were okay after I found him and held him all the way home. I didn't realise that somewhere in all of this he's decided to let me go. It's what scared me all along, that I'd lose another thing, and someone like Dan isn't going to be an easy loss to move on from.

"Don't leave. Don't give up on me. Please." My voice breaks on my final plea.

Dan's head drops and his shoulders shake. He crumples like a wet piece of paper and collapses onto the floor, leaning against the side of my bed. He's sucking in great heaving breaths, like he's trying not to cry.

My body screams at me, but I fold myself until I can sit on the floor beside him. I reach out, only hesitating for a moment before my hand slides into his curls and I tug him towards me.

"I don't know how to be the person you need me to be," he says, his voice muffled by my shoulder.

He keeps saying things like this and I don't understand why. "I know I'm difficult, and so messed up, but I don't need you to be anyone but yourself," I say. His hands stay in his lap and I try not to feel hurt that he isn't reaching for me, that he doesn't want to touch me. He's letting me touch him though, and for now I suppose that's a win.

"You told me you didn't want this." It's a whisper, but I hear it like he's yelled it right in my face.

"I don't – I don't remember saying that. When did I say that?"

"Tonight, after Nicole rang me. Before I left. You said you didn't want me."

Oh. My little outburst seems so long ago, and so irrelevant in light of what has happened since. But that's not what I said at all. "I said…" I take a shaky breath and try again. "I said I didn't want it … at the start. I was scared. Scared of what it would mean, of having to be out, scared because last time I let myself be seen by someone it all went horribly wrong. I'm scared of what else I might lose, especially if I let myself have you. What would happen to me if I lost you? You're not someone who'd be easy to get over."

He finally turns to face me, his brown eyes locking on mine and studying me closely.

"I'm scared all the time too," he whispers. "About Nic, about losing her. I'm always scared she's going to leave me." A deep shuddering breath as a tear streaks down his cheek. "She tried to leave me."

I reach for his hand, willing him to accept the gesture. He slips his fingers between mine until they're laced tightly together. The relief washes through me. We're not out of the woods yet, but we're close. We can make it.

"No, she didn't try to leave you," I say, fierce in my belief. "She tried to leave the pain because it got too much. She called you because she didn't want to leave you." Another tear tracks down his face. "You saved her life. I think you've saved a lot of lives, Danny."

He shakes his head as if to deny it.

"You have. You've made mine so much better. I couldn't have done all the things I've done these past few months without you."

He snorts. "I didn't do anything."

"You did. You were there, you believed in me. You treated me like I could already do these things. You make me feel like I can do anything I want. You opened the door to possibilities I didn't know were there anymore. You showed me how strong I can be."

Dan doesn't say anything to that. He sits there and stares up at me as I reach out and swipe a tear from his cheek.

He shivers violently and I realise how frozen he still is. In the dim light of my room I haven't noticed until now that his lips are tinged blue. It felt too confrontational to turn on the overhead light, so there's only the warm orange glow of a salt lamp in the corner, a gift from Kristen.

"Come on, we need to get you warm and I need to lie down."

He jumps to his feet, shock on his face. Shock and guilt. "I'm so sorry. Your back. Why are you sitting on the floor?" He looks horrified, but it's not his fault. He's got so much going on in his head.

"I'm okay, Dan – or I will be. Help me up?"

He reaches for me and gently lifts me to my feet. I'm unsteady, but his hands land on my waist, helping me balance. It's so reminiscent of earlier tonight at the ball, that I have the urge to step into him, to kiss him and hold him close.

But we aren't there yet.

His turmoil is too fresh, our emotions still too scattered. I'm not even sure he wants this.

"Do you want a shower or anything before we go to bed?" I'm still fully dressed and I start to slide my jacket off.

He shakes his head. "No, but let me help you." He reaches for the buttons on my shirt.

"Danny, I'm supposed to be looking after you." I sigh when his fingers brush my neck as he slides the first button free.

"I don't need looking after."

"Yes, Danny, you do. Everyone does. You know something I've learned the last few months? It's okay to let someone help you. Even if you don't think you need it, it's still okay to let them."

"I'm fine, though."

"Maybe, though after tonight it's okay not to be. You spend

so much time taking care of other people. Sometimes we want to do the same for you."

He starts to argue, so I place my hand over his mouth. He licks it and I pull it away as he laughs. The sound is so unexpected, so delightful, I can't help but grin at him.

"I'll let you help me," I say, smoothing his hair back from his face, "if you let me help you."

"We can help each other," he says. "Okay."

CHAPTER 44

Dan

LUKE'S BED is something else.

We're lying side by side, Luke flat on his back, me curled on my side facing him. He let me finish unbuttoning his shirt, then slid it from his shoulders. He even let me help remove his brace. But he baulked at me helping with his pants, which honestly is probably for the best.

"I don't have any clothes," I whispered after realising I had no idea where my bag was. Probably still in my car, but the rain had started again and I wasn't in any mood to drag all my stuff inside.

Luke handed me a pair of shorts. "You have to do this part on your own. I've got to eat something so I can take some painkillers."

I headed for the bathroom and finished changing. By the time I got back Luke was lying on his bed, also wearing dry shorts, eating the sandwich.

"I thought you weren't supposed to eat lying down," I said, crawling onto the bed beside him. "Was that just a lie my mum told me as a child?"

Luke smiled. "Tell that to my back," he mumbled through a mouthful. "My mum told me the same thing, but I've perfected the skill by this point. Still can't drink like this though, which is a shame. Sitting up to take those pills is going to be a bitch."

"I'll help you," I said.

"I know you will."

He ate his middle-of-the-night meal, then I helped him to sit up to swallow his meds.

Once he'd swallowed the pills he pushed himself to standing. He was shaky and clearly exhausted, but he placed his hands on my shoulders, the heat of them branding my bare skin, and pushed me onto the bed. From there he proceeded to tuck me in like a small child. But I couldn't argue, because it felt nice to have someone take over. It felt especially good when he lay down beside me, reaching out and wrapping his fingers around mine.

Now, here we are, both exhausted but unable to sleep.

I think over what we've talked about tonight, how what Luke said paralleled what Jake said. I can't understand why everyone keeps telling me helping people is bad.

I turn away from those thoughts and return to something else Luke said earlier. Something that's been sitting in my heart, a little glowing ember. "Earlier, you said you didn't want it, didn't want this … at the start. And now?"

I hold my breath. Hold it tight, as if it's the only thing protecting my heart, which I've just handed to him, along with a sledgehammer.

"You totally missed the rest of what I said, didn't you?" he says, slowly lifting his gaze to meet mine. I stare blankly at him, because he's right. His grey eyes are locked with mine and he draws in a breath. "Now," he says, that voice raspy, "is totally different."

I let the breath out. The tiny ember sparks. "What else did you say?" A little squeak. It's the only voice I can find. He's holding my heart in his hands, the sledge hammer still hovering.

He thinks for a moment. "I can't remember for sure, but it was something along the lines of everything I've done to keep you at a distance was a waste of time and I've…" He pauses.

"You've what?"

"I've fallen for you so bloody hard, were the words I think I used."

The ember bursts to life in my heart. The cold ache of worry for Nicole lingers in my chest, but Luke's words and his warm presence here beside me help to thaw some of that pain.

I lift our hands, bringing them to my mouth to brush a kiss against his knuckles. "You know," I say, "the feeling's mutual."

I wake sometime in the early morning. There's a soft grey light filtering in the window on the back wall of Luke's room, so I know the sun is only just beginning to rise.

I know it's Luke's room because of all the mountain bike posters on the wall, the collage of photos and the shadow of the drum kit in the back corner. Everything else is a little foggy. This bed is so comfortable I never want to leave, and it smells like coffee and chocolate. Like Luke.

I roll over and there he is, sprawled beside me, still asleep. His hair is all messy, lashes dark against his cheeks (which are alarmingly pale considering his naturally brown skin). Even in sleep there's a pained twist to his mouth, and I remember the way he moved last night after pushing his body beyond its limit.

Because of me.

I shouldn't have caused him that pain. But … Nicole.

Her phone call comes hurtling to the forefront.

She's okay. She's safe. I repeat the mantra.

I slow my breathing and take a few minutes to remind myself that everything is okay, and while I do, I study Luke.

My eyes trail down his body. The sheets are tangled around his waist and I can't help catching my breath at the sight of him. He's beautiful. I wish I'd got to undress him properly, but maybe … maybe we'll have another chance. He was so determined last night that I let him look after me. Maybe it was more than obligation.

Luke shifts beside me, a small groan slipping from his lips. His eyes flutter open and his head tilts towards me. A soft smile plays at his mouth as those sleepy grey eyes take me in.

"Hey," he whispers, voice husky with sleep.

"Hey." I rest my head against the pillow, facing him. I want to take in as much of his face as possible, to memorise it.

"This is really not how I imagined so many of our firsts happening," he says.

I flinch. It's not how I imagined it either, but everything that happened last night was because of me. "I'm sorry you didn't get the night you wanted," I say, the regret washing over me.

He reaches towards me, then stops with his hand suspended between us and grimaces. His hand lowers to the bed. "That's not what I mean. I had an amazing night. I had imagined though, that things would have been slightly different the first time I shared a bed with you." The blush is back on his cheeks and my heart twists at how adorable he is.

I reach my hand out towards his, hesitant. I don't know if he wants my touch. I don't know if he wants me here, or at all, or if I'm only here because he knows I have nowhere else to be. He told me he wanted me last night, but things might be different in the cold light of day.

His gaze tracks my hand and when I pause, a breath from making contact, he lifts his fingers to graze mine. I place my hand over his and he closes his eyes briefly, the relief evident on his face.

"It's not how I imagined it either," I whisper.

"Maybe next time," he says, a glint in his eye that makes me swoon.

"I might hold you to that," I say.

"Please, please do."

"You want this? Us, I mean?"

"More than anything I've ever wanted in my entire life."

I roll towards him, slide my arm around his waist and crash my lips onto his smiling mouth.

CHAPTER 45

Luke

WE LIE in bed together for what feels like an eternity.

It can't be, because Mum would have come to check if we were alive or at least not doing something she deemed inappropriate … which crosses my mind occasionally, especially when his gaze travels down my body and lingers.

Instead we lie there, staring at each other across the pillows. It's like heaven. A warm, cozy haven from everything that happened last night. Neither of us has forgotten Nicole, but in each other's company the pain and worry feel more manageable. At least, they do for me.

I revel in the way Dan's gaze drifts over me and the way his hand feels in mine as our words from last night echo between us.

I've fallen for you so bloody hard, were the words I think I used.
You know, the feeling's mutual.

I lie there until I can't anymore because I so desperately need the bathroom. "I need to get up," I say, disappointed and filled with dread at the thought of having to make my body move. I slip my fingers free of Dan's and try to roll over. I can't help the groan that slips from my lips as I do.

In a flash Dan is up, moving around the bed towards me. "Do you want—"

I cut him off with a nod and explain the easiest way for him to help me sit up. It involves him looping his arms around my torso and lifting and I try *very* hard not to think about his hot skin meeting mine. Another first time I imagined playing out differently.

But I'm sitting, then with a little more help I'm standing. Both crutches in hand, I shuffle for the bathroom.

By the time I'm back Dan is sitting cross-legged on my bed, wearing one of my shirts. My heart skips at the sight of it. I could so easily get used to this.

"I hope this is okay?" he asks, sheepish. His curls are a tangled mess, which makes him look like a small mischievous boy – except for the way the muscles in his forearms flex as he twists his hands in his lap, and the sharp edge of his jaw I have a desperate urge to run my teeth along.

"Of course," I say, a smile playing at my lips as I try not to think about the sound he might make if I did that thing with my teeth and his jaw. I lower myself onto the bed beside him.

"How badly does it hurt?" he whispers, taking my face in his hands. His fingertips smooth the skin around my eyes.

"Pretty bad," I admit. It's been a while since it was this bad – since the ache was ever-present and every movement caused spasms of pain.

"I'm sorry you're hurting," he says.

"I'm sorry you're hurting too," I whisper back, as I reach up and trace along his cheekbone.

He bites his lip. "She'll be okay, though?"

I nod. "She'll be okay, and so will you."

"And so will you," he echoes back to me, before he leans in and presses his mouth to mine.

It's soft and sweet and utterly perfect.

And cut short by the sound of car doors slamming outside my room.

A moment later Jonathan and Hollie stride into my room from the direction of the house. They must have completely ignored Mum. Then I realise she's trailing them.

Hollie falls to her knees on the bed, reaching immediately for Dan. They wrap each other in a tight embrace as Jonathan sits carefully beside me, resting a hand on my shoulder. I lean into him, shoulder to shoulder with my best friend who's arrived just when I need him. Because of course he has.

"Why are you here?" Dan croaks against Hollie's hair. She pulls back, studying him carefully, watching fresh tears run down his cheeks.

"We came to take you home," she says.

Dan stares at her then turns his head to stare at Jonathan. "You came all this way to pick me up?"

Jonathan nods. "Hollie will drive you home. I'll take the other car. There's no rush though. Whenever you're ready."

"God, I love you," Dan says, pulling Hollie in for another hug. Those words. Could I ever hope for him to say them to me?

"I love you too," Hollie replies without hesitation, her grip tightening on him further.

"Come have some food," Mum says from the doorway. "It's ready when you are."

I nod my thanks and she disappears back to the kitchen.

Hollie detangles herself from Dan's grasp and sits back on the bed, studying him. "Why did you never tell me about Nicole?"

Dan slumps, like the question is too heavy a burden. "Because … because I always, always want to make you feel better, not worse. I want to make you happy. And telling you about Nicole would mean telling you about all of it, and much of it isn't happy.

"I don't want to tell you how scared I am all the time that I'm going to lose her. I didn't want the heaviness of all of that to come between us, like it has before for me." He hesitates.

"Jake?" Hollie asks and receives a nod in reply.

"It wasn't really his fault. He didn't realise what was going on, or so I discovered this week." A small smile.

"This is why you're so good with me?" Hollie asks, and Dan shrugs. "It's how you knew what was wrong with me?" He nods, looking sheepish, like he doesn't believe he's helping her at all. "Danny," she says, her voice turning slightly away from the soft tone she's been using. Her hands find the sides of his face, forcing him to hold her gaze. "You know I absolutely adore you, but you have to know that I don't only want you for the good times and the bad jokes. You're my best friend and it's a two-way street. You carry all my heavy loads for me. Let me – let us –" she waves towards Jonathan and me "– carry your heavy loads for you, too. The dark bits don't scare me, Danny, just like mine don't scare you."

He nods slowly. "Okay," he says.

I reach over and take his hand, pulling it into my lap as I tangle our fingers together. Our palms meet, a perfect fit as always. "She's right. Let us in. You're always there for everyone else. Let us be there for you. We *want* to be there for you."

He doesn't say anything, but he squeezes my hand so tight it makes my heart skip.

Jonathan nods beside me.

"Can we eat first? Then I'll tell you everything?"

Hollie laughs, Jonathan snorts and I simply smile at this gorgeous boy sitting beside me, finally letting us in to help him.

CHAPTER 46

Dan

I CAN'T BELIEVE Hollie and Jonathan came all this way to pick me up. I don't even know what time they would have left this morning to get here this early.

Although, I guess it's not exactly early; Luke and I just haven't been able to drag ourselves out of bed yet.

I didn't want to leave the safe comfort of lying there with him, of being so close to him in our little bubble, away from the reality of everything outside these walls.

Alone in his room, just us, I felt safe, like nothing could go wrong, not when he was holding my hand and telling me he'd fallen for me.

Reality arrived, as it was always going to, but not in the way I thought it would. I imagined a long, solitary drive home wondering how all of this was going to affect my family and how I'd deal with Jake when I got home and found him still in my house.

I never expected that Hollie would walk through the door, and when she wrapped her arms around me so tightly I could barely draw breath, I thought I might shatter into a million pieces right there. I would have if she hadn't been holding me so tight.

Luke's mum has piled so much food on the table in front of us that I don't know where to start. She must have been cooking all morning. There's pancakes and French toast and bacon and at least five different kinds of fruit. She had to have known Hollie and Jonathan were coming, because there's more than enough for them.

Hollie holds my hand and leads me to the table before nudging me into a seat. I watch as Luke uses both crutches to get to the kitchen and groans as he lowers himself into a chair, his eyes fluttering closed in a grimace of pain as he does.

I'm sure his pain is my fault – both the physical and emotional pain I put him through. I can't believe I ran out on him last night and didn't even explain what was wrong. My mind had frozen, and no words seemed like the right ones. I can't balance the person he needs me to be with the person my sister needs, and the person Hollie needs, and who my parents need me to be.

I still don't know what I'm supposed to tell them all after breakfast. They asked for me to let them in, to let them help share the load. But I don't know how to do that.

I wish Luke and I could go back to our little bubble of coziness and I didn't have to have this conversation.

Instead we eat and eat and eat, and Luke takes a range of different pills, then we retreat back to his room.

I sit at the head of Luke's bed, my legs stretched out in front of me as I lean against the wall. Luke lies flat on his back with his head in my lap and my fingers naturally find their way to tangle in his hair.

Hollie and Jonathan are still in the kitchen, clearing up our mess, but I'm glad they're not here yet.

"I'm so sorry about last night," I say. Luke immediately tries to sit up and I press my fingers into his shoulder to keep him still. "Stay there," I say, my voice soft.

He grunts, like he's unhappy that he can't sit up and face me. "You don't have to apologise."

"Maybe in your eyes, but I think I do. I shouldn't have taken off like that. I should have explained. I shouldn't have left you there like that. I'm sorry."

He reaches up and wraps his fingers around my wrist – an echo of that time he taught me to play the drums. "Thank you, but no more apologies. I understand that you were scared. I've been scared, Dan. I know what it's like when you can't think through the fear. It's how I almost lost Jonathan. You need to know though, that you don't have to go through this alone."

"I don't know how to be the person everyone needs me to be."

"You keep saying that, but Danny, the only person any of us need you to be is yourself. Only you."

"Everyone already has so much to deal with, so much to worry about, I don't want to make them carry all my shit too." I hate saying these words out loud. I don't even like to think them in the solitude of my mind. I want things to go back to how they were before I completely fell apart last night. Then Jake's words echo back to me, and I realise that maybe he had a point, maybe Luke has a point, and maybe it's time to give up the fight to always be self-reliant.

"You know, helping someone we care about isn't a burden. You must know that, right? Because you're so good at helping other people. Do you feel like Hollie's a burden when you help her through a tough day? Do you think Nicole's a burden because she's struggling with things? Do you wish I didn't open up to you about the hard parts of my life? Do you wish I hadn't leaned on you when I needed help?"

I immediately open my mouth to deny those claims. How could I ever think three of the people I care about most in this world are a burden, or wish they hadn't come to me?

Then it hits me, and I wonder how I could have been this stupid for so long.

"Of course I don't think that," I whisper, my voice all scratchy. "But I see your point."

"Good," he says. "I don't ever want you to struggle, but when you do I want you to come to me, or Hollie, or Jonathan or your Mum or even Jake. We want to be able to help you because we care about you, just like you care about us."

"Okay. Jury's out on Jake caring, though."

Luke chuckles as I lay my hand across his chest. He lays his over the top, sliding his fingers between mine.

He squeezes tightly, and when Hollie and Jonathan finish in the kitchen and come to find us, I open my mouth and I talk.

CHAPTER 47

Luke

I TOOK heavy-duty painkillers with breakfast, and as I lie flat on my back with my head in Dan's lap, his palm pressed against my chest and his simple "okay" echoing through my head, they start to kick in.

I don't know where he got it into his head that help is only for other people, but I'm relieved he seems to be starting to understand that it's not the case.

Hollie and Jonathan have finished doing whatever they were doing in the kitchen and have settled onto the end of my bed, waiting to hear Dan's story.

He strokes his fingers through my hair as he talks about his sister, about her history and her struggles. When his voice wavers his fingers stop moving and I reach up and hold them tight.

Hollie sits leaning against Jonathan. His arm slides effortlessly around her, and when her emotions come to the fore and a tear falls on her cheek, Jonathan pulls her even closer, wiping away the moisture. Seeing him so effortlessly comfortable with another person always fills me with contentment, to know that despite everything, he's come out of this okay. Like I have and like Dan will, too.

Dan talks about Jake and the collapse of their friendship, how he'd needed his friend who wasn't there for him, and how neither of them had understood why until two days ago. He talks until he runs out of words.

My eyes are closed but I keep my hands moving against his, light brushes of my fingers, a squeeze now and again, so he knows I'm not sleeping.

Silence falls. His fingers resume working through my hair. My eyelids grow heavier.

I fade in and out as Hollie, Jonathan and Dan begin talking quietly again. I catch the occasional word or sentence, with Hollie making the same assurances I have, but I can't stay focussed enough to reiterate the message. The stupid medication has made me drowsy. It's been so long since I've taken this super strong one that I forgot it knocks me out.

"Sweetheart," Dan says, leaning down to murmur close to my ear.

"Hmm?" I slowly drift back into consciousness.

"I'm so sorry, but we need to go."

A hand smooths over my cheek and I reach to grab it. I hold it against my skin, willing myself to remember this moment, the feel of him.

"I know," I say. "But I don't want you to."

He slides out from underneath my head, lowering me down onto a pillow instead. "I don't want to go either," he says, kneeling beside the bed so he can be at my eye level.

I turn to face him. Somehow I find the energy to lift my hand and place it along his jaw. I trace the shape of his eyebrow, the curve of his mouth, the straight line of his nose.

"Please don't give up on me," I whisper. "I know I'm a mess, and I don't know how I can ever make this work, but please, don't give up on me."

"Oh, sweetheart," Dan says. If he calls me that again I might never let him go. "I'm not giving up on you, not unless you give up on me first. I don't know how it'll work, but it will. We'll figure something out … together. We'll help each other figure this out."

"Hey." Another voice. Jonathan. I glance over to see him and Hollie coming back into my room. "Sorry guys, we've really got to get going."

He makes his way towards me and Dan slides back a bit.

I try to sit up but Jonathan rests a hand on my shoulder. "It's all right," he says as he kneels beside me, in the place Dan was a moment ago. "We'll come back and see you soon, all right? Get Kris or Mum to bring you down to visit. Any time you want."

I nod.

"I'm so proud of you, man," he says. "To do what you did last night, and everything else. Getting back to school, the riding. Nothing's going to keep you down. You deserve all this." He tilts his head towards Dan. "I'll see you real soon, okay?"

For the first time since my accident I don't want to go back to before it happened. Yes, everything is different now, but different doesn't necessarily mean bad. If my accident hadn't happened I wouldn't have met Dan, Jonathan wouldn't have met Hollie. I wouldn't have Tyler as such a significant part of my life. I wouldn't have discovered exactly how strong I can be.

Jonathan starts to rise, but I grab his arm. "Johnnie, so you know for sure, I love you, all right?"

His mouth tugs into a smile and he ruffles my hair like some jerky older brother would do. "Love you too, man."

Hollie steps into the space Jonathan leaves and drops a kiss onto my head. I feel so useless lying here, but they don't treat me like I am. And maybe I need to take my own advice and let other people look after me from time to time. Not always, but sometimes.

"We'll look after him," Hollie whispers, for only us to hear. I smile at her.

"I know you will. Thank you."

She's gone again and my eyes close for a heavy blink. When I open them, Dan is back, his eyes deep pools of sadness.

"I promise we'll make this work."

I nod. "I'll do whatever I can," I say. My eyes are growing heavy again and I curse that medication.

"I'm going to see you so soon. We'll talk, and there'll always be our emails."

I tug my mouth into a smile. "I love our emails."

"I do too."

"Say hi to Nicole for me. Give her a hug for me and let them look after you." I nod towards Hollie and Jonathan.

He nods. "I will."

I'm fighting with the drugs, fighting to stay awake because I know there's something else I need to clarify before he leaves me here. Something I need him to know, even if it means pushing myself so far out of my comfort zone it feels like falling off a cliff.

"Danny," I whisper and force my heavy, heavy eyelids to remain open so I can watch his face, "so you know for sure … I love you."

They're the same words I said to my best friend, but the meaning is completely different this time and Dan knows it.

His expression freezes and my heart seizes with it. I've pushed too far. My timing is wrong. I shouldn't have said anything.

It's only a moment, though, before he sweeps in and kisses me. Swift and fast and a little desperate.

"I love you too, sweetheart. Have a good sleep and I'll see you real soon."

He moves away, his fingers dragging down my jaw until they finally slip away. I miss his touch immediately, but I'm cradled in a cocoon of blissful contentment that has absolutely nothing to do with how immensely comfortable my bed is.

It doesn't matter what chaos life throws at me next, I'm going to be able to handle it. And I don't have to do it alone because I have the best people in the world by my side.

Before the door closes behind Dan, I'm asleep, dreaming about love and all its possibilities.

***

I sleep for hours and when I wake up there's an email waiting for me. My heart skips and soars.

It's a photo of Dan and an older girl with his same tangle of curls. It's clearly Nicole. She's curled into him, both tucked into a bed with a fluffy pink blanket pulled up around them. The girl's face is pale with dark circles under her red-rimmed eyes. Both their faces are drawn but lit with soft smiles.

There are only a few words.

Nic says hi back.

I love you, sweetheart.

Resources

Some of the topics in this book can be confronting.
If you need assistance, please reach out for support.

New Zealand:

Depression Helpline: 0800 111 757 or free text 4202
Youthline: 0800 376 633 or free text 234
The Low Down: Text 5626

Australia:

Beyond Blue: 1300 22 4363
Kids Helpline: 1800 55 1800 (ages 5-25)

United States:

Teen Line: 800 852 8336 or text 839863
Mental Health America: 1 800 985 5990 or text Talk-WithUs to 66746

United Kingdom:

Give Us A Shout: Text 85258

SANEline: 0300 689 5652

If these numbers don't apply to you, please google your local mental health support line, or reach out to friends, family, or your school.

Acknowledgments

It's always weird for me when I get to this point, because I want to thank everyone in my entire life for helping me live my dream as an author! You really don't want to read all that, so I'll try to narrow it down.

First, I've dedicated this book to Kelsey and Natalie, my best friends for over twenty years. (I'm not counting how long it's really been, because I feel old enough as it is!) I know how to write great friendships because of the two of you. I can't encapsulate what you mean to me in a few simple words, so just know that I love you.

A massive, huge, enormous thank you to my husband, Chris, and daughters Charlotte, Taylor and Isabelle, for your constant support, love and cheerleading.

My family: Mum, Dad, siblings and in-laws. You help make all this possible. Special thanks to Alyssa for making me promise I wouldn't make Luke's story too sad. I think I did okay there.

I've met some truly incredible friends through Bookstagram and other book-related things. Your support, motivation and celebrating of my success has made all the hard parts of this venture absolutely worth it. Extra thanks to Mon and Georgia for always managing to talk me down from the edge. I'm so excited we're all friends IRL now!

Sarah W: you know you need a special mention. I'm so grateful the internet brought us together and I appreciate you in so many ways – from our mocktail dates to your vast supply of knowledge you're always willing to share with me, to our endless exchanging of the most random memes and reels.

To my publishing team: Kaycee, Patricia and Jennifer. I can't thank you enough for your incredible services in beta reading, editing and cover design. You've been brilliant to work with as always and have made this book the best version possible.

My Street Team: Thank you for being my super fans! It means the world that you all love my books enough to want to shout about them to everyone.

Thank you to the booksellers, librarians and other champions of young adult books, New Zealand authors and independent authors who've seen fit to include my little indie published books in their stores/collections/work.

Last of all, my readers. Wow. There is no greater joy for an author than seeing someone connect with their stories, so for every one of you who has read, reviewed, posted, shared or talked about my books, thank you so much!

Lynda Tomalin lives in a small town in New Zealand, where she writes sweet, swoony books about teenagers finding their place in the world.

She is a mum of three girls and a farmer's wife, and when she's not daydreaming about her fictional characters and trying to find space for all the books she keeps buying, she works in administration (but mostly only to fund making books).

Find her online:
www.lyndatomalinauthor.com
Instagram and Facebook:
@lynda.tomalin.author

Email:
contact@lyndatomalinauthor.com

Also by Lynda Tomalin

THE STARS BURN BRIGHT

A sweet, swoony YA romance about discovering and celebrating your worth.

Seventeen-year-old Essie is looking forward to her summer holidays.

It means weeks of dedicating herself to her sewing business while her parents are busy working. Sure, her jerk of a brother is home from university, but he's mostly working too, so it's easy to stay out of his way. She can be herself – whoever she wants to be, without expectation or judgement or always being told she's over-dramatic.

It's going to be amazing.

Until Jackson Sherwood, her brother's childhood friend, comes to stay.

Jax. Essie has no time for the smug jerk who's always smirking at her, like he's so much better than her.

Jax's arrival threatens to ruin her plans for a peaceful summer, but as their situation forces them to spend time together, Essie starts to see a hidden side of the unwanted guest, and starts to learn about herself: who she is, where she fits in the world … and what she's willing to stand up for.

Also by Lynda Tomalin

FLYING AND FALLING

Hollie is learning to live with depression.

She's working hard to put the darkest days behind her. She's got a job she loves, friends she cares about, and she's coping. In fact, she's doing pretty well.

Then a mysterious – and gorgeous – new boy shows up at school.

Jonathan is running away from his past.

Weighed down by a guilty secret, he's fled to his aunt's rural property under the guise of helping out on the farm.

As Hollie and Jonathan are unexpectedly thrown together, a growing mutual attraction scares and excites them.

But the past isn't so easy to escape, and they both have to decide if it's enough to keep hiding, from themselves and from each other.

Or can they risk hoping for more?

Winner of a Storylines Notable Book Award 2023

Shortlisted for the 2022 Storylines Tessa Duder Award

www.ingramcontent.com/pod-product-compliance
Lightning Source LLC
Chambersburg PA
CBHW032358310726
48973CB00007B/2076